PENGUIN BOOKS

THE WINNING STREAK

Arnold Grisman is the Assistant to the Chairman for Creative Resources at J. Walter Thompson. He has worked in most major U.S. cities at a variety of things, including assistant director of Broadway musicals. His hobbies include languages, carpentry, book collecting, and horticulture.

THE WINNING STREAK

Arnold Grisman

PENGUIN BOOKS

PENGUIN BOOKS
Viking Penguin Inc., 40 West 23rd Street,
New York, New York 10010, U.S.A.
Penguin Books Ltd, Harmondsworth,
Middlesex, England
Penguin Books Australia Ltd, Ringwood,
Victoria, Australia
Penguin Books Canada Limited, 2801 John Street,
Markham, Ontario, Canada L3R 1B4
Penguin Books (N.Z.) Ltd, 182–190 Wairau Road,
Auckland 10, New Zealand

First published in the United States of America by
St. Martin's Press 1985
Published in Penguin Books 1987

LIBRARY OF CONGRESS CATALOGING IN PUBLICATION DATA
Grisman, Arnold.
The winning streak.
I. Title.
[PS3557.R536W5   1987]   813'.54   86-15123
ISBN 0 14 00.9369 9

Printed in the United States of America by
Offset Paperback Mfrs., Inc., Dallas, Pennsylvania
Set in Times Roman

For Rita

"God does not play at dice."
      —Albert Einstein

THE
WINNING
STREAK

One

The dice jumped from his fingers like speckled mice, hopping and scooting over the green felt, darting, tripping, sliding, tumbling, until, running into the rail, they came back, one flying, the other scrambling, and turned up seven.

Goldberg was well acquainted with the feeling that started somewhere near his heart and blew down his arm like a trumpet call; it had betrayed him regularly for the past twenty-four months. Maybe, thought Goldberg tentatively, big and bent, only halfway out of his crouch, wearing a safari jacket, white pants, torn Adidas sneakers, still a man people noticed.

"Seven," said the stickman, bored. "Shooter wins."

Two o'clock on a Monday morning in Las Vegas is the pause between a week gone and a week coming. Dust flowers sprout in the carpets. Dealers dream at empty tables. The gamblers have a leftover look—as though they had been accidentally abandoned in the Sunday night rush for the planes. Two o'clock on a Monday morning is the time losers come face to face with their losses.

The casino was like a town where the young have gone off to war, thought Goldberg with a familiar ache. When the last plane of the weekend left, the age level rose like some moon-drawn tide.

There were three gray men at the dice table and a Clairol blonde from Kansas City whose ex-husband owned a Buick agency. Billy the Shit, she called him whenever anybody would listen.

The gray men bet wrong, the grass widow right. When Goldberg and the grass widow collected, she shot him a glance of complicity he did not find pleasing. His sympathy was with the Buick dealer.

Taking the dice from the stickman's rake, Goldberg rolled a four, made his point in two passes, and collected again. The three gray men woke up, one thin and papery, acquiring a little touch of pink above the cheekbones. The Clairol blonde chuckled and moved closer, her perfume filling his nostrils with cheap promises. Don't crowd me, thought Goldberg fiercely, but he said nothing. He had six hundred dollars in chips in the slot in front of him and the trumpet call was blaring out of his chest along his arm. He was beginning to concentrate. Little red mice, he said to himself, knowing it was important not to change anything. He felt the sweat roll out of his armpits down his ribs.

He came out of his crouch easily now, no longer Goldberg, the dice degenerate, but Goldberg, the new Sid Luckman, rising from the huddle to place himself behind his wall of blue. Christ, how long ago was that? Who would have believed then that Lou Little could die? The red mice danced a seven on the come-out and Goldberg's rack was filling with chips. Tension began to tease at the Monday-morning doldrums. The dealers both had bright blue eyes they hadn't seemed to have before. The stickman was tall and thin, a Giacometti man with a stick like a lance. The two boxmen, whose job it was to see everything, switched to a new plateau of alertness. Suddenly there were six more players at the table and the morning, summoned from its temporary death, was alive.

2

Goldberg was pressing now, jumping his bets with less and less caution, riding the two red mice to a paradise where all percentages had been warped in his favor.

In ten minutes he won six thousand dollars behind the mice. News of the streak was sucking in gamblers from the slots, from roulette, from twenty-one, from baccarat, from beds and other hiding places, until they stood three deep around the table.

Goldberg was an expert on the odds. The odds against four consecutive elevens are 104,976 to 1.

Goldberg threw four consecutive elevens.

He had thirty-two thousand dollars, which isn't enough for breaking such odds. It's something that will happen to you only once in your life—if then. You should have bet your house, both cars, the houseboat, the savings account, the stocks and bonds, the Christmas fund, the little woman's mink coat, the table silver, the diamond rings, the diamond earrings, the piggybank, your sister-in-law's inheritance, the gold football. But Goldberg didn't have any of those things anymore, not even the gold football, which he had hocked in a fancy hockshop on Fifty-seventh Street and never redeemed. He didn't care that he had none of those things to bet, because he didn't need them; he was far enough into his streak to realize how real and deep it was.

If you've never had that feeling, you may dismiss it as simple greed, but it's more like a religious revelation, the sudden discovery that somewhere in the universe there is a power that can and will reverse the odds in your favor.

Goldberg's arm had done well by him on other occasions. The New York *Daily News* had described it as golden on the day in 1941 when he threw six touchdowns against Harvard straight in the face of all the oddsmakers. "Nick the Greek Meets the Golden Arm," said one of the headlines.

His arm felt good now, loose and strong and tireless, but he didn't want to spoil things with the two mice. Give credit where it's due, Goldberg's mother had always told him when she was instilling the laws of life. A penny saved is a penny earned, was also one of hers. Early to bed, early to rise, makes a man healthy, wealthy, and wise. Bananas are gold in the morning, silver at noon, and lead at night. She was a Jewish Ben Franklin. The love of a good woman is a man's anchor in life—I was always your father's anchor. That was as near to the birds and the bees as she ever got.

The stickman's chatter had emerged from some depository where he had been saving it for another night, hustling the suckers into the hard way, "Ladies and gents, place your bets on the hard way. Get yourself nine to one on the hard six or the hard eight."

Somewhere in his toes Goldberg smiled; the little red mice were reversing all the odds. He rolled the hard eight and made his point.

The cocktail waitress was living at his elbow now, offering him drinks he wouldn't drink but welcomed nevertheless because she had been there before. When you've got a streak as deep and true as this one, you don't change anything. The cocktail waitress, who had once been a secretary in Salinas, understood that and wasn't going to spoil it.

Somewhere around the forty-two-thousand-dollar mark Goldberg noticed that the Clairol blonde had disappeared, seduced away by some unimaginable opportunity. In her place was a red-headed girl in a white evening dress. Goldberg was six-foot-two; the girl was no more than three inches shorter. She might have been a showgirl but she had a look to her showgirls rarely have; she looked as though she knew that sooner or later the house percentage always

4

gunned you down and was amused more than discouraged; you have to be very tough for that, the way a scalpel is tough, or a diamond, or Goldberg.

It had taken Goldberg fifty-six years to get there, but the girl didn't look more than twenty-five; they learned everything faster these days. He sent the red mice out on another mission and, in three rolls, they won for him again.

Although Goldberg was riding the mice to the biggest high a gambler can get, he could not break a longtime habit of watching everything that went on around him.

It was only ten percent of him that watched the telltale movement of eyes, signals that hands made, the tremors of intent, the unconscious withdrawals, but ten percent was enough to tell him that the girl in the white dress had made a difference from the moment she entered the game. In a town where beautiful women, dressed and undressed, are as commonplace as trees at Christmas, she commanded attention in a way that could not be explained by red hair, white skin, green eyes, good bones. There was a mystery in the green eyes, a smile at the corner of her lips that said you'll-never-find-me. She shared the electricity at the table with the shooter even as she shared his prosperity, betting the front line, riding the red mice alongside Goldberg.

At the end of half an hour Goldberg still brooded over the dice table, swinging his passer's arm in long loose arcs that sent the red mice on sortie after sortie. Ninety times. A hundred times. A hundred and one. Chips overflowed from the table into the pockets of his safari jacket where they hung and bulged like automatic pistol clips. He was living the dream gamblers pursue in vain all their lives, that mystic reversal of the facts, like gravity suspended, and even as he lived it the dream was somehow fading at the edges. He forced himself to concentrate, trying to feel only his arm, see only the dice, feel and see them the same way each time in an endless instant replay. Every time his attention wavered memory flooded in.

Childhood ends. Reputation erodes. Love disappears. Courage fails. Life passes. Ecstasy is hard to maintain even when it comes riding behind two red mice. The only thing that persists is memory, carrying back like a river all those other ends, erosions, disappearances, failures, and passings.

Goldberg remembered the moment of his son's death, not when it happened but when he heard about it, which was when it happened to him. What he remembered first was the sound of sobbing, deep, raucous, a shameless Old Testament grieving that filled the room as persistently as though it had been traveling there for centuries; second he remembered his own surprise when he realized that he, Goldberg, was doing the sobbing.

He hadn't cried since he was seven years old, not when he broke his shoulder in Baker Field, not when the German took his legs out from under him with the machine pistol, not when his own father and later his mother died. The infantry captain who was the Department of Defense's official messenger of death looked away in embarrassment, muttering Vietnamese place names that had existed previously for Goldberg only in *The New York Times*. When the captain turned back, he automatically threw up one arm to protect himself from what he saw in Goldberg's face.

"The shooter's point is six," intoned the stickman, who had taken over as the messenger of Goldberg's fate.

By now Goldberg's luck was something even Goldberg couldn't spoil; it was an affair between his arm and the red mice that were building his pile of chips with the relentlessness of destiny. He had long ago lost track of winnings—by now numbers mattered less than direction and the direction was always higher, spiraling upward toward some point Goldberg could not anticipate.

Although he had not had a drink in twenty-four hours, he felt himself entering a state he identified with a certain kind of drunkenness, a top-hat-white-tie-and-tails kind of euphoria in which all he needed was Ginger Rogers in order to become Fred Astaire—Fred Astaire as he had been in the forties and fifties, which Goldberg now recognized as his own prime although he had not realized it then.

Goldberg looked over at the girl in the white dress. She was watching him gravely as though she had detected something even Goldberg didn't know about.

The only thing Goldberg understood about himself was that he was undependable. He had been undependable ever since the moment when he realized who it was that was filling the room with sobs and, finally comprehending, rushed at the captain as though he could wipe out the news by wiping out the messenger. It was like the pulling of a pin that had kept together the neatly ordered parts of Goldberg's hitherto proper life. Once he had been very dependable; now even he didn't know what to expect from himself from moment to moment. Somewhere in the back of his head he tapped up an endless staircase, top hat in hand, tails flying, patent-leather shoes tap-tap-tapping their way toward a rendezvous with an infinitely blond Ginger Rogers who was as small and sugary as the bride on a wedding cake. Even Goldberg's fantasies weren't very dependable anymore.

Now that his arm had gone into business for itself Goldberg watched it with a certain respect, remembering all of the good things it had done for him, throwing footballs, putting an end to the German with the machine pistol, holding a child, beginning that mysterious silken journey under a strange woman's skirt that could end in delight or despair, or more probably, both. The arm kept going at the business of making him rich, if not beyond the bounds of avarice, certainly into one of the closer suburbs.

By this time the news of Goldberg's streak had traveled up and down the Strip. People who had been asleep when it started forty-five minutes earlier had received the news in darkened bedrooms a mile away, dressed, and were crowding their way to the table where Goldberg's arm performed its miracles. Even if you couldn't get close enough to gamble, you could get close enough to say you had been there when the event passed into gambler's legend.

At the one-hour mark the red mice hesitated, stuck trying to make ten, rolled again and again as they danced their way miraculously past the fatal seven, until finally they made the point and regained their irresistible rhythm.

At three-thirty, an hour and a half after he had begun, Goldberg saw on the periphery of the crowd a face he remembered from an earlier time, equipped now with jowls and horn-rimmed spectacles and a cover of gray hair like steel shavings. It was one of the men he had come to Las Vegas to meet; Goldberg somehow expected him to be younger. That surprise set up all kinds of jangling in Goldberg's now-undependable head, alarm bells, tocsins, burbled warnings: a man who had found some luck could use it all up at once and never have any more. Astonished that he still cared about hoarding luck or anything else in the aftermath of his life, Goldberg looked over at the girl in the white dress.

She shook her head, at least he thought she shook her head, although she may have been merely moving her hair around. Whatever it was that she did was enough of a sign for Goldberg.

"I'm putting it to bed," he said, pulling back the arm that had cocked itself to shoot again.

There was a moment when nobody understood that he was stopping, followed by a gasp, a titter, and a sound that was very like a hiss from the outskirts of the crowd. Somebody clapped—there was a minor rattle of applause that was an embarrassment to the true gamblers.

Goldberg, who had no need for celebrity, stuffed his chips in a shopping bag supplied by the management, and began pushing his way through the crowd toward the cashier's cage. Behind him echoed the stickman's cry, "Next shooter."

When he reached the cashier's cage, the girl in the white dress was right beside him, carrying her own winnings, which she brought to the adjoining window.

Goldberg exchanged his chips for one hundred forty-five thousand dollars in hundred-dollar bills, which made a brick approximately six inches high, six inches long, and a little more than two and a half inches wide, weighing nearly three pounds. About the same as a small chicken, thought Goldberg, putting the brick in his shopping bag.

"How does it feel?" asked the girl at his elbow.

Because she seemed genuinely interested, Goldberg did not answer immediately. The only thing he felt was sweat turning to ice in his armpits. He'd cashed in the euphoria along with the chips; all he had now was a package of money weighing about the same as a small chicken. He was sorry he had stopped. "Mostly I feel hungry," he said. "Also thirsty."

"I'll buy you a steak and a martini in the King Arthur Room," offered the girl in the white dress.

Goldberg looked at her, wondering what kind of commitment he was being asked to make. She didn't look as though she had ever needed either money or a friend for the night. That small tidy smile was working at the corners of her lips again.

"What's funny?" he said.

"You are," she said. "You carry that shopping bag as though it were eighteen seventy-five worth of groceries. What's your name?"

"Goldberg," he said.

"No first name?"

"Just Goldberg," he said.

"Have I seen a picture of you somewhere?"

"Not unless you read thirty-five-year-old newspapers."

"That's funny," she said. "I could swear I've seen you somewhere before. It's not a common face."

"Take me to the King Arthur Room," said Goldberg who knew exactly how uncommon his face was and didn't want to talk about it.

"My name is Hall," said the girl, grinning her pirate's grin as they walked past swords, shields, and escutcheons en route to the King Arthur Room.

Goldberg's left hand—the throwing, shooting, touching hand—brushed against her thigh and the contact sent him spinning once more into the past, remembering girls' names, girls' faces, his wife's name, his wife's face. It was part of the undependability of Goldberg's head that it would not stay very long in the present; everything that happened to him was an occasion for memory.

"You're here alone, aren't you?" The girl twisted slightly to stare into his eyes, green eyes against hazel, green eyes that always seemed to be coming from laughter or heading into it.

"In a manner of speaking." Goldberg swung his shopping bag in a slow thoughtful arc. He remembered a girl from a long time away who had had that look; he had found her in a tree where she had been hiding from a German patrol and brought her back through the lines. They had been together for three weeks before she had disappeared again. Sooner or later, it occurred to him, everybody disappeared. "I came to attend a reunion." he said.

The maitre d', unaware of Goldberg's triumphs, either recent or past, sat them at a table in the corner where they both drank vodka martinis on the rocks with a twist in a silence that had become so much a part of Goldberg's life he did not find it in any way unnatural. The girl in the white dress allowed him his silence through the third martini when it started to bore her.

"Remember me?" she said. "Name's Hall. We came in here together."

"Yeah," said Goldberg. She had already become part of the past and therefore retrievable: remembering the moment when he first saw her at the table, he realized that for a fraction of a second she had been part of a present that was just starting. "When did you come in?" he asked.

"You'd just made eight the hard way, looking like you owned the dice table."

"What do I look like now?" he asked, partly curious, partly because it was a long time since he had maintained a conversation for any distance and he wasn't sure yet how to keep this one going.

The girl smiled, realized the question wasn't a joke, and thought about it, studying Goldberg's face like a gypsy scrutinizing a tea leaf. "You came to the right place—I've been watching men's faces since I was seven years old." She smiled sourly at the memory. "It started as a kind of

11

survival science, trying to figure out what was on my handsome daddy's mind, whether he was going to kill Mommy, close the bedroom door and make love to her, or just disappear. Turned out he was going to just disappear."

She shifted slightly, her green eyes fishing for the place where she would start, withdrawing, darting, suddenly cautious. "You said I might have seen your picture in a thirty-five-year-old newspaper," she said reluctantly. "A big football player thirty-five years ago?"

Goldberg nodded.

"Boola boola," said the girl, who never surrendered her right to be angry. "I once had a boyfriend who ran back footballs for the L.A. Rams. You play pro ball?"

"You've changed the subject," said Goldberg.

She nodded. "Suddenly I don't want to do this anymore. Order me another drink. Hate your nose, love your eyes."

"Like," said Goldberg.

"That's another thing." The girl turned another corner into anger that never seemed very far away. "You're a goddamn pedant. You put an enormous investment into worrying about the wrong things."

"You read that in my face?"

"Forget it. I didn't come here to read faces." She hesitated, smiling as though about to tell him why she had come but thought better of it and went on. "Tell me when you knew the dice were hot."

He shrugged. "I know it every time I pick them up."

"But this time you were right—there had to be a difference."

Goldberg didn't understand why there had to be, but he also knew that, having started, he wanted to go on talking to this girl. He told her about the trumpet call that went from his heart into his arm and how the red mice danced for him, turning the odds against the house, point after point, until he knew there was no way he could lose.

Remembering the play of the game down to the last throw of the dice, he started to recite it for her, apparently without any danger of boredom, for she shared the memory as enthusiastically as she had shared the fact. Midway in the recital, the basic unreliability of his head threatened to take over as he remembered the aggrieved look on the captain's face, falling, the messenger paying for his message with a damaged jaw.

"You need a first name," he said abruptly.

"And you don't?"

"No." He wondered again what it was she wanted from him, sure only that he hadn't figured it out yet and probably never would.

"Call me Barbara." Her grin invited distrust; out of some vanity he did not understand she preferred not to be believed, a dangerous red-haired lady, flaunting her duplicity.

That was all right with Goldberg; what he wanted from her right then was not to have to call her Hall. He stood up, staggering slightly, the handle of the shopping bag threaded through the fingers of his left hand. "I'll tell you what it was like," he said, "it was like an hour and half free-fall. I'm sorry I stopped. It's a son of a bitch being back on earth."

He left her there, waiting to pay the check, half feeling he'd made a bad mistake but hewing to a course he knew was his; Goldberg was too busy paying for his sins to pay for anything else.

He was in bed a half hour later when she knocked on the door. "Nobody ever walked out on me before," she said, neither complaining nor wondering, merely stating a truth.

She pushed her way into the room and started taking off

13

her clothing as matter-of-factly as though they had been undressing in front of each other for twenty years. "You're on a streak," she said. "You think it's over, but I know better—you saved it by stopping when you did." She smiled the crooked grin he was beginning to think of as her trademark. "I'll make a deal with you right now. The minute your luck runs out so will I."

Two

Goldberg sat up in the king-size bed, talking at first with the hesitations of a man speaking a foreign language after six weeks at Berlitz, and then more and more fluently.

Strewn around the room were sixteen books on World War II that Goldberg had been trying unsuccessfully to read.

In the other king-size bed the girl listened. She was a careful listener. Propped up on six pillows, brilliantly naked, she paid attention with her whole body.

Goldberg was edging up on his subject. He was telling her about the Yale game in which his shoulder had been broken although he no longer had any serious interest in the event. If she had smiled the enigmatic smile that was her trademark, he would have stopped, but she was as careful as he was. When Freud's beard popped into his still-unreliable head, he rejected it out of hand, but not before the girl started to move tentatively on her own king-size bed; realizing that he had been staring at her where she was bearded, Goldberg rejected that, too.

Her body had exploded on his sight when she first pulled the white dress over her head, and he was still dazzled whenever he looked at her. She amazed him in every way including the way she made love; there was a solicitude in it that astonished him, for it seemed in no way in keeping with the rest of her personality. When she took off her clothes, she became a Sister of Sexual Mercy. Dressed she was another person whom Goldberg did not understand. He had once made a profession of suspicion and every instinct, every remnant of his training, drove him to speculate about who she was, what she was. While he wondered, he went on talking; he was not sure he could have stopped if he had wanted to, but he did not want to. If he stopped it would mean that conversation was no longer possible; he had to go up, down, out, around, through to the other side; for better or worse, he could no longer stay in the place where he had been.

He talked for an hour and a half, circling around his true subject, or what he thought was his true subject. He left football, which had for a time been a large part of his life, and dealt with girls in the late thirties and early forties. He told her about his first bad girl, who had been rather pleasant, and his first good girl, who had been unnerving. He told her the names of twelve girls he had known in London during the Blitz.

"That was before I was born," she said, the enigmatic smile working but something else going on, too, that Goldberg perceived as disdain.

"I'm giving you my little collection of memories," he said. "It's not polite to smile at the dust."

15

She kept on smiling a couple of seconds longer to prove she was not intimidated, but then she put the smile away in an effort at conciliation that did not seem a regular part of her character. "I'm not smiling," she said meekly.

"Reminiscence interruptus is a cruel and unnatural act," said Goldberg, the flippancy more in his voice than in his head, which was still full of flying bricks and London girls. He made the same kind of effort to focus on Barbara Hall he had made when he was concentrating on the red mice.

"Please go on," she said.

Goldberg wondered about the *please* coming from a woman who did not seem to have had much use or need for it. A body the Greeks dreamed for their goddesses, a monument to desire. The face, bold, intelligent, cynical. Gown by Halston, watch by Piaget, shoes by Gucci, gold by Goldberg—she had to have at least twenty-two thousand dollars in her purse as a result of last night's winning.

Goldberg had had too many problems of various sorts to consider himself irresistible. What had drawn the girl to him? Even she had felt it necessary to supply a reason—the hot streak. Goldberg knew gamblers too well to dismiss the possibility that that was all she wanted, but then he began to consider a series of small signs and signals she had been giving out ever since she entered the room. She had the covert watchfulness of an agent in enemy country—the look thrown over her shoulder down the corridor, the starting and crying out in her sleep, the intensified listening when the doorknob rattled, the way her hand shook when she lit a cigarette.

"You smoke too much," he said.

"I'm glad you brought that to my attention." She sneered at him through a veil of smoke, amber fingered, shaking, strung out.

"Why are you afraid?" he asked.

She tried her cynical smile but didn't quite make it. Her right hand, reaching automatically for a pack of matches, started stripping them onto the bedsheet with a blood-red thumbnail. "Is it as obvious as all that?" she said finally. "I've always prided myself on a poker face."

"Poker is a game of cards," said Goldberg. "You're holding something worse than a busted flush."

"You worried I'm going to get you into trouble?"

Goldberg thought about that for a while: it had never occurred to him. "If you've got a new kind of trouble, I might be able to use it," he said. He watched her face call up new reserves of inscrutability. "Official trouble?" he said.

"About as unofficial as you can get." She half covered herself with the sheet, automatically grasping at any form of concealment that was handy. "That's all I can tell you. If it bothers you, I'll get out."

Goldberg grunted. He considered telling her who he was, or at least who he had been, but he decided that might worry her more than ever. "When it gets too much for me to handle, I'll let you know."

"Just give me a little notice," she said.

He stretched and scratched his head, flexed his right arm, touched the biceps with his fingers, surrounding the question he was about to deliver with casual gestures. "I think I'll take a shower," he announced. "I'm getting hungry. You want to eat in the room or downstairs?"

"Is that the first test?" She was flustered, angry, and at the same time beginning to find her situation, whatever it was, somehow funny. "I've always been very good at tests," she said. "The less I know the better I do at them."

"Sooner or later everything seems funny to you, doesn't

17

it?" said Goldberg, interested. "Just make sure you're not laughing when you should be running."

"Who says I should be running?" She challenged him with jewel-green eyes that moved from mood to mood with a celerity that was itself a disguise.

"Last night you seemed comfortable enough in the casino and later in the restaurant. We've only been separated for fifteen minutes since then, but now you're as jumpy as a cat. Did something happen in the fifteen minutes?"

She shook her head. "Not really."

"Do you want to go downstairs for breakfast?"

"I don't have anything to wear for breakfast."

"Tell me where your clothes are and I'll get them."

The green eyes were changing again; she was not incapable of caution, but it came and went with a frequency that could be dangerous. "You don't want to go where my clothes are," she said.

"Why not?"

"It's too far away." She tried to change the direction of the questioning. "Who are you?" she asked. "Outside of being one-name Goldberg, what do you do for a living?"

"I'm retired," said Goldberg curtly.

"Don't complain about me then—you're not exactly an open book yourself." The challenge was back in the changeable green eyes. "You talked about yourself for an hour and a half, and, as far as I know, nothing's happened to you since 1945. What are you retired from—World War Two?"

"That's a thought," said Goldberg, "although not the right one."

"You're the one that's running," said the girl. Getting out of the other king-size bed, she wrapped the sheet around her like a toga. "Maybe I could wear this down to breakfast," she said, lighting a cigarette with fingers that

18

were no longer trembling. "Look, every once in a while I spook myself. Maybe there's a man I should be running from, but I'm not. Maybe there's a man who should be chasing me, but he's not. At least not yet. If he ever decides to and you're still around, I'll let you know because I'll be needing all the help I can get."

"Didn't your mother ever tell you to be careful about the company you keep?"

"No, Daddy. My mother was no one to talk. She was the one who found my father."

Goldberg wondered what his own daughter would have to say about him, and where she was. The trouble with parenthood was it was too important to be left to amateurs but there were no professionals. He picked up the phone. "I'm ordering breakfast. What would you like?"

What she liked was a trucker's breakfast, which she ate, when it was delivered, dressed in the sheet. She ate it down to the last egg-soaked piece of toast with a relish that did not seem to be even slightly impaired. They breakfasted in silence, two hungry conspirators who had finally found something to do that didn't require suspicion.

When breakfast was over, Barbara Hall started to talk about the boyfriend who ran back footballs for the L.A. Rams. "I was managing a place on Sunset Strip. It was a pretty good deal—I was going to UCLA during the day. The owner was a guy named Harry who thought it was good for business having a college girl on the premises. He'd quit school in the middle of the fifth grade and he put a lot of stock in education. He used to go bankrupt at least once a year. I guess he figured there was something he didn't know he could have found out in college. Anyway one night this guy comes in, Spider Kemp. You ever hear of him?"

Goldberg shook his head.

"Nobody ever heard of him except ten minutes that night he was all over the TV. He'd run back a football fifty-five yards for the L.A. Rams and he was famous. He came in in the middle of a crowd and people asked for his autograph. They'd never asked for it before and they'd never ask for it again. Years later they'd find it written on the back of a menu from the Passionate Poodle, and they'd wonder who the hell Spider Kemp was, but that one night he was a football hero. The house bought him drinks. In all his life Harry never bought anybody a drink, but nobody famous ever came into the Passionate Poodle before. He probably figured higher education was beginning to pay off.

"After a while the Spider Kemp crowd drifted away, but Spider stayed with me, drinking at a table in the corner. He was cooling off fast from one of the shortest fits of glory in history—it couldn't even last out the night. It was as though he could see what was coming and it scared him. I went home with him because I was sorry for him. Whatever you think, I don't generally go home with people—and never because I'm sorry for them. Spider was my only experiment in pity. He'd bounced around the league on special teams—the suicide squad—running back kickoffs, and never quite good enough. He was a little too light, a little too fragile, and he was trying to make up for it by taking crazy chances. That was his style—kill me if you catch me—and generally they caught him.

"I stayed with him about three months and it was like watching a doll that belonged to a careless kid—every week he was a little more chipped and broken. He had to know what was happening, but he wouldn't talk about it. He kept concentrating on that second when he was going to break away again and be all over the television news for another ten minutes. Finally I couldn't stand it anymore

20

and I walked out. He kept coming around for a while, always a little more busted, with that crazy loser's look in his eye, the original Mr. Whistle-in-the-dark. I got out of the Passionate Poodle, I got out of L.A. That was the end of Spider Kemp as far as I was concerned except for seeing him once on a street in New York. He didn't see me. He kept looking up as though he were expecting a football to fall out of the sky into his hands. He'd been All-State at some crazy high school in Texas."

"Do you still live in New York?" asked Goldberg.

"You ask too many questions. I never lived in New York. I was just visiting."

She leaned back in the chair, restoring the toga to the places from which it had fallen away.

"What's wrong?" said Goldberg.

"I hate people who pry."

"You're the one who told me about him."

"Let it go at that. I told you what I wanted you to know. That's all you're entitled to."

"Didn't you ever want to get married?" asked Goldberg.

"Is this a proposal?" One bright eyebrow made a circumflex. She was amused. She was not amused. She was amused again.

"I've been married," said Goldberg.

"Congratulations. So have I."

"My wife said I wasn't very good at marriage."

"Did that hurt your feelings?"

"No. I think it surprised me. I come from a long line of good husbands. It was kind of a family tradition, like wine making or running for the presidency."

"Poor baby," she said. She smiled her secret smile, which was different from her cryptic one; it took longer and seemed more genuine. "When she grows up, my daughter is going to be one of the richest women in America," she said.

"I have a daughter, too," said Goldberg.

Barbara did not want to hear about Goldberg's daughter. The hand that held the cigarette was shaking; whatever went on behind those sea-green eyes was starting to spook her again. "I save every cent I get my hands on. I invest it. I happen to be a shrewd investor."

"Where does all that money come from?" asked Goldberg, knowing now that he was prying and ready to take the risk.

"You'll never know, football player," she promised him, the hands shaking harder than ever.

Three

Goldberg had always mistrusted reunions although at one time in his life he had gone to them conscientiously. Heroes with potbellies, coming together to celebrate the past, could only betray it; better to preserve it intact in memory. The inseparable companions of twenty or thirty years ago were strangers now, seeing in each other's faces only their own death marks. At least new friends reminded you of nothing.

If he hadn't won at the dice table Goldberg wouldn't have gone to this reunion even though he had traveled three thousand miles to attend it. It was listed on the hotel bulletin board between the Podiatry Council and Darling Industries Annual Sales meeting—Company D 2788th Regiment, OSS. The name was as deliberately enigmatic as it had ever been, for it described neither a company nor a regiment and it had never been intended to. Whatever it had been, it was meeting now in the Dragon Room where Goldberg was headed.

Schoyer would be there, the man he had seen at the dice table. For a few seconds that made Goldberg thoughtful; privacy had been his personal foxhole too long for him to abandon it easily now and Schoyer knew more about him than he liked.

The books scattered around his hotel room were a principal reason Goldberg was going, or so he had convinced himself. Although he believed the books had it all wrong, he was determined to test the validity of his own memory against the memories of those who had been there with him. World War II had always seemed to him a different war, now being diminished by footnotes and the endless appetite for novelty; doctors of philosophy in search of clay feet were trampling on the best part of Goldberg's life.

In light of that, whatever Schoyer knew did not seem sufficiently important to keep Goldberg away from the Dragon Room, which was long and green but otherwise had nothing to do with dragons. It had a dais on which Goldberg would not be sitting, and tables set for about two hundred men, most of whom were now struggling for drinks at either of two bars set up on opposite sides of the room. Goldberg was startled to discover that so many people had gotten so old all at once. He had probably never known more than half of them; Company D had been an organizational fiction manufactured out of a series of small

23

detachments that spent most of their time in the field where they had died in surprising numbers. It was not a line of work that allowed much leeway for mistakes, and there had always been plenty of mistakes. As a matter of fact, Goldberg was amazed to find so many survivors.

Goldberg apparently had changed less than the others because several men recognized him instantly, supplying their own names when he still could not remember; even then he had trouble associating the names with the faces: eyeglasses, gray hair, and fat were better disguises than he would have suspected.

Schoyer spotted Goldberg almost the minute he came into the room; he must have been watching for him.

"Hello, there, quarterback," said the man with the steel-wool hair and horn-rimmed glasses; Goldberg would have recognized him anywhere in any disguise. "Somehow I didn't think you would show up," said Schoyer, giving Goldberg a look that promised Goldberg secrets about himself even Goldberg didn't know. At least Schoyer hadn't changed—he was as easy to dislike as ever.

"You're not drinking?" said Schoyer skeptically.

"I've given it up."

"When did that happen?"

"About five minutes ago," said Goldberg.

Schoyer, who had always considered flippancy one of the seven deadly sins, perhaps the deadliest, grinned resentfully. "I saw you winning at the dice table," he said. "Must have been at least a hundred grand."

"You have a romantic imagination, Schoyer."

"What do you mean by that?"

"If the facts don't match your imagination, you make your own facts."

"You telling me I'm a liar?" Schoyer's normally pasty

face took on a touch of dusty rose. "You always were a smart-ass, Goldberg. Maybe that got you into trouble as much as anything else."

Goldberg knew that smart-ass was a recent development, but he wasn't about to tell Schoyer, who liked humility in other people almost as much as he liked secrets, particularly if the other people were Goldberg. For a moment, Goldberg wondered whether Schoyer had found out about the girl; that would really drive him crazy.

Spoons drummed against water glasses as the managers of the reunion tried to get it started. "I had it in mind to warn you," said Schoyer, turning away to find his seat, "but now you can simply go fuck yourself."

Goldberg, who placed no value in Schoyer's warnings, either given or withheld, found his way to table nine where Seaver, now a high-school principal in Wyoming, was wondering for the thousandth time why the girls in Leghorn were the prettiest in Italy. "I don't know whether it's even true anymore," he said sadly. "Have any of you guys ever been back?"

Nobody had.

"Maybe it was never true," somebody suggested.

"It was true all right," said Seaver, remembering. "It had something to do with the water."

Two old warriors at Goldberg's table were exchanging pictures of their grandchildren. Charlie Procter, the shyest man Goldberg had ever known, was studying his fingernails with the intensity of a magician trying to make himself disappear. Charlie had been the jumper ahead of Goldberg the night they landed, through the navigator's misreading of grid coordinates, on the roof of the SS barracks. He and Goldberg were the only two who had lasted out the night.

"Goldberg," said Fred Winkler, "you sly son of a bitch,

you look young enough, you must be wearing makeup."

Before Goldberg could answer, Bill Brombeck, the master of ceremonies, banged his glass with a soup spoon and the evening's ceremony was under way.

The preliminaries went quickly: a few bitter CIA jokes—for, not against, since everybody on the platform was a founding father—some nostalgia, and a handful of statistics on what had happened to the members of Company D. The main business of the evening was giving Tom Marston a Silver Star for something that had happened thirty-four years ago—the screw-up with the partisans outside Milano where so many were killed and everything would have been completely bungled if it hadn't been for Marston. At the time it had all been too secret and too many important people had been at fault for any medal giving, but Jumping Jim hadn't forgotten; he was there in his general's suit and decorations for the bestowal. He had wanted it to be a Congressional Medal of Honor because the stakes had been so big, but somehow he couldn't negotiate it, and he was a little savage about that.

When it came Tom Marston's turn, he trundled to the front of the platform where he gave a graceful little speech, hanging in the hoops that attached his arms to the stainless-steel pipes. He became a little sentimental about the old days when his legs still worked although he didn't mention that, and he called up the names of distant places and even more distant events that had code names like Derringer and Split. Once his eyes brushed against Goldberg with whom he had been quite close and a puzzled frown moved across his face as though he had remembered something that saddened him. Goldberg wondered just what he knew, or thought he knew; Goldberg wasn't important enough for many people to be aware of what had happened to him.

It was then that Goldberg started drinking, Scotch at first and finally, because the Scotch wasn't working, martinis. Goldberg was traveling back to the time when he got all his wrong ideas, or at least confirmed them; it had taken him twenty-eight years to become suspicious of the truths that harbored in the big words like honor, country, fidelity, courage. The larger the word the more closely it demanded inspection; Goldberg was overwhelmed by a sense of the danger of abstract nouns.

He looked over at the table where Schoyer held forth to a group of men who did not seem to want to listen to him. Goldberg, by now drunk enough to do whatever came to mind, said good-bye to his own table and moved to Schoyer's, carrying a chair. When he reached Schoyer's side, he planted the chair and sat on it.

"Schoyer," he said, "you have the air of a man expounding large truths. Expound me a large truth, Schoyer."

"Smart-ass," said Schoyer, easing his chair away from Goldberg.

Goldberg noticed Petrakis, who was somewhat older than the rest of them and had once been rumored to be the world's greatest flute player. Goldberg had always liked him. "You still play the flute, Petrakis?" he asked.

"Only for my own delight," said Petrakis. "It turned out the world has a very limited need. For fifteen years I have owned a seafood restaurant in San Francisco." Petrakis old had a Homeric cast he had lacked when young; then he had been merely large, now there was the dignity of Agamemnon. It would have been very easy to believe that Petrakis was wise as his placid olive eyes moved from Schoyer to Goldberg and back again. "Schoyer tells us you have been cast out by the Secret Service. Is that true, Goldberg?"

Goldberg enjoyed Petrakis, who moved through the

27

earth's thickets and snares with the imperviousness of an early land monster. "That is true, Petrakis," he said gravely. "I was cast out for the unreliability of my head. You can trust Schoyer in that although not in too many things. He was the one who cast me out."

"It was a departmental decision," said Schoyer severely.

Goldberg looked around the faces at the table. He knew them all; except for Schoyer, he had once liked them all, and even Schoyer he had only started to dislike later. It seemed to him he could remember sitting with this same group, years ago, talking.

Goldberg drank some of the martini he had brought along with the chair to Schoyer's table. "Let me tell you when my head got unreliable," he said, surprised at how easily the words came out after all the time they had been bottled up inside him. "For years I was so reliable people set their clocks by me. I was a model citizen, a model father, a model employee. I coached Little League baseball, and voted regularly for the candidate of my choice, who, out of tribute to FDR, was always a Democrat. I believed firmly in the Declaration of Independence, the Constitution of the United States, Thomas Jefferson, Nathan Hale, and Patrick Henry. If I had met Benjamin Franklin, I would have recognized him as my mother. I read regularly *The New York Times,* the *National Geographic,* and anything the Book-of-the-Month Club suggested. I bought a color television set as soon as one was available. I listened to the news on the car radio every morning. In short, I was well informed. If there was a fly in the ointment, it was that I wasn't as successful as everybody had always predicted I would be, but on the other hand, I had a comfortable house in a comfortable suburb, a lovely wife, a handsome, intelligent son, a darling daughter, and a Labrador Retriever whose dam had won best-of-show in Madison Square Garden. It was all as pretty as a picture postcard when along came a war *The New York Times* had trouble explaining to me in a place the *National Geographic* had regularly ignored. At first it didn't seem to have much to do with my affairs—I was too old to enlist, my son was too young, and the rest of my dear ones were exempt by reason of either sex or species."

"Smart-ass," muttered Schoyer.

"Let the man talk," said Petrakis.

"How did I know that it was a war without a beginning, a middle, or an end, and that it would go on forever? One day my son came to me and said he would either enlist or run away to Canada; to just sit things out in college was a cowardly evasion. To the young it is very important to stand up and be counted; it never occurs to them that perhaps no one is counting."

When Schoyer's chair creaked, Goldberg felt the unreasoning anger rise like some deep subterranean force that had just been tapped by a prospector's drill. Putting both hands out to grip the table, he hung on. "What the hell did I know? Perhaps I had two wars confused in my head, or maybe I always marched to the big words without knowing what they meant. I told him about Thomas Jefferson, Nathan Hale, Patrick Henry, and his grandfather, my father, who was gassed at Belleau Wood. I told him about Tom Marston up there on the platform even though he hadn't got his medal yet. Two days later my boy enlisted. Six months later he was in Vietnam flying a helicopter. Six weeks later a man wearing captain's bars came to me and told me my son was dead. I had filled him with pap, shoveled it in the way I'd shoveled in the pablum when he was a baby, and by that fatherly act I killed him." Goldberg released the table's edge and drove both hands down on the plate in front of him with a force that shattered it. Glasses danced and tumbled everywhere.

"Easy," said Petrakis.

"I killed my son," said Goldberg.

"You didn't kill your son," said Petrakis.

"When the Army's messenger gave me the news, I hit him," said Goldberg. "I'm not proud of what I did, but I did not hurt him badly. I have been hurt worse in the name of sport."

"A hairline fracture of the jaw," said Schoyer punctiliously.

"It did not break any teeth?" inquired Petrakis.

"No teeth," said Schoyer, who, after his own fashion, was an honest man.

"That is good," said Petrakis. "The jaw, after all, heals itself. With teeth that is not the case."

"The unprovoked attack on an army officer in the performance of his duty was only one incident," said Schoyer, angered now that he had been so right and was being so widely misunderstood. "The department really had no options."

"He's right, Petrakis," said Goldberg. "I became entirely unreliable. I drank, I gambled, my wife left me, taking our daughter with her to Lima, Ohio, where her family owned a bank. I am not presenting myself as an injured party. I'm just telling you what happened because you were once my friends."

"Old friendships never die," said Petrakis.

"Everything dies, Petrakis." Goldberg looked around curiously at the faces of the men who had been his friends. Carter. Johnston. Percy. Evans. Petrakis. O'Brien. Thomas. Hoffman. Adamson. Secondari. What had happened to them that had changed them so? Petrakis owned a restaurant. Thomas was falling asleep. Secondari looked as though he had been kicked in the belly regularly every day for the past thirty years. "Last night I won a hundred forty-five thousand dollars at the dice table. Maybe that's a sign I should start a new life. Anybody got a recommendation for a new life?"

"In the words of Socrates," said Petrakis, "first you must know thyself."

"In the words of Goethe," said Goldberg, "if I knew myself, I'd run away."

Thomas was asleep. Carter looked embarrassed. O'Brien, who had once studied for the priesthood, tried to remember what he had been taught that might apply to the starting of new lives. "Another thing," said Goldberg, "Schoyer has a warning for me but he refuses to deliver it."

Thomas opened his eyes. Evans forgot his embarrassment even as Secondari forgot that he had been kicked in the belly regularly every day for the past thirty years. They all came alive momentarily as though hearing the sounds of a game they had once been good at.

"Do you care to discuss the warning in front of all of us?" asked Petrakis magisterially.

"No, I don't." Schoyer leaned forward toward Petrakis. "Where the hell did you get that habit of talking like the Pope? You're Petrakis, the flute player—you must have fucked every woman under fifty in Vienna."

"Not every one, Schoyer," said Petrakis, "only those who were interested in baroque music." He bestowed an old man's smile on the memory before turning back to Schoyer. "What makes you so angry, Schoyer? We all owe each other something even if it is something as cheap as a warning."

31

Schoyer thought about that; he was not enjoying the hostility of his former comrades. "If he wasn't such a smartass, I would have told him in the beginning." Leaning forward in the chair, hands locked under his chin, he deliberately settled himself into the manner in which he delivered official reports. "I arrived in Las Vegas about six o'clock yesterday evening. Since I do not particularly like Las Vegas, I went immediately to my room where I took a nap that lasted until one o'clock in the morning. By then I was hungry for the dinner I had missed, so I showered, went downstairs, spent about an hour on dinner, which brought me to two-thirty. By then I wasn't sleepy in the least and started to wander, thinking maybe I would meet some of you, have a drink or two, and then be able to sleep. It turned out you were all in bed, or in hiding. The only one I saw was Goldberg, it had to be Goldberg, I thought. He was standing at the dice table with more chips in front of him than the dealer, and every time he threw the dice the pile got bigger. I don't think Goldberg saw me although he can tell you that better than I can. About three-thirty Goldberg cashed in his winnings and went to the King Arthur Room with a girl in a white dress. Better looking than any of your girls, Petrakis—she was a raving goddamn beauty."

"In this life the most beautiful girls do not always adore baroque music," said Petrakis regretfully. "It is a situation that I hope will be corrected in another, better life." He leaned forward. "By this time you were following Goldberg—is that correct? Had he committed any fresh offenses against the Secret Service? Would you explain that to us?"

Schoyer shrugged. "I had nothing better to do. Perhaps I was curious what a man in as much trouble as Goldberg would do with that kind of money. I calculated it to be at least a hundred thousand dollars—he has told you the exact amount. At any rate, while I was following them at some distance down the hall to the King Arthur Room I noticed a man a few paces behind me. I did not realize yet that he was following Goldberg, but I observed him anyway. He gave me a distinct impression of being from out of town."

"Everybody in Las Vegas is from out of town," said Petrakis.

"Not as far out of town as this guy," said Schoyer. "He was wearing English riding boots."

"At three-thirty in the morning?" said Petrakis.

"You got it," said Schoyer. "Dove-gray riding pants, a gray and white houndstooth tweed jacket, a pearl-gray silk ascot. He had a gun on under the jacket."

"You saw it?"

"Felt it when I bumped into him a little later." Schoyer was becoming impatient with the interruptions. "If you'd shut up for a while, Petrakis, I'll tell this through to the end. Then you can ask any questions you want, and, if I can, I'll answer them. Now where was I?"

"En route to the King Arthur Room," said Petrakis, "Goldberg and his girl ahead of you, the man in the English riding boots a few steps behind you."

"Goldberg and the girl went in. I stayed outside. So did the man in the English riding boots. That was when I really began to observe him. If you remember the position of the King Arthur Room, the door can be watched from the edge of the casino floor. Riding boots and I wound up at adjoining slot machines, watching the entrance to the King Arthur Room. I lost twenty-five dollars in nickels, which is a lot of nickels, before Goldberg came out alone. Riding boots followed him. By then I was more interested in the girl. She came out in about five minutes, went to the desk where she got the number of Goldberg's room, and went up to the room. I followed her down the hall, passed the room after the door had closed. At the other end of the hall, in the cul-de-sac where they keep the ice machine, riding boots was buying ice. If he had followed Goldberg up, as he undoubtedly did, he must have spent ten minutes buying ice."

"Could you describe the man in more precise detail?" asked Petrakis. "By now he may have taken off his riding boots."

Schoyer could describe him and did with considerable satisfaction. "A hair under six feet, couldn't have weighed more than a hundred and fifty-five pounds, very thin but not frail, as though he had been put together with steel wires. Narrow shoulders, small bony head, aquiline nose, prominent cheekbones, blue eyes, platinum-blond hair neatly cut, a little on the long side but not obtrusive. Not much more than thirty years old. My grandfather had a walking stick with a man's head for a handle. This man had a face like that, like it had been carved out of the wood of an ash tree. Everything about him was very hard. When I bumped into him to feel the gun, I felt the muscles of his upper arm. Hard as steel. All bone and muscle, nothing wasted."

"How did he like being bumped?" asked Petrakis.

"I apologized, but he didn't seem to think that was enough. Blood on the floor was more like his idea. Only he had other business. He looked like a guy who always got his priorities straight." Schoyer grinned at Goldberg, showing the gold in his rear teeth. "A pro. I don't think I would want him chasing me."

Four

Goldberg was a little drunk when he left Petrakis, with whom he had spent a half hour after the reunion. Petrakis had invited him to San Francisco, which he recommended as an excellent place for the starting of new lives, pointing out his own conversion, instant and painless, from flutist to restaurateur. Goldberg promised to think about it and he was doing that as he started to cross the edge of the casino in the direction of the elevators. His daughter might be in San Francisco, he thought, idly dropping a coin in a fifty-cent slot. While he had no particular reason for thinking that that was where she had gone, it was one of the places young people ran to, the only American city ever confused with Paradise. He had no idea what he would say to Debbie if he found her—he had never said anything yet that seemed to make any difference—but this time something might work.

Next to Goldberg a woman with a leather-palmed driving glove on her right hand was playing four machines in tandem, moving from one to the other in a clockwork shuffle, the left hand sowing quarters, the right one reaping handles.

Goldberg, who had been standing with one arm upraised throughout the course of his reflections, brought the arm down suddenly, carrying the handle with it. Almost instantly there was the crash of a falling jackpot. For a second the woman was convinced the crash belonged to her and scampered among the machines looking for it. When she realized the jackpot was Goldberg's, she stopped next to him.

"How do you do that?" she demanded suspiciously.

"The secret is not caring too much," explained Goldberg. "It loosens up the arm motion."

"Show me," she said, handing him a quarter and pointing at her nearest machine. Goldberg inserted the quarter, pulled the handle, and turned away. Behind him there was the definitive "klump" of a jackpot. Once more he felt the intoxicating sense of omnipotence that had held him at the dice table, Goldberg the newly invincible, his luck still holding.

The feeling carried him across the casino floor, past the bank of cigarette machines at the entrance to the elevators, up the elevator to the door of his room. When he put the key in the door and turned the lock, the feeling was still with him. It lasted a few seconds longer while he examined the room from the doorway.

The dress was gone, the purse and shoes were gone, the girl was gone. In their place was the confusion of an intense, angry search, mattresses upended, sheets in balls, drawers empty, books out of their jackets. At the center of the confusion, on the aquamarine vinyl couch, sat the man Schoyer had been following, unmistakable although he had changed out of boots and jodhpurs into canary-yellow trousers and a white linen jacket. In his right hand he held the gun Schoyer had detected beneath his armpit; there was a silencer attached to it now.

"Entrez," said the man.

"Isn't that a little pretentious?" asked Goldberg, rocking slightly in the doorway.

"Get your ass in here before I shoot it off," said the man.

"That's better," said Goldberg, closing the door behind him. "A spade is a spade is a spade." Walking a little more unsteadily than was strictly necessary, he advanced into the center of the room, hands hanging loose and relaxed at his sides. He still had the feeling of his luck with him. On the bed table, not far from his left arm, was a heavy crystal ashtray that accurately thrown would make a considerable dent in his visitor's high-boned arrogant head.

"Stop walking, cowboy," said the man on the green couch. "I want to talk to you more than I want to shoot you, but I'll shoot you if it's necessary." On the surface his voice had the nondescript quality of a man who had lived in many places and adapted to all of them, but underneath Goldberg could still hear what he construed as the wah-wah-wah of Nebraska, flat, nasal, like the twanging of a one-string guitar.

"Bet you've spent more than one night in Omaha," said Goldberg, still manufacturing drunkenness.

The eyes were as flat as the voice, an impenetrable metallic blue very close to the color of the gun: they glared a prohibition against any speculation about where he had spent his nights or days. "Keep your betting for the tables," he said. "All you'll lose there is your shirt."

"The money's in the office safe," said Goldberg, bluffing.

"I'm not here for your money, cowboy."

Too bad, thought Goldberg—that would have been simple.

The gun moved a fraction of an inch, finding a point slightly higher on Goldberg's belly. "You come with a name?" asked Goldberg, not quite sure why he was pushing but pushing anyway as he swayed closer to the ashtray.

The man didn't want to mention his name any more than he wanted to talk about Omaha. With that kind of aversion to small talk he'd be a hell of a problem at a party, thought Goldberg. "Colt," said the stranger and promptly fell in love with his own wit. The small pinched knotty face extruded a laugh like gears clashing; the narrow body writhed snakily. "You can call me Mr. Colt, cowboy."

The party's warming up, thought Goldberg. He'll make a little joke, I'll make a little joke, pretty soon we'll be giggling out our most intimate hopes and dreams.

"Where is she?" demanded Mr. Colt, abandoning his laughter as suddenly as he had assumed it. He screwed the gun in the air on a line with Goldberg's belly button.

"Who?" said Goldberg, relieved that the stranger had to ask the question.

"You ever been shot in the balls?" inquired Mr. Colt.

"Kicked, never shot," admitted Goldberg.

"Shot is worse," Mr. Colt assured him, recalling some episode that made the blue metallic eyes glow.

"Las Vegas is full of girls," said Goldberg.

Mr. Colt looked at the gun in his hand as though asking it for advice; it must have advised patience, because he sighed and started again. "You ever thought of putting together a routine, cowboy? You could be pissing away a fortune. Yeah, Las Vegas is full of girls all right, but this one you picked up at the dice table, took to the King Arthur Room, and brought up here. She spent the night, the next day, and part of this night. You remember that girl?"

"The girl in the white dress," said Goldberg.

"You're hot," said Mr. Colt. "Keep it up."

"If you know so much tell me her name," said Goldberg.

"There you go," said Mr. Colt. "What the fuck's this

38

business with names? You writing a telephone book?"

"You her husband by any chance?" asked Goldberg.

The gun twitched once and then held still, rooted in Mr. Colt's lap like a supplementary penis. The eyes crackled with some private joke. "You notice any horns? You drunk fuck. Who would marry a broad like that?"

"If I knew where to find her, I might marry her myself," said Goldberg.

Mr. Colt looked at him in amusement. "You probably would," he said. "When I find her, I'll tell her. It'll be something nice for her to think about." He wiggled the gun. "She'll need something nice to think about."

"What the hell did she ever do to you?" asked Goldberg.

"Purely a matter of business," said Mr. Colt. Reminding himself of that seemed to calm him down. "Business makes the world go 'round," he said, returning to the manner that had made such a big impression on Schoyer, crisp, contained, as efficient as a switchblade. Canary-yellow pants. White linen jacket. Pale yellow sport shirt. A .38-caliber Colt with a silencer on it growing out of his lap. "What's your line of work, cowboy?"

"I'm retired."

"You're too young to retire."

"Early retirement. There's a big rage for it these days."

"What did you retire from?"

Goldberg suspected that the truth might not advance his case with Mr. Colt. "I was in the car business in Des Moines."

"What kind of cars?"

"Buicks."

"Shitty cars," said Mr. Colt. "People used to paint lemons on them."

"That was only one year," objected Goldberg. "And

39

only one model, the Special. Hell, that was a long time ago. Except for you everyone's forgotten about it."

"What did you talk about?"

"In the car business?"

"In bed, you schmuck. Don't tell me you spent forty-eight hours saying goo-goo and kitchy-kitchy. People talk in bed, they talk their fucking heads off. Half the secrets in the history of the world were given away in bed."

"She said she studied sociology at UCLA."

"Who cares?" said Mr. Colt. "What else did you talk about?"

"I asked her who was chasing her."

Goldberg had Mr. Colt's attention now. He pointed the gun after which he had named himself in the direction of Goldberg's stomach and moved his head in a series of quick confirmatory stabs. "What makes you think somebody was chasing her?"

"She was jumpy as a bedbug."

"Bad conscience," said Mr. Colt.

"More than that, she was scared."

"She had reason," said Mr. Colt with satisfaction. "Did she tell you the reason?"

"She's a close-mouthed lady."

"Totally untrustworthy," said Mr. Colt. "I could tell you stories about her would make your hair stand on end." Mr. Colt relaxed behind his gun, which still pointed at Goldberg's belly. He seemed to have made a deliberate decision to relax. He had also decided to be casual and friendly. He was about as casual and friendly as a king cobra sliding across a lawn in Larchmont. "Take my advice, if you ever see her again, turn and run."

This change of pace was making Goldberg uneasy. Although he was still farther from the ashtray than he would have cared to be, he started leaning toward it inconspicuously.

"You got a clean suitcase," said Mr. Colt, still engrossed in his own joviality, "cleanest suitcase I ever saw. It could belong to absolutely anybody. You got about as much identification as a newborn baby."

It was at that moment Goldberg chose to make his move, but even as he made it he knew he was too late and too far. The gun was rising and when it reached the top of its rise it made a sound softer than the popping of a champagne cork.

Goldberg did not know where he had been hit, but even as he was falling he remembered what the girl had said: she would leave him when his luck ran out. It was running out all over the floor.

Five

The phone was busy, then it wasn't busy, but no one answered. The bell was now in Goldberg's head; even when Petrakis finally picked up the phone the bell wouldn't stop ringing.

"Shot," mumbled Goldberg. "In the head." Suddenly he was embarrassed. "I don't think it's bad but it's bloody," he said apologetically.

It was the note of apology that made Petrakis listen.

"You," he said. "All night it's been childishness. What is it with you, Goldberg?"

"What do I have to do to convince you I'm shot?" complained Goldberg. "Bleed into your ear?"

"*Coraggio,*" said Petrakis, making up his mind. "What's your room number?"

Goldberg gave it to him.

Three minutes later Petrakis came through the door, big and calm as a stuffed moose. "I called Doc Harris," he said, looking at the blood on the floor and the towel around Goldberg's head.

Goldberg swayed like a drunk.

"Lie down," said Petrakis.

"I'm looking for something," said Goldberg.

"Sit down," said Petrakis.

Goldberg shrugged and sat down. "It's gone," he said. "I don't have to look."

"You mean you kept it here?" said Petrakis, olive eyes darkening as he realized what Goldberg was looking for. One hand went to the long silver horn of his mustache, which he fingered like a hair flute. "Didn't you ever hear of a hotel safe?"

The bell in Goldberg's head had started to ring again. "Get me a fresh towel," he said, trying to change the subject, but Petrakis wouldn't quit.

"What the hell were you thinking of?"

Goldberg pondered. No answer, no towel. "It was a highly professional hiding job," he said.

"One hundred and forty-five thousand dollars?" said Petrakis. "Mr. Mosler makes the only professional hiding places for that kind of money."

He brought Goldberg a fresh towel, but he still wanted an answer he hadn't gotten. "Freud said there are no accidents," announced Petrakis.

Putting a little tuck in the fresh towel, Goldberg decided that the most he wanted from life right now was to shut Petrakis up. "You are saying I wanted to lose the money?"

"Ahhh," said Petrakis gloomily, "self-knowledge is the beginning of wisdom."

"You are obviously wise, Petrakis. What was the peculiar bit of self-knowledge that set you on the road?"

"I discovered that the Bank of America and I were not natural enemies."

Goldberg shrugged. "I was on a winning streak, Petrakis. The feeling is better than anything you can buy over the counter, or from the world's fanciest pusher. You can get away with anything when you're hot."

"Do you have anything left?"

"Three thousand dollars. It's in my pocket. You want to count it?"

"You are insane," said Petrakis, still playing a tune on his mustache. "Even a Goldberg should have a better explanation than that."

"I'll work on it," said Goldberg. "Meanwhile, I need another towel."

There was a knock on the door. It was Harris, wearing a baby-blue leisure suit and carrying an Adidas bag. A short man who bounced as though he resented gravity, he ran a big hospital in Boston, but his thoughts were more and more of tennis.

He bounced across the room toward Goldberg, stripped away the towel, and whistled.

"Bad?" said Petrakis.

"Son of a bitch's got a head like a block of granite," said Harris.

"What about the blood?" asked Petrakis.

"A thirteen-year-old virgin loses more every month," Harris assured him. He grabbed Goldberg's arm, dabbed it with alcohol, and stabbed him with a hypodermic needle. "Roll over," he said. "Next one's in your ass."

Goldberg felt the coldness of alcohol again and a second deeper stab. Blood trickled onto the pillow in front of his eyes.

Harris pulled a box of Kotex from his bag. "Compliments of a friend," he said, beginning to clean out the wound.

When he was done, he taped a fresh supply of Kotex to one side of Goldberg's head. "Anybody else would be due for one mother of a headache. If it bothers you, try Scotch. See your regular physician—and don't mention my name. Tell him you fell down drunk and opened your head on a bedpost."

"I should tell you," said Goldberg.

"Don't tell me anything," said Harris, starting to bounce toward the door.

"Thanks," said Goldberg.

Harris turned, his round, muscular, blue-eyed face as impersonal as the front of a hospital. "I don't know who shot you or why, but you're too old for that. Grow up, Goldberg. The rest of us are grandfathers."

And he was gone, Adidas bag flying behind him.

Petrakis started to laugh. It was a three-part laugh, stifled at first, then trickling out of his lips in a series of whinnies, and finally erupting into an Olympian boom. Petrakis, who had been only nominally Greek in his youth, was now deriving himself from Homer.

"Are you a grandfather, Petrakis?" asked Goldberg.

Petrakis shrugged his shoulders. "There is always that possibility," he said. "As far as formal arrangements are concerned, I married two years ago a Greek-born girl, young, lovely, of an excellent family. I will have to wait to become a grandfather."

"Son of a bitch," said Goldberg, "I don't know whether I'm dying, or being born again." He raised one hand in a salute to the Kotex on his head. "I don't think I'm dying."

Petrakis sat down in the yellow and white–flowered armchair. "Rebirth is a very painful process," he said. "Come to San Francisco. It is a fine place to be reborn. I will teach you the restaurant business."

Goldberg shook his battered head carefully. "I don't think so, Petrakis. I'm not ready for the restaurant business, but I'll remember the offer."

"You are going after the girl?"

"She took my money."

"How do you know the man didn't take it?"

"I'm not sure, but I don't think so," said Goldberg. "I seem to remember having the feeling that it was gone when I entered the room."

"If you are so lucky, win some more," said Petrakis.

"I have to know why she stole from me," said Goldberg stubbornly.

"You are in love with a girl you found at a dice table?" Petrakis's eyebrows were smaller versions of his mustache—bushy, gray, horned. They twitched a message of incredulity. "It is fine to be born again, Goldberg. But must you be reborn so young?"

"Maybe that's the only way," said Goldberg. "The least I can do is find her and ask her why. If I don't like the answer, I will take back the money."

"I will guarantee a loan with the Bank of America," said Petrakis. "You will have your own restaurant. San Francisco is full of beautiful, sexually frustrated young women. You can be born again three or four times a week. Even five if that is your inclination."

Goldberg's head was now buried in the pillow that rose

45

around his ears and muffled them in foam rubber.

"Goldberg," said Petrakis in the distance, "do you hear me?" But Goldberg did not answer because he did not know. It was a good question.

Six

The airport slot machines have a different music.

In the casinos jackpots drop like thunder; at the airport they give a miserly, tinny ring. Money was not meant to leave Las Vegas except in armored cars, thought Goldberg, lingering in the airport lounge, dazzled by the light of the desert that poured upward from the ground, flooded from the sky, ricocheted from aluminum wings.

He had tried the ticket agents at every counter with descriptions of Barbara Hall and Mr. Colt, but nobody had seen either one of them. To tell the truth, they hardly saw Goldberg standing in front of them; all gamblers look alike in Las Vegas.

Was he in love with the girl, or did he simply want his money?

It would have been easier to believe he simply wanted his money.

But something had happened between them in the hotel room that Goldberg could not account for.

The Romans explained love's surprise by blaming it on

Cupid; to Goldberg it was more like falling off a curb: you had never expected to, but there you were. It seemed unreasonable that he could love her because she had loved his winning streak. Perhaps it was just that he had met her at the moment when he was being born again, an imprinting from which he would never be free.

Sauntering past the cocktail lounge, Goldberg saw the Buick dealer's wife at the bar, drinking and staring. As he hesitated, her stare met his. He went into the bar.

"Have a drink, big shooter," she said in the high-pitched jeering voice Goldberg remembered from the dice table; it turned even an invitation into a kind of argument.

Sliding in beside her, he ordered a vodka martini.

"What've you been doing to your head?" she asked.

"Opened it on a bedpost," explained Goldberg.

"I'll bet." She studied the bandage as though she knew something about bandages. "I'm Fran Castelli," she said finally, offering her hand.

"Goldberg," said Goldberg, taking the hand.

"You remember me?" she asked with that same jeering note, a woman who was never sure anybody remembered her and protected against insults by doing the insulting first.

"Of course. The dice table. The Buick dealer's wife."

"Ex-wife."

"Join the club," said Goldberg, "I'm divorced myself."

That seemed to give Fran Castelli a moment's cheer, but the cheer didn't last. "Walk out on her for some twenty-six-year-old popsicle?" she asked, the lined vinegary face defiant under the false blond hair. Her arms and shoulders were surprisingly youthful, fresh and round and tan; all the bitterness of her body had flowed to her face.

"She walked out on me," said Goldberg. "Her popsicle wore pants, a beard, weighed two hundred pounds, and an-

47

swered to the name of Ed. Had his own insurance company."

"She must be a good-looking woman."

"I always thought so."

"You want to talk about it?" The Buick dealer's wife ordered another Scotch sour. She looked at her watch and settled expectantly onto the bar stool.

He'd better talk about it, thought Goldberg. It would be safer to postpone what he wanted to talk about until after the next Scotch sour.

He found it easy to give away memories of his wife; he gave them away anywhere, in bars, on busses, in the street to perfect strangers.

"It was a storybook romance," he said. "I was a war hero. She was a homecoming queen."

"Which war?" demanded the Buick dealer's wife surprisingly.

"WW Two," said Goldberg.

"You don't look old enough," said the Buick dealer's wife.

"I was a mere baby," said Goldberg. "Wars are usually fought by babies," he added and stopped himself; that was enough of that. "We were married for twenty-four years. It was a kind of progressive misunderstanding. I had no life strategy—I just went along from day to day doing what I thought was expected of me. It turned out later what she expected of me was to be a great man. She thought we looked like JFK and Jackie. If we did, that was the end of the resemblance. I realize now that our children were raised in an atmosphere of disappointment—hers really, not mine. I thought everything was fine. When she left, she said I must be a man's man—I certainly wasn't a woman's. She said she was giving me back to the boys."

"You're not a fag, are you?" asked the Buick dealer's wife suspiciously.

"I don't think that's what she meant," said Goldberg.

"Sounds like a real bitch."

"In all fairness, I should point out she would probably tell the story differently."

"You ran around?"

"I was one of the fifty-one percent of American husbands who are faithful to their wives," Goldberg assured her.

"Son of a bitch," said Fran. "I sure wound up with the wrong forty-nine percent."

Goldberg looked into the bottom of his glass, occupied now only by ice and a sliver of lemon. He knew she was going to tell him and he knew he had to listen. People now exchange divorce stories the way they once exchanged war stories, he thought. Maybe someday there would be reunions—the Veterans of '78, or they could organize by law offices, or county court systems, and exchange reminiscences of combat in the courts.

"Listen to this," she said excitedly, "that son of a bitch cheated on me on my honeymoon."

"How did you find that out?"

"Listen." She looked at her watch. "I don't really have to catch that plane. What are you doing for the next twenty-four hours?"

"Doctor's orders," said Goldberg, pointing defensively at his head.

"Listen." A diminutive tear rolled out of one red-rimmed eye. "I don't know what's happened to men," she said to her drink. "It's the new American disease."

Goldberg looked at his own watch, wishing he had not seen the tear; pity was more than he had bargained for. "It'll work out," he said.

"The hell it will." Fran Castelli shook away her single tear and returned to what she had been before. "You came in after me—I didn't send for you. What do you want?"

Goldberg wasn't sure what he wanted. "There was a girl in a white dress at the dice table."

"There sure was." Fran Castelli remembered the girl in the white dress without pleasure. One hand went automatically to the bridge of her nose in a gesture of concealment that Goldberg suspected had been with her since childhood.

"A woman would notice things a man wouldn't," said Goldberg.

"And vice versa I'm sure." She signaled to the bartender for another drink. "What makes you so interested?"

"I'm conducting an investigation," said Goldberg, bending toward her and whispering.

"For whom," asked Fran Castelli, sarcastically, "the Department of Public Works?"

"Keep your voice down," whispered Goldberg urgently. "I don't like the looks of that guy at the end of the bar."

Looking down the bar at the potbellied stranger in the cowboy hat, she was impressed in spite of herself.

"What the hell did you expect me to notice?" she whispered back. "That dress must've cost somebody a thousand dollars. She poured out chips like they were water. What did you expect me to notice?"

"Keep going. You're doing fine."

"She was the best-looking woman in the casino, but she didn't care."

"What do you mean by that?"

Fran Castelli shrugged. "I don't know. She wasn't on the make. A couple of high rollers tried to pick her up, but she couldn't've cared less. Something else was on her mind."

"Did she talk to anybody?"

"I told you she wasn't interested." The Buick dealer's wife hesitated. "One guy. It wasn't much—hello and a wave. A tall skinny guy."

Colt, thought Goldberg.

It wasn't Colt.

"Wore a tux like maybe he worked in the casino. Looked like John Carradine. You could've cut paper on his jaw-bone."

"Just hello and a wave?"

"That's all I saw." Fran Castelli was looking at her watch again. "This is your last chance," she said. "It's up and away for old Fran."

"I'm really sorry," said Goldberg, touching his bandage apologetically.

Seven

The man who looked like John Carradine drifted through the casino like a swimmer treading water, lingering in place, then carried slowly forward by an invisible current that swirled him relentlessly back and forth across the casino floor in a series of crisscrosses so leisurely they seemed to have neither pattern nor purpose.

His name was Davis. He had been drifting this way for nearly nine years and he was totally bored. The soles of his feet were bored with the feeling of the carpet. The fingers that hung out of the tuxedo sleeves were bored with each other. Boredom glazed his eyes, coated his tongue, dulled his nostrils, but nothing happened on the casino floor without his noticing it. He was a hired watcher, a professional spotter, a detector of every trick, device, or sleight of hand ever devised to cheat at gambling.

His qualifications were extraordinary: before he lost his nerve, he was the Michelangelo of card mechanics, the cheater's cheater, genius of his trade. Now he lived inside his boredom as though it were a high-collared overcoat from which he spied with the contempt of a connoisseur on the shabby shifts and dodges of amateurs.

Goldberg tracked him for an hour until his shift was up and then slid in beside him at the coffee-shop counter.

The thin man ate with the intense concentration of absolute need. Without the five lumps of sugar in the coffee you had the feeling he might have died before he got to the sweet rolls, the fried eggs, the bacon and home-fried potatoes, and buttered toast. The lantern jaw worked, the teeth ground, the tongue licked—it was survival eating, requiring all his attention and energy. The dark, nearly black eyes lurked in their deep sockets, all watching suspended, as though they, too, were devoted utterly to this intaking of nourishment. It was not until the final moments of swabbing the plate with the last triangle of toast that the lurking eyes picked up Goldberg on the adjoining stool and began to notice him.

Goldberg let him get used to the idea of his presence before he started to talk. "Slow night," said Goldberg.

The thin man sighed, whether for the food gone or the conversation coming, it was not quite clear.

"Mr. Goldberg," he said.

"You know my name."

The thin man sighed again. His eyes had come back to the exterior world, restored by eggs, sausage, and sugar, and they watched Goldberg all at once, the big feet under the counter, the big hands on it, challenging him to do something the thin man could not detect. "You're a famous man, Mr. Goldberg," he said, deep voiced and thrifty with his words. "Around here at least. For a week at least."

"You saw me win," said Goldberg.

The thin man smiled as thriftily as he spoke.

"I'd like to buy you a drink," said Goldberg.

"Why?" asked the thin man.

"I'm trying to find a girl."

"Management doesn't like me to drink with gamblers."

"Does that bother you?"

"No," said the thin man who had lost his nerve but not all of it. "I don't drink. Why do you need this girl so badly?"

"It's a personal matter."

The thin man smiled his thin smile.

"Somebody is trying to kill her," said Goldberg. "She should be warned."

There had been a time when people tried to kill this man; he lost a degree of his professional indifference.

"I think she's a friend of yours," said Goldberg.

Davis looked thoughtfully at the agile fingers because of which people had once sought to kill him; for a second he could have gone either way, then he made up his mind. "What's it worth to you?" he asked. "My time is valuable."

"A hundred bucks."

"Two hundred."

"Two hundred," agreed Goldberg.

"I have to get these duds off," said the thin man. "I'll meet you in fifteen minutes at the Diamond Slipper."

The Diamond Slipper was a cab ride away down the

53

Strip. Goldberg was waiting for the thin man when he showed up in blue slacks and a yellow knitted sport shirt that showed every bump, knob, and nodule in his bony torso.

Sitting down at the table the thin man ordered a double Johnnie Walker Black without bothering to explain his retreat from abstinence.

"Who's this friend of mine?" he asked after a giant swallow that sent the Adam's apple bobbing in his throat like an escaped balloon.

Goldberg described the girl in the white dress who had smiled at and greeted Davis during the winning streak.

There was a moment of light in the dark eyes. "That one?" said the thin man. "Somebody wants to kill her?"

He did not seem entirely surprised.

"I've watched her for about a year," he said, thinking about that year all over again, wandering through it for hints and signs he might have missed the first time. He shook his head. He drank some Black Label. He shook his head again. "She was off schedule your night. Saturday night was when she came. I remember the first time, last April. She came in about nine o'clock, bought twenty thousand dollars worth of chips for cash, spent the next couple of hours losing them, quit, cashed in the two thousand in chips she had left. Lady, I said to myself, that's the last we see of you for a good long time. I was wrong. Next Saturday there she was again. Same routine. Twenty thousand worth of chips, lost eighteen, cashed in two. Two losing weekends back to back and she didn't bat an eyelash." The Adam's apple bobbed. The nearly black eyes sparkled wistfully. The thin man's fingers tilted against each other on the table as though hungry for a cold deck. "This used to be a *place*," he said wistfully. "Stakes would blow your

54

mind. Now it's a goddamn A&P, ribbon clerks betting the grocery money. This chick was a diamond in a dime store." His nostrils spread reminiscently. "She even smelled different." He shook his head like a tolling bell. "The way this country is going pretty soon there won't be anything left—they're even running out of gas."

"Every Saturday night," said Goldberg, "twenty thou a shot?"

"You got it," said Davis. "Three months of that and then it went up to forty." Even the memory was enough to peel away the boredom that normally covered him like a crust. "I would have worried about her, but I never saw a broad wanted worrying less. When she held the dice, it was a sight to see—she was like a queen in charge of the world."

"You got any idea where the money came from?"

The thin man scowled; he seemed to resent having his memory either interrupted or challenged. "Even at twenty thousand a pop she would be losing over a million a year. And she only stayed at twenty for three months. No, I don't know where the money came from." He shook his head and sighed. "You don't ask where money comes from in Vegas. There are some questions that could be dangerous to your health. Besides, who cares as long as it's there? You wouldn't ask Niagara Falls where the water comes from, would you?"

"Was there ever anybody with her?"

"She was purely alone. Plenty of guys went after her, but she was in town to gamble. She might as well have been a nun for all the care she gave the guys."

Davis was pleased. So was Goldberg. They were like two elderly uncles celebrating the chastity of a niece.

"It was funny," said Davis. "You know what a gambler is like when he digs himself deeper and deeper into a losing streak. It's like running into a tunnel that goes no way but down. Something's going to change. Something's gotta change. But it doesn't change and when you can't stand it any longer you'll bet the Empire State Building knows how to waltz if the odds are good enough. A guy on a losing streak should carry a bell like a leper—he's dangerous to everybody. Not this lady. She lost money like she was spreading confetti at a wedding. She was happy. I never saw anybody have such a good time at the dice table."

Goldberg felt better about the disappearance of his winnings; confetti was devoid of emotional significance. "She never won?" he said.

"She never left soon enough," said the thin man. "She wasn't the kind to quit on a party." He rolled a coaster between his magician's fingers. "Maybe she won somewhere else. It's hard to believe the way she played."

"What the hell?" said Goldberg. "She gambled other places?"

"Does the night have stars?" asked the thin man of his fingers. "There are seven nights in the week—and if you get up early enough there are the days, too."

"She said she gambled other places?"

"She didn't say much." The thin man shrugged. "My owners got no prejudice against losers as long as they pay. It wasn't my business to find out where else she gambled." The coaster danced among his fingers. "There were nights I saw her out on the Strip. This car she drove, a yellow Ferrari, was hard to miss, especially with her in it."

"She didn't live in town?"

"If she did she sure kept it a secret. And this is a town it's not easy to keep secrets in. She was in and out, in and out. There's a lot of places in the United States to gamble. I never figured she gave us all her trade."

Goldberg's hundred forty-five thousand was beginning to

sound like pin money; he wondered why she had bothered to take it.

"You never saw her talk to anybody else?"

"Sometimes she ordered a drink. She'd say thanks to a dealer when she tipped him."

"That was all?"

"Probably she talked to me more than she talked to anybody else—and that was practically nothing. Hello. Goodbye. How you feeling? It was mostly the way she looked and smiled and played—it was good to watch."

When the thin man frowned, the bite of the lines into his face was alarming; you thought he might be doing himself some permanent damage. "There was once," he said. "In over a year there was once. A black woman came into the casino. You don't see too many black people in the casino—and even if you did you'd remember this one. She was the biggest woman I ever saw. The way she walked around staring in faces you knew she was looking for somebody. When she got to the dice table, she stopped staring because she'd found what she wanted. For a couple of seconds it looked like the girl was in trouble, then she settled down and it was over. The black woman took her arm and they walked away together. It still looked like some kind of trouble, but now it was the kind of trouble that was nobody's business but her own."

"You know the black woman's name?"

"I heard the girl call her Martha."

Davis hesitated, reluctant now to reveal the extent of his own involvement. Uninvolvement was his natural state; involvement was a violation of some internal principle that he found embarrassing. "It was late," he said. "The black woman checked into the hotel. I got her name from the desk clerk. It was Martha Weir."

Eight

Goldberg had grown careful with his luck, not so much doubting it as hoarding it.

He won eight hundred at blackjack; then, satisfied that the cards were falling his way, added another six hundred before driving down Interstate 15 toward the Los Angeles Freeway. In his pocket he had Martha Weir's address, which he had bought from a desk clerk for twenty dollars.

He was on the outskirts of Los Angeles when he remembered Gardena and felt his right foot slacken on the gas pedal. Gardena was where they had the poker palaces—a city of small homes, small businesses, straight streets, and the sweet rustle of cards on the evening breeze. When the state legislature decided poker was a game of skill rather than chance and no more illegal than ice skating, Gardena recognized the opportunity and grabbed it. With six public cardrooms working night and day every day except Christmas, Gardena was the draw-poker capital of the world. While it was no Las Vegas, it was only fifteen miles south of downtown L.A. Suddenly Goldberg was headed there as though the Avis Ford had a mind of its own.

Around nine o'clock in the evening he pulled into a large parking lot next to a cinderblock rectangle that announced its business with a neon arrow in perpetual motion. He got

58

out of the Ford and walked past rows of personalized license plates that were their own announcements, a kind of gambler's dictionary. ACES, BETCHA, RAISE, BLUFF.

The sharks were in town tonight, thought Goldberg, looking for the smell of blood. He felt the stiffness disappear from his lower back into the thin night air and at the center of his chest he felt the excitement that meant the winning streak was getting ready to go.

He went past a wooden sign, into the interior of the building, past the guard table, toward the enormous *U*-shaped rail that seemed for one confused moment to be the purpose of the whole operation. Goldberg's side of the rail was the spectator's side, but there were so many spectators and they were so busy they were a game in themselves. Beyond the rail stood the poker tables under clouds of smoke that hung in laminations, fresh curly smoke at the bottom, stale early-morning smoke at the top.

Behind Goldberg in the direction away from the rail there was an enormous blackboard coded with paint numbers and initials in chalk. The man next to Goldberg on the rail was small and round and hairless except for eyebrows like twin mustaches. He was amiable enough, but in no hurry to start a conversation; he had the air of a man with not much to do and a lot of time to do it in, and he was trying to spread that little as far as it would go. "Stranger here?" he said finally.

"Yes," said Goldberg.

"Didn't really have to ask," said the man. "Just being polite. I could tell you everybody here who's been here before." He looked around the room as though he had it in mind to start the telling, but something in Goldberg made him stop.

"Name's Eames," he said, putting out his hand, "same

59

name as the chair, rhymes with screams. First name Harry, Harry Eames."

"Goldberg," said Goldberg.

"First name?" said Harry Eames.

"No," said Goldberg.

Harry Eames thought that over. "I'm seventy-two years old," he said as though it was important for Goldberg to know.

"You don't look it," said Goldberg, because he was expected to.

Harry conceded the point with a shrug that was as leisurely as everything else about him. "Everybody says that. I'm a retired poker player. What's your line?"

"I gamble," said Goldberg.

"Thought so." Eames was pleased with himself. "I can spot a pro from fifty feet away just the way he walks into a room. Matter of fact, now I think of it I seen you around, Vegas, Reno, Tahoe, somewhere."

"I doubt it. I've just got one of those faces everybody thinks he's seen before. But I'm new in Gardena. How do I get a table?"

Eames pointed a strong stubby forefinger at the blackboard behind them. "You get the boardman to put down your initials." He looked around the playing field. "No seats now at any table you'd want to play at. You see everything here's set by law. This side's all scared money, one dollar and two, like that. Drive you crazy. High stakes are all in back, up to one hundred and two hundred. You want some action put yourself down for table twenty-seven. Doc Giordano leaves at ten-thirty like clockwork, or his old lady's going to come and get him. She used to be his nurse, pretty girl, turned mean as a snake the minute he put on the ring."

"Ten-thirty's an hour and a half," objected Goldberg.

"The restaurant ain't bad," said Harry Eames. "You could buy me dinner. Or I could buy you dinner," he added defensively. "I've got a book on every regular poker player in Gardena. It would be worth your while. It takes a lifetime to build a book like that. I'll tell you what every twitch means, the players at table twenty-seven. Like what it means when Jake Willoughby turns that big gold ring on his left hand. Jake don't know he does it, but I know."

"Sure." Goldberg looked down into the faded blue eyes of the anxious ex-pro, wondering how good he was before he got anxious. "Old age is a shipwreck," was what De Gaulle said before he got there himself, and he'd always had the words whatever else he had. "Where's the restaurant?" asked Goldberg, feeling the bugling in his chest subside and wondering whether it had gone for the night. Golden years, shit, thought Goldberg, taking the old poker player by the elbow.

Eames started to lead Goldberg along the right side of the rail, pausing to nudge him in the ribs and point at a skinny man trying to pass as an accountant. "Local juiceman," said Eames, "shylock, loan shark. Two years ago he stopped seeing me like all of a sudden I'd gone invisible. Probably was the best thing ever happened to me. If the juice don't get you, the plagues will, like it says in the Bible, boils and bumps and broken legs. Bet you've never known what it's like to be invisible."

"Don't bet too much," said Goldberg. "How's the food?"

"You like California food you'll like the food here. No booze though. This is a hometown place and they like to keep it hometown. Poker without sin is the aim of the city fathers. But you could go outside and throw a rock blindfold and never miss a bar. You thirsty?"

"It'll hold."

Goldberg followed Eames into the restaurant, a modest room with a plastic sheen and hometown girls waiting tables. It was, as Eames had promised, conscientiously respectable.

"They got a TV room, too," said Eames after he had placed his order. "It's a regular home away from home. Personally I prefer a slight flavor of sin, it kind of puts an edge on life even if you don't do anything but watch. You sure you don't want a drink? I got a little bourbon in my hip pocket could kinda sneak into your water glass without no trouble at all."

While they sipped bourbon, Eames started to deliver his book on table twenty-seven. "Doc Giordano, I won't bother with him because you're going to be taking his place. Generally he feeds the game, he's a real contributor. They tell me he's the biggest gynecologist in Beverly Hills. Those Beverly Hills ladies must be having some kind of problem because he carries a roll would choke horses. Shame you're going to miss him. For a real poker player he's like a magic bank, you don't have to make deposits only withdrawals. When he leaves, a Hail Mary goes around the table he lasts out another night on the freeway."

A neon-blue leisure suit came to the door of the restaurant and the man inside it surveyed that modest room as though it concealed something he wanted badly. He found what he wanted and headed for it. It was the table next to Goldberg. He sat down at it as though he had just taken it by storm.

Although the leisure suit was meant to hang loosely, there was no hang to it at all; instead it was swollen with muscle that had been developed lifting weights or punching something heavy, maybe bags, probably people. The face that went with the muscle was not so much emotionless as incapable of emotion, broad cheekbones, sunken eyes, a red beefy forehead under close-cropped, pale yellow hair. He was about twenty-six, twenty-seven, somewhere around there. He put his hands down on the table like a pair of plates and examined Goldberg as though he was thinking of having him for dinner.

"Something wrong?" said Eames.

"You know the guy at the next table, the blue suit staring at us?"

Harry Eames shifted his eyes from Goldberg to the stranger and back again. "Never seen him before," he said with a slight shiver. "Never want to see him again. He a friend of yours?"

"Doesn't look like he's ever been a friend to anybody," said Goldberg.

"Jesus," said Eames, "you owe some people money?"

Goldberg laughed. "Don't worry your head, Harry. Whatever he wants, he wants it from me. Finish your steak."

Eames, who had been working on the T-bone with relish, seemed to have lost his taste for it. "What are you going to do?" he asked.

"I'm not going to do anything. He's going to do whatever it is he's got in mind, and then I'll know what I'm going to do."

"Jesus," said Harry Eames.

"Tell me more about the table," said Goldberg. "Tell me about the guy who turns the big gold ring."

"That's Jake Willoughby." Harry Eames put down his knife and fork. It was easier to discourage him from eating than from talking. "More than anybody else he's the guy you've got to watch. You'll know him right away, big guy in

63

a five hundred-dollar suit and a big gold ring, serpents and diamonds. He's earned his living playing poker for twenty years and it's been a nice living, easy six figures. With no cut for Uncle Sam that's still pretty good money. He's a real strong player, he don't get tired and he don't get rattled. The only thing he's got is this funny little business with the ring." Harry paused, giving his insight room to breathe and gather admiration. "When he's about to bluff, he turns the ring. Just once. It's no big deal, you gotta watch for it. One little turn of the ring and you know he's playing cards he don't hold." Harry looked at Goldberg to make sure he appreciated the value of the gift being bestowed. "Not too many people coulda noticed that, or old Jake would never have stayed in six figures all these years. But, like I told you, I got the book on everybody. When I was going good, there wasn't much I missed."

Goldberg thought about Harry's book while the old man sneaked some more bourbon into the two water glasses. "There are people who see things," Goldberg said finally, "and there are people who don't. You've got the gift, Harry."

The statement seemed a little grand to Goldberg after he had made it, and he wondered whether he was getting drunk, but the old man didn't find it in the least too grand. He ran one hand across his eyebrows, combing them en route. He was very pleased.

"You've spent a lot of time in Vegas, Harry. I want you to think back. Did you ever see a girl in a white dress? The most beautiful girl you've ever seen?"

"Las Vegas is full of beautiful girls," said Harry. "Next to the gambling it's what the place is about."

"This one's nearly as tall as I am."

"Showgirls run big," said Harry Eames. "There's something about tall beautiful girls that encourages a gambler's natural ambition. What's so special about this one? You stuck on her? I was stuck on a showgirl once. I thought I was going out of my mind. I couldn't look at a queen of hearts without seeing her face on it."

"This one was not your garden-variety showgirl. She was always where the action was and she never seemed to run out of money. Very beautiful. Very tall. Always wore a white dress. There couldn't be too many girls like that even in Las Vegas."

Harry sighed. "Must've been after my time. These days Las Vegas is a long way away for me." Old age came over his face like a shadow as he contemplated all the things that were after his time. He took another slug of bourbon to stir his memory. "Maybe," he said slowly, dipping his tongue once more into the bourbon, "I remember one time at Santa Anita, about a year and a half ago, I ran into a couple of old gamblers who were drinking and talking and there was mention of a girl they called the Angel." Returning memory washed the shadow from his face and once more he did not look his age. "Always wore a white dress, it was kind of a trademark. Nobody said she was beautiful." His glance was a little skeptical; there was even a touch of reproof in it as though Goldberg had been leading him astray. "You sure you got that right about her being beautiful? They said a big girl in a white dress with all the money in the world. That was what they really talked about, the money."

"Why'd they call her the Angel?"

"She staked busted gamblers. She called herself the lender of last resort."

"Where'd the money come from?" asked Goldberg.

"Nobody said. Where does money come from in Vegas?

It could grow out of the desert like cactus for all anybody cares. What's important is it's there. When you're tapped out, you'd take a stake from the devil if he was lending."

"Did any of your gambling buddies raise a stake from her?"

"I'm not real sure," said Eames regretfully. "They wasn't too clear about it. It's possible they just heard it around. It seems sometimes you could find her and sometimes you couldn't. She was kind of a floating bank." He peered across the table a little woozily. "That's why you're looking for her? It ain't a torch—it's a stake."

"Not exactly." Goldberg was watching the man in the neon-blue leisure suit again as he slashed the meat on his plate and pretended not to notice he was being watched.

"You find her you let me know now," said Eames, touching up his eyebrows. "If ever a man needed a stake, you're sitting with him. You know where to find me. You call the club they'll call me. Everybody knows my name. You don't have to worry. The kind of money the Angel's got there's plenty for everybody."

Goldberg looked at his watch. As the minute hand moved to the bottom of the dial, Goldberg's initial was announced over the public-address system. He motioned to the hometown girl for his check and, familiar with the urgencies of gamblers, she brought it instantly.

"Jesus," said Eames, "I haven't given you the rest of the book."

The man in the neon-blue leisure suit, who was undoubtedly some kind of legacy from Barbara, was pulling out his wallet now and dumping bills on the table without waiting for his waitress to finish her addition.

Goldberg tried to recall being followed out of Vegas, but there had been too many cars. A gunmetal-gray Corvette had hung in his rearview mirror for quite a while about an hour outside the city limits, and he remembered wondering why it was spending so much time there. It was probably the Corvette, he thought. "Don't worry your head, Harry," he said with a smile. "I'll just keep my eye on the gold ring and let the cards take care of the rest."

With Eames at his side and Little Boy Blue trailing a little behind, he picked up five thousand in chips at the cashier's cage and went to claim Doc Giordano's seat, which was pointed out to him by the floorman.

"Name's Goldberg," he said as he sat down.

The seven players at the table didn't seem much interested; they were probably still mourning the departure of the good gynecologist.

Jake Willoughby, who had just cracked open a fresh deck, was shuffling it with the steady authoritative rhythm of a threshing machine. He was as big as advertised and the five-hundred-dollar suit came with a vest. Thick lips. A full round face. Dark eyes that had spent a lifetime giving nothing away. "Jake Willoughby," he said. "The game's high draw, jacks or better to open. Joker's wild with aces, straights, and flushes." The guarded eyes took in the chips in front of Goldberg. "I see you came to play."

Goldberg nodded, looking around the table. The only woman at the table smiled a greeting and then withdrew it quickly as though it had been a mistake. She was a tall lean soldierly lady in her mid-fifties with square shoulders, a straight back, and long large-knuckled hands devoid of rings. She didn't look as though she made too many mistakes of any kind.

Willoughby sent the cards skimming over the green field of the card table like flights of angry hawks. As each card dropped, Goldberg moved his eyes to the nearest sets of fingers, the drummers, the graspers, the conscientiously cool.

In Goldberg's early estimate Willoughby was the strength of the table, with the woman probably a surprising second. It was a grim table, no smiles, three chain-smokers, one tattoo, one set of bloodshot eyes, Willoughby, the woman, Goldberg. Only Goldberg and Willoughby waited until the deal was complete before picking up their cards.

Goldberg had come to play luck rather than his skill, of which he had no high opinion, but he was beginning to suspect he had left his luck in the parking lot. His hand showed two pair, tens up—with odds about eleven to one against making a full house after the draw.

On the rail Little Boy Blue hung by his elbows, concentrating his full glare on Goldberg's shoulders and not shifting it when he met Goldberg's eyes. It was possible there weren't going to be any bugles blowing for Goldberg in Gardena.

Ahead of Goldberg the woman opened, two chain-smokers and the tattoo stayed in, one player folded. Goldberg raised, the next player dropped, and Willoughby came out charging like a bull, meeting Goldberg's raise and raising back. Everybody ran from the game except the woman and then Goldberg raised again.

"Way you throw it around that better be Texas oil money," said Willoughby with a grin, meeting Goldberg's latest raise. Willoughby had very large, very white teeth. When he exposed them as he did now you got the feeling they were a warning of trouble to come.

Goldberg kept his tens and drew three cards.

Willoughby stood pat, the teeth on display again, the thumb of his left hand nestled against the pinkie ring. Goldberg read him as puzzled. All victims are welcome at the poker table, but Goldberg's craziness needed further exploration.

Goldberg looked at his hand. He had picked up another ten. Goldberg bet. Willoughby, after a second's hesitation, called and, when he saw the third ten, lit a large cigar to calm himself.

"You're a lucky son of a bitch," he said, blowing a protective cloud over the pot.

"Sometimes," said Goldberg cautiously, not wanting to put too much faith in that third ten.

The next hour and a half was the winning streak turned inside out. All of a sudden Goldberg was playing the cards and not his luck, running and ducking and maneuvering and losing steadily. Willoughby and the woman were the big winners, but even the tattoo and two chain-smokers were taking money from Goldberg.

This was the first time since it had started that the winning streak had really died on him and Goldberg began to wonder whether the loss could be permanent. He remembered what it had been like before the streak started and suddenly deep inside his left knee he felt a familiar ache that brought with it the face of the big Princeton tackle who had put the ache there in the first place, O'Meara, O'Mara, something like that, hands like watermelons and a shark's grin. O'Meara-O'Mara had a red mustache that seemed to sprout fiery wings as he moved in on his quarry. He'd gone on to play for the Chicago Bears, but it turned out he wasn't mean enough for the pros. Goldberg's knee, however, remembered him in the days of his glory.

Goldberg bought more chips from the chip girl who dug them out of her apron with a motherly smile, cookies for Goldberg. He smiled back and returned a fifty-dollar chip. Good Goldberg.

Around twelve o'clock the winning streak came back without preliminary notice. By twelve-thirty he had raked in ten pots for a total of eighteen thousand seven hundred, leaving table twenty-seven in the grip of the unnerving suspicion that they were the victims of some outrageous but impenetrable fraud. Two chain-smokers left. Willoughby summoned fresh cards for the third time in twenty minutes; once he left the table to speak to the floor manager who now hovered discreetly over Goldberg's shoulder.

The woman with the West Point shoulders dealt and Goldberg's cards dropped in front of him as neatly as homing pigeons, one for Goldberg, two for Goldberg, three for Goldberg, four for Goldberg, five for Goldberg. They sat in front of his chips in a disarray that tempted his fingers, but he held back on the fingers, raising them from his lap only far enough to attach them to the end of the table. The tattoo opened. Goldberg, his fingers still locked to the table's edge, raised.

"You're not going to look at your cards?" said Willoughby. His teeth were remarkably like those of O'Meara-O'Mara. If he had known about the pain in Goldberg's knee, he would have enjoyed it, but not much; there wasn't a knee anywhere big enough to hold all the pain he wished on Goldberg. He picked up a tower of chips and slid five off the bottom. "If I paid you, would you look at your cards?"

"No," said Goldberg. "I'm not playing the cards. I'm playing the luck."

"You smell it?" said Willoughby, who did not believe in luck, his own or anybody else's. "That how you know it's there?"

"Bet," said Goldberg, keeping his hands in plain sight on the edge of the table. He remembered sitting like this years

70

ago, in kindergarten, for fingernail inspection. While Willoughby did his own fingernail inspection on Goldberg's hands, Goldberg remembered the teacher's name, Miss Wilson, a tall frantic woman in her late twenties, afflicted with a nose much too large for her face. Goldberg suspected it was the nose rather than a natural vocation that had brought her to pedagogy. "I give you fair warning," he said, "this is your last shot at me. I leave at the end of the hand."

Willoughby counted out chips one-handed and dribbled them into the middle of the pot. His skin, normally the creamy ivory of a cue ball, had turned a flatter paper white. He was a man who lived by a code and he'd broken his own code, not by seeming angry—anger was one of the tools of his trade—but by letting the anger become real.

The hooked fingers dispensed four more chips into the pot. "And once more," he said.

The military lady, looking cynically from Willoughby to Goldberg and back again, said, "My daddy always told me to stay clear of private fights," and tossed in her hand.

Showing his openers, the tattoo followed her out of the game.

The remaining chain-smoker studied his cards, sighed, and stayed in, but he wasn't happy with his decision.

"And two hundred," said Goldberg automatically, tossing two chips into the pot and replacing his hands on the edge of the table. All sensation of the streak was gone now; it had been replaced by an awful tedium that reminded him of the way he had been not long ago, perpetually ensnared in the emptiness of his days and nights, talking to ghosts.

Willoughby blew a large half-speed smoke ring, placed a smaller faster one in the middle of it, and called without looking at Goldberg, who was concentrating now on the man in the neon-blue leisure suit. There was no sign of him at the rail anymore, but he would be somewhere, waiting.

The military lady, the deck poised in her left hand, glanced expectantly at Willoughby. Now that she was a by-stander she had taken off her poker face. Her eyes had a slight shine to them. The tip of her tongue moved along her lips. "How many cards would you be asking for, Jake?" she inquired. Hearing the touch of brogue in her voice, Gold-berg wondered what route had brought her to Gardena, what countries she had known, what lovers she had had, and why she played poker in Gardena night after night. Goldberg's head was adrift in idle speculation.

"It's kind of you to ask, but I think I'll be staying with these," said Willoughby and somewhere in the tone of his voice, in the slight mockery of the brogue, Goldberg heard that the gambler and the soldierly lady had once been lovers and were not anymore. With this piece of informa-tion Goldberg now turned to the reading of Willoughby's face.

One of the nice things about poker is that it is utterly shameless. Invented by riverboat gamblers as a device for fleecing the innocent, it has retained from its beginnings a quality of unabashed aggressiveness close to war and with the same generous interpretation of permissible behavior. It is one of the few human activities in which eight people can sit and stare at each other not only with impunity but with a sense of absolute propriety. Goldberg stared at Willoughby for a good thirty seconds without wavering. The face was featuring its cat-that-ate-the-canary look. It could mean Willoughby had an unbeatable hand, or it could mean he had no hand at all. This was the second time he was standing pat. The first time had been pure bluff.

Goldberg did not think he would be trying to bluff now.

The chain-smoker stubbed out his cigarette and asked for one card. When he received it, he seemed pleased with it. Again possibly nothing. The chain-smoker lit another cigarette and pulled the smoke into his lungs with a long low whistle.

Goldberg gave himself three choices: stand pat without looking at his cards, look at them and then decide what to do, or discard up to five cards, still without looking at them, and call for new ones.

He had the sudden unnerving conviction that the streak had left with the man in the neon-blue leisure suit.

If the streak had still been working for him, he would not have needed to question what he should do; he would have been swept along like a river in flood, no questions, all answers. His special relationship with the laws of probability required a lover's obsessive concentration, which once surrendered might be gone forever. There was no guidance in poker wisdom, for everything he had done from the beginning of the hand made no poker sense at all. The only thing left to do was whatever would irritate Willoughby the most. Goldberg tossed all five cards, still unexamined, toward the dealer. "I'll try a refill," he said.

Goldberg had never regarded himself as a superstitious man during the days when he thought he understood everything that happened to him, but now he was in the grip of something he admittedly did not understand and he was trying to move with the mystery rather than against it. The streak could be like a talent you lost if you abused it. He should have quit when his concentration went, but now the problem seemed to be to escape without embarrassment. As the fifth card fell in front of him, he tapped his fingers on the edge of the table and shook his head regretfully, knowing he did not want to see what was on the other side of his cards. Then for a moment the concentration returned and there was a message in the back of the cards that said with the unmistakable force of the streak, get out, get out, get out now. Without hesitating he started to gather his chips.

"You leaving?" growled Willoughby.

"Is there a rule against it?" Goldberg was on his feet, his hands and pockets full of chips. "It's been a pleasure taking your money," he said, glancing at his watch, "but if I don't stop playing before the stroke of one I turn into a pumpkin."

As Goldberg reached the rail and passed through the opening in it, he saw Willoughby pick up his discards, in violation of the house rules, and look at them. What he saw there Goldberg would never know, but it was enough to bring Willoughby halfway out of his chair before he slumped back into it and slammed Goldberg's abandoned cards down hard on the table.

Goldberg cashed in at the cashier's cage, and moving fast, found Harry Eames in the television room, where he shoved two thousand in hundred-dollar bills into his hands. "There's your stake, old buddy," he said.

People were staring at Goldberg as he loped toward the door, but he was in a hurry now for whatever was going to happen to happen.

Nine

When Goldberg drove the Avis Ford out of the parking lot, the Corvette was waiting for him by the curb, lights off, engine running. As he passed it the lights flicked on and the Corvette slid into position about fifty yards behind him.

Instead of heading directly for the freeway, Goldberg did a series of right- and left-angle turns through the streets of Gardena until he came to a gas station and pulled into the circle of light. The Corvette lurked on the edge of darkness. For a moment he thought he might have lost it, but when he crossed the station into the street beyond it, the Corvette screeched around the corner and resumed its place on his tail.

There was no chance he could outrun or outcorner it and no place to hide in the checkerboard pattern of those perfectly laid-out streets, but the truth of the matter was he didn't really want to, because somehow it was tied to Barbara. There were no other connections in his life strong enough for anybody to want to follow him.

He caught a glimpse of the driver of the Corvette in the beam of a passing car and recognized the thick neck and close-cropped blond hair of the man who had been staring at him from the rail of the cardroom. Little Boy Blue and Mr. Colt. He was being hunted along these anonymous streets by an anonymous man who thought he knew the way to Barbara and intended to follow him there. While a shrewder man would have made some attempt at secrecy, the driver of the Corvette didn't look as though shrewdness played any part in him. You pointed to him and he ran through walls. He would not be afraid to die, because it had never occurred to him that he might.

Goldberg drove toward the freeway with the Corvette behind him, windows closed, air conditioning on low in an effort to minimize the smog. When he burst onto the nearly empty freeway, the road was bright all the way to the City of Angels—a bomber's moon—and hunter and hunted raced in a dreamlike harmony, eighty miles an hour, fifty yards apart.

Goldberg remembered walking alone, half-drunk, through the streets of Florence years ago, hours after it had been retaken from the Germans, at about the same time of another moonlit night, through streets that were like tunnels between steel-shuttered shop windows and ancient gray stone, Goldberg wandering through history, hearing the shuffle of feet that had walked there before him on private and public business for the better part of two thousand years, Guelfs and Ghibellines, Medici warriors, Michelangelo with marble dust in his hair, and girls of a beauty so rare men were struck dumb by the sight. Or so Goldberg had been led to believe, and with his head suddenly filled with the beauty of those unknown women he had stopped.

He stopped his feet but the sound of footsteps continued for another two beats. Start and stop, he repeated the process half a dozen times, sometimes catching the footsteps, sometimes not. He was being stalked through the streets of Florence by somebody who might be a native Florentine, or might be a leftover German, but was certainly no ghost, and for the first time in his life Goldberg felt the hair rise on the back of his neck. The footsteps followed him then the way the Corvette was following him now with the difference that in Florence so long ago whenever he turned he saw nobody. He had had a long way to walk, into the hills of Fiesole, and with no idea of the purpose of the game that was being played with him, but he had been convinced that the longer it continued the more dangerous it would become. He pulled the .45 from its holster and turned abruptly, knowing that he was inviting a shot if shooting was what the stalker had in mind. Perhaps Goldberg was the only one of the two with a gun although that seemed unlikely; Italy was full of guns, bought, stolen, surrendered, lost and found. Whatever the reason, when Goldberg started to walk again, the pistol hanging from his right hand, the footsteps no longer followed him. The game was over.

As Goldberg watched the Corvette in the rearview mirror, he realized that a major difference between the two situations was that he no longer had a gun and he decided to pick one up the first chance he got. He changed lanes and the Corvette changed with him. When he changed back again, so did the Corvette. He was being hunted as openly as he had been in Florence although on the road to L.A. he thought he knew why.

About ten miles outside the city limits the Corvette pulled to the right, coming up alongside Goldberg. For a couple of seconds the two cars ran side by side, while Goldberg saw the driver's face through the dimness of two windows as a lighter shade of darkness. Then the window of the Corvette slid down, and the face was a little more distinct, but not nearly as distinct as the gun that glinted in the moonlight. Goldberg swerved and the Corvette swerved with him. He swerved again and the Corvette was still there, with the gun poking out of the driver's window. In the flash of a passing headlight Goldberg caught a glimpse of the face behind the gun. It was the face of a man who had lived his whole life for the fraction of a second in which he would kill Goldberg.

The face fell back into darkness, but the gun was still visible. Goldberg saw the barrel kick up as the bullet thudded into the Ford somewhere behind his head. He jammed his foot down on the accelerator pedal and momentarily outdistanced the Corvette, which overtook him quickly, swaying slightly from side to side as the driver fought to control the wheel and the gun at the same time.

Fast was better, thought Goldberg, it made aiming harder. The only trouble was the Ford ran out of fast sooner than the Corvette, and pretty soon the cars were running neck and neck again. The second bullet pierced the rear side window and buried itself in vinyl. Goldberg swerved once more to the left, quickly followed by the Corvette, but this time instead of straightening his wheels Goldberg turned them right in a feint at the other car. The Corvette, surprised, just managed to get away in time, while a homeward-bound Cadillac zoomed by both of them screaming its outrage in a long, drawn-out horn blast that wailed its way into the distant dark.

Goldberg knew the duel of the freeways couldn't last much longer, for he was driving the slower and less-maneuverable car and sooner or later Little Boy Blue was going to catch him with a bullet. They were running parallel again now with the gun between them shifting from side to side as it probed for a target, a number of which would do, either in Goldberg or in his car.

Goldberg brought his left foot into position over the brake pedal, while he relaxed the pressure on the accelerator. Right foot up, left foot down, he reduced speed with an abruptness that shocked the Ford into a shudder and the beginning of a skid, but he managed to keep it in lane while the Corvette, taken completely by surprise, sped ahead of him. As the Corvette struggled to decelerate, its rear wheels came even with the Ford's front wheels, and Goldberg tramped on the gas again, shooting forward while the Corvette was still slowing down. This time Goldberg was not trying to get away, but there was no way the other driver could guess that. The Ford roared ahead briefly until Goldberg was sure his own front wheels were clear; then he spun his steering wheel to the left, the recipe being not too much and not too little, hoping he had the timing right and the judgment, and the Ford did exactly what he wanted it to do, nudging the Corvette with its rear end almost exactly behind the Corvette's front wheels, sending it into a clockwise spin while the Ford jumped out of the top of the clock.

Goldberg raced on toward Los Angeles with the Corvette revolving in his rearview mirror, scattering light across the freeway in a series of crazy arcs.

The hunter was out of the hunt, and with him the secret of his intentions. Why would he want to kill Goldberg if Goldberg was supposed to lead him to Barbara Hall?

Ten

At eight o'clock in the morning he was in Echo Park, looking for Martha Weir's house. He found it on a corner on Hyperion Avenue, a small Victorian castle rendered in brown shingles, with two tower rooms staring across the rooftop at each other. There were rust stains on the white trim, but otherwise the house was without blemish.

When he turned into the driveway, Goldberg saw the red MG in the shed that served as a garage. The house was quiet the way houses in Los Angeles are quiet—as though the owner had left forever a minute before.

He rang the doorbell. Nothing happened for a while; then he heard feet shuffling toward the door, and someone began to inspect him through the peephole. A minute passed with Goldberg on display on the front porch trying to find an expression for his face that would open doors. He wound up smiling at the closed door as though he were asking it to dance. When the door finally opened, he was stuck with the smile on his face.

The woman was as tall as he was, but broader and deeper, dressed in a white nurse's uniform. One hand was behind her back. She was in her fifties, he guessed, but she had probably always looked the way she did now, ageproof, weatherproof, shockproof. She was black and she didn't want him on her porch.

"State your business," she said. The accent was British, the rhythm calypso.

"Martha Weir?" he said.

She wasn't afraid. She didn't look as though she had ever been afraid of anything, and she wasn't about to start now, but she was more than normally bothered by a stranger on her porch.

"I'm looking for Barbara Hall," he explained.

She brought the hand around from in back of her. It had a gun in it. "I'll bet," she said.

The gun moved up the center of his belly until it found the spot it wanted and stopped. He put the smile back on his lips. "You don't shoot somebody for standing on your porch."

"Depends on why they're standing there."

She had a face left over from some ancient kingdom that pursued its own laws without fear or favor. His smile wasn't doing him any good at all. He took it away. "You know Barbara," he said.

"Who sent you?" The face changed now for the first time, letting the contempt shine through.

"Nobody sent me. I'm a friend of hers."

The contempt deepened. "She always had funny taste." Martha Weir looked him up and down as though he were a chicken she was thinking of buying and finally concluded that as a chicken he was no worse than most.

"Somebody's trying to kill her," said Goldberg, "almost killed me instead. She needs all the help she can get."

"Where is she now?"

"Running. I don't know where she is."

Martha Weir used the gun as a pointer. She pointed him inside with it. "Keep remembering I've got this and we'll get along just fine."

She followed him through an archway of yellow oak,

81

carved in a leaf pattern, into the living room. The living room was a small square museum dedicated to Martha Weir's obsessions. Four walls were lined with glass shelves, on which animals swarmed in ceramic, wood, and metal herds.

"I'm night nursing supervisor at Cedars of Lebanon," explained Martha Weir, "and when I come home it's restful to look at things that go on four feet."

She pointed the gun at the chair in which she wanted him to sit. He sat. The table next to him was covered with photographs in frames, different ages of Barbara. A thick leather photograph album rested on a shelf under the table.

"That's the other way I rest my eyes," said Martha Weir, who took it for granted she knew what was going on inside his head. "Pictures of how it was once."

"You've known her a long time?"

"I'm her mother," said Martha Weir. "That give you a problem?"

Goldberg shrugged.

"I adopted her, picked her up on the road out of San Diego. She was nine years old and running away, because her father had left and the mother's boyfriends were starting to look at her funny. We worked out the adoption proceedings between us without the help of the sovereign state of California. She was mine for eleven years. Then she decided she belonged to herself. Now you tell me somebody's trying to kill her."

The elegant British syllables developed an edge and caught in her throat. She glared at him. "So far I've done all the talking. You talk Mr. . . . ?"

"Goldberg."

"Mr. Goldberg. What do you do when you're not sitting in my living room, Mr. Goldberg?"

Goldberg hesitated. "Gambler," he said finally.

The dark eyes looked into his head and drew their own conclusions. "Do you have children, Mr. Goldberg?"

"Two," he said. "A boy and a girl."

She was surprised. "That's all you have to tell about them?"

"The boy is dead." It occurred to him that this was the first time he had said that aloud to anybody. "He was killed in Vietnam."

"So," said Martha Weir. It was less a statement than an escape of breath. "Would you care for some tea, Mr. Goldberg? I would offer you something stronger, but I don't keep it in the house. My father was a drinking man." She paused as though she had said enough, but she was relentless even with her own memories. "The last time I saw him he was lying in a puddle of his own making."

"I'd like some tea."

"You will excuse me, Mr. Goldberg. Before I put away my gun, I must make sure you don't have one of your own."

Standing, Goldberg held his arms above his head with the elbows crooked. She patted him deftly wherever a gun might have been and nodded for him to sit again. "You're a strong man," she said when she was done. She put her hands on her hips and looked him over thoughtfully from head to foot. "Don't get me wrong, I don't even need a man to carry out the garbage. You stay in your place, Mr. Goldberg, and I'll get the tea."

While she was gone, Goldberg picked up the leather-bound photograph album and riffled through the pages. When Martha Weir returned with the tea, he asked her why there were no pictures of the daughter Barbara told him about.

She cleared a space on the table next to Goldberg's chair without answering. She put down his tea cup. "Sugar and cream," she said. "Also lemon. What do you take, Mr. Goldberg?"

"Lemon," said Goldberg.

"I have always preferred sugar and cream," said Martha Weir. "I could never understand lemon." She filled her cup with cream until there was just enough room for the three spoons of sugar, her lips pursed in calculation as the last spoonful slid into the cup. "I'm too big to diet," she said. "If I weighed fifty pounds less, nobody would notice the difference."

She settled in the chair across from him as though she had forgotten his question and sipped her tea with careful pleasure. "It appears you don't know my Barbara very well," she said finally.

"Oh?"

"Strangers in bed are still strangers," said Martha Weir, fixing him with her dark surgical eyes. "I suppose you've been to bed with her?"

Goldberg was silent.

"I like that," said Martha Weir. "Nowadays everybody tells everybody everything. You find that to be true in your line of work, Mr. Goldberg?" She finished her tea and leaned forward. "Just what did you say your line of work was?"

"Gambling."

"Of course, I must have forgotten. I have these little lapses." She looked as though she had never forgotten anything and didn't expect Goldberg to believe she had. "Somehow you look official," she said. "Like you expect people to jump when you say jump."

"I'm not official. Once. Not anymore. What makes you say I don't know Barbara?"

"If you knew her, you'd understand she keeps Miranda to herself like she was the secret to the back door of heaven. Nobody's supposed to know about Miranda except Barbara. Once there were pictures in that album. She took them all out and would never let me take another." She leaned back, resting the teacup in her lap, and studied the inside of her left hand. "Exactly what kind of official were you, Mr. Goldberg?"

"I was in the Secret Service." He saw the question in her eyes and answered it. "Department of the Treasury. Protects presidents and chases counterfeiters. I was fired for hitting the army captain who brought me the word of my son's death. There's a longer explanation, but that's what it was all about."

She thought about this for a while, ducking her head periodically to mark some conclusion for or against. In the end she folded her muscular hands together on the great white shelf of her belly and gave him the shine of her teeth. "You tell me now why you think somebody's trying to kill her," she said encouragingly.

"A tall man," said Goldberg, "as tall as I am but thinner. Wore English riding boots, a hacking jacket, and riding pants, but not as though he's ever been near a horse. High cheekbones, long thin nose. His eyes were bad-news blue. When he turned them on you you knew you were in for trouble."

"I know the eyes," said Martha Weir.

"He was looking for her in my room in Las Vegas and when he didn't find her he shot me instead. That's why the bandage."

Her hands came apart on her belly and started to tap, first against each other and then against the great roll of flesh inside the white nurse's uniform. "That's Doc Holliday in every respect," she said. "I never saw him wearing riding boots, but he dresses for whatever's going on in his head that day. You take his name. Holliday's what he got from his family. It was his own idea to put Doc in front of it. Even when he was a kid he liked to think of himself as a killer. You did something he didn't like, he'd point his finger at you and say, 'Bang, bang, you're dead.' It was supposed to be kidding. I never took it for kidding."

The hands had settled down again in her lap, two sets of fingers hanging on to each other for dear life. The dark eyes were remembering what it had been like with Doc Holliday. "When he first showed up Barbara was fifteen, he was a couple of years older. I don't know where kids find each other, they go off someplace like they've gone off a hundred times before, and then one night they come back with somebody and it's never the same again. After he'd been hanging around for about six months, they told me they were married although the only evidence I ever saw of that was the baby. By then Doc Holliday was gone. Bang, bang, we were all dead as far as he was concerned—and God be thanked for that. We were a family again except that now there were the three of us. It lasted like that until Miranda was about five years old when something happened to Barbara. I never knew what it was, but whatever it was after that she was different."

The fingers locked together in her lap and when she turned her head toward Goldberg, her eyes were burning with suspicion. "Tell me something, Mr. Goldberg. Did she take your money when she left?"

He hesitated.

"Ahh," she said bitterly, "all you're after is getting your money back. I should have known that."

He was losing her, thought Goldberg, and once lost she would be gone forever. "The money has nothing to do with it. I make money like turning on a faucet."

86

"You present yourself as a very unusual man," she said sarcastically.

"I started a winning streak the night I first saw Barbara. Before I stopped rolling the dice I was nearly one hundred fifty thousand dollars ahead."

"That's a lot of money, Mr. Goldberg."

"Not if you win it in two hours."

"You're telling me you always win when you gamble?"

"More often than not. If I don't feel it, I don't play. The minute I start caring about the money the streak will stop."

"Where did that rule come from?" she asked drily.

"All I know is what I've seen, and I've thought about it a lot. If I cared, the whole thing would stop." She was as bullheaded as Schoyer, thought Goldberg, beginning to lose his temper. "What the hell do I have to do to get you to believe the truth, bring witnesses? Follow me around and you can see for yourself."

He looked over the small crowded room with its stucco walls and meager fireplace, and it reminded him of the houses he had spent his young manhood in, pinched for room and short of cash. "When I first married I paid attention to money like everybody else. Money could straighten crooked teeth and turn kids into concert pianists and Supreme Court justices. It turned lawns green, laundry white, and lit up the sky with fireworks on the Fourth of July. Paradise was just around the corner and money was going to get us in. I admit it, I cared about money then, like everybody else. No more. No less. Now I've got no use for money at all and it pours in like spring rain. You think I worry about it, or care about it? What could it buy me? An extra pair of socks? I'm wearing all the socks I need." He stood up. "Look, we're both wasting our time with this conversation. I thank you for the tea and the cookie."

"Sit down, Mr. Goldberg."

He continued to stand, filling the room with his height and his bulk. "I'll drive you to Gardena," he said. "Watch me play poker. I'll put what I win in a garbage can, or you can have it for your favorite charity."

Suddenly he felt the sensation in his chest and arm that meant he was going to win and he had trouble keeping himself quiet.

"If you don't care about money, why do you gamble?"

"People don't gamble for money," said Goldberg impatiently. "You gamble to win. You can make money working in a bank." He glared down at the swollen body caught between the arms of the overstuffed chair and felt the muscles in his hands twitch with the need to shake her. "If it were a matter of the money she took, I wouldn't have followed her out the door and I wouldn't be here and I wouldn't have gotten myself shot in the head."

"All right," she said quietly, "so you're all in a huff now. Go ahead and huff. Just you get this one thing straight. Whatever she's done to me, I'd never do anything to hurt her. I'd die first. And I don't die easy. You come in here with your wild stories and think you can open up my head and everything'll pour out. Not so fast, Mr. Goldberg, not so easy." She patted her thighs with her flattened palms to settle herself down. "If not the money then, why? What makes you go to all this trouble to keep her from being killed?"

As he confronted those skeptical eyes, he knew he would have to offer them more than he had offered yet. "I was next to dead for a long time," he began reluctantly. "You've heard about the walking wounded, I was the walking dead. Two things woke me up when I expected nothing ever could. The dice and your daughter. Maybe I feel obligated. Maybe I just need to see how it all comes out. Take your pick."

Martha Weir thought about that for a while. "I can tell you where she lived," she said slowly. "I kept phoning and there was no answer. I drove over and there was nobody there. I couldn't find any sign of where she had gone, but maybe you can."

She hesitated as though she had something else to tell him, but she wasn't ready yet. "Start with that," she said. "Then we'll talk some more."

Eleven

The Avis Ford, bullet marked but as ambitious as Gene Autry's horse, wound its way along Laurel Canyon, rising steadily toward the California sky that this afternoon was all blue and gold, a pioneer's heaven left over from the world before smog. Goldberg paused to give it the attention it deserved and then returned to the subjects that preoccupied him a good part of the day and in his dreams all night.

At that first dice table in Las Vegas the past had drained out of his head, leaving a vacuum in which the mysterious present rose obsessively. Sometimes guilt, sharpened by the sense he was betraying his own grief, drove him to remember what it had been like before, but the memories were thin and unreliable, diminishing a little every twenty-four hours. For the most part his head was busy with the streak and Barbara. He tried to understand the streak; he talked to Barbara.

He handled the winning streak with a certain reluctance; there are some things better not talked about even to yourself. In the beginning the explanation had been easy: even gamblers' dreams came true on occasions. Luck was the exception that fed the machines. But luck had moved in with Goldberg; Job had developed a hot hand, and he had to wonder why. Goldberg preferred not to wonder why. When the Lord told Abraham to sacrifice his only son, the good God had provided a substitute for the knife. That was as far as Goldberg cared to go in that direction. It was better to think of the streak as a prolonged accident, but an accident that required cultivation. When things were going right, you kept them going with small gestures in which you did not believe but performed anyway. Different people handled it in different ways, baby shoes, rabbits' feet; Goldberg knew a fighter pilot by the name of Conrad who wore his lucky baseball cap through three cycles of fifty missions each, and was shot down, still wearing it, on his hundred fifty-first mission. Who could say it hadn't worked? One hundred and fifty missions was a long time to survive. The real mystery, perhaps, was why the baseball cap had stopped working.

About one-third of the way up Laurel Canyon you come to Willow Glen, a rustic trail so minor you can easily miss it. Turning into it was like plunging from the tawniness of the canyon wall into a wilderness of green leaves and shadow and secret bubbling wells. About half a mile in Goldberg found the house he had been told was Barbara's, a majestic brown-shingled building with a deep porch in a clearing in the woods.

Goldberg brought the Ford to a stop on the dirt road that curved around the house. There was no sign of life anywhere until curtains moved on the second floor. A woman's face peeked between the curtains, but withdrew quickly when she saw Goldberg looking at her. Goldberg waited, thinking she might come down to meet him, but there was no further movement from the house. Finally Goldberg unfolded his legs from the bullet-nicked Ford and walked quickly up the path onto the front porch. When he pushed the bell button, he heard chimes echo inside with the deep-toned authority of a cathedral bell. The chimes made more of an impression on Goldberg than they did on the woman who had been examining him from the upstairs window; at least they didn't bring her to the door. Goldberg gave the sound time to echo and die within the house before he played the chimes again, still without any acknowledgment from the woman inside. Patiently he repeated the process five times, each time allowing an interval for response and each time getting none until at last he began to blend the end of one ring into the beginning of the next, creating hills and valleys of resonance that rolled through the house with the threat they would never stop. When she couldn't stand it anymore, she opened the front door, a big young woman, somewhat over five-foot-ten, wearing a bikini that had slipped down over her appendectomy scar. Her navel, buried deep in the roundness of her firm young belly, had a slight squint to it. Her breasts were splendid, her lips sulky, her green eyes glazed as though they had been a long time sleeping. She had straight brown hair that hung down over her shoulder blades. There were streaks of dirt on her arms and legs. Her feet were bare and in her right hand she carried a medium-sized crowbar.

"You crazy?" she demanded.

"Don't be afraid," said Goldberg soothingly.

"Do I look afraid?" she inquired with a sneer, brandishing the crowbar like a baton. The tip of the crowbar was covered with white powder, probably plaster. The powder, whatever it was, had also made white freckles in the division between her breasts.

"Who the hell are you, the town boob-inspector?" she demanded. "Inspection's over."

"Sorry," said Goldberg. "I'm looking for an old friend."

She started to close the door. Goldberg put his foot in and leaned his weight against the panel. "Don't tell me I look like your old friend," she said. "You never seen me before in your life, and if you don't take your foot out of the door I'm going to pry you loose from your toes with this little ole crowbar."

"My old friend owns this house," said Goldberg.

"Then you go tell her she charges too much goddamn rent," said the woman with the crowbar.

"Relax." Goldberg leaned harder into the door. "If you don't watch that thing, I'm going to take it away from you and spank you with it."

"Bet you'd enjoy that, wouldn't you, you old bastard?" She withdrew the crowbar from the vicinity of Goldberg's toes. The thought seemed to amuse her. She held the crowbar in both hands across her muscular thighs and leered at him. "The minute you shoved your legs out of that old piece of junk I figured you for a spanker. Tell me what you want and get the hell out."

"How long have you been living here?"

"Weeks. Months. Who knows? Out here one day's so much like the next how do you keep count?"

"Who did you rent the house from?"

She shrugged her shoulders. "My husband does all the business. All I know is it costs too goddamn much and the pollen is murder." She had a sneezing fit to prove her point.

"When do you expect your husband back?"

"Whenever he good goddamn pleases to come back. That could be anytime this century."

"Thank you." Goldberg removed his foot from the door-sill.

"Fuck you too," she said and slammed the door.

Inside the house he heard the tramp of heavy feet on the floorboards as she returned to her domestic chores, whatever they might be. When Goldberg backed the Ford onto the road, she was watching him again from the upstairs window. He drove a short distance in the direction of the canyon road, then he turned around in a small clearing and went back along Willow Glen, past Barbara Hall's house, down the road to the nearest neighbor, a sprawling ranch with a swimming pool beside it and a skinny little girl in the swimming pool, doing laps. Getting out of his car, Goldberg watched her churn through the water like an Olympic contender. When she came out of the water, pulling off her cap and shaking out long lank blond hair, Goldberg said, "Nice going."

"You ought to see me when I'm really trying," she said, putting on horn-rimmed glasses that transformed her into a scholar-mermaid.

She was about eleven, thin and supple and just on the edge of everything. She was a funny little girl with braids and an air of self-possession so natural she must have been born with it.

"Would you join me in a Coke?" she asked, accepting him the way she seemed to accept the whole world, as a friend, or at least an interesting curiosity.

Removing two Cokes from a portable cooler, she handed him one. "My name is Mavis Carlson," she said, wiping her mouth with the back of her hand.

Goldberg gave her his name in return. "I once had a little girl like you. Good swimmer, too. Blond hair. Wore glasses."

"What happened to her?"

"She grew up."

Mavis seemed to find the idea of growing up attractive. She smiled at the prospect.

"How long have you lived here?" asked Goldberg.

"In this house? All my life. At least ever since my mother and father brought me home from the hospital. He's an orthopedic surgeon. He used to be captain of the Stanford ski team. My mother plays the piano." Goldberg thought he detected a slight note of disapproval. "My mother's the one who taught me to swim. She's a fantastic swimmer."

"You must have known the Halls down the road."

"Barbara and Miranda. Miranda used to baby-sit me." Mavis adjusted the cushions on two white metal beach chairs beside the pool. "Why don't we enjoy our Cokes sitting down?" she said, pale blue eyes inspecting Goldberg with interest through the oversize lenses. "Her mama didn't like the idea much, I don't think, because it made it look as though they needed the money. Miranda said her mother was a terrible snob, but she never looked snobby to me. More worried than snobby."

"What did she worry about?" asked Goldberg.

"That's an interesting question, I've thought about it a lot. Mostly I think she worried about Miranda, having to leave her alone in that big house with the Mexican maid when she went away."

"Where did she go when she went away?"

Mavis seemed enraptured by Goldberg. She took inventory of his scars, bumps, and less obvious contusions. "Are you a private eye?" she asked.

"Kind of."

"I thought so." Mavis took a fresh slug of Coke as though regretting it was not bourbon. "What's the rap?"

"No rap. I'm just looking for them, they seem to have disappeared."

"Nearly a month," said Mavis with satisfaction. "Gone without a trace. Although she was six years older, I regarded Miranda as my best friend in the world. She was . . . incandescent, a very exciting person to be with. Maybe that's what worried her mother."

"Why would that worry her mother?"

"You know mothers. They want their daughters to be little girls forever. They remember what *they* did when they were young and they're afraid. Probably that's why Barbara sent Miranda away to school."

"And when did that happen?"

"Must've been nearly four years ago."

"Then you haven't seen her in four years."

"Summers. Vacations. Not like the good old days, but Miranda was incandescent, a little time with her was better than a lot of time with most people."

"Do you know where she went to school?"

Mavis removed the Coke bottle from her pursed lips and examined him with some skepticism. "For a private eye you don't know much."

"It's just the beginning of the investigation," protested Goldberg. "Give me a break."

Mavis squinted at him in this new light. "To tell you the absolute truth I don't know where she went to school. She never told me. She said her mother didn't want her to tell anybody. Usually that wouldn't stop Miranda for a second, but this time she did what her mother told her, she seemed scared not to. She did say it was very fancy, like an English

95

lady school, tea in the afternoon, and curfews. Miranda claimed it was kind of a rich girl's pen."

"Pen?"

"Penitentiary," explained Mavis, pitying Goldberg his innocence.

"That must have been very expensive."

"Money was never their problem." She leaned forward in her chair and pointed the half-empty Coke bottle at Goldberg. "Miranda once showed me a Pan Am bag full of hundred-dollar bills. Brand new. Must've been a million dollars in that bag."

"Probably less," said Goldberg.

"I just said it for emphasis. It was a lot of money—and I was very young at the time. Barbara always had a bag like that when she went on her trips. It never seemed to get empty." Mavis leaned forward again, looked around for eavesdroppers, and lowered her voice. "Do you think they've been murdered?" she asked, unawed by the possibility.

"Most people who disappear haven't been murdered. They just go away somewhere."

Mavis sighed. "That's good to know."

"Tell me about the new tenants," said Goldberg.

"New tenants?"

"The people who are in the house now."

"Oh, them. They drove up in a chocolate-brown Mercedes early this morning. First time I ever saw them. She's kind of good looking in a hooker sort of way, but he's really grungy."

"I've just seen the woman."

"Wait'll you see the guy."

"I can't wait." Goldberg stood and put his empty Coke bottle down on a small white table. Mavis rose with him, holding out her hand. "Thanks for the information and the drink," said Goldberg. "If I can ever return the favor, just let me know."

"I'd love to see Miranda again. You ever find her tell her to call, she's got the number. Tell her I miss her."

"Sure thing," said Goldberg, feeling the delicate bones of her hand nestled in his palm like a small bird.

As he drove away, she stood very straight, her face alive with delight in the wonderful world that had washed him up beside her swimming pool, bringing news of deadly strangers and the mysterious disappearance of her best friend.

Goldberg drove slowly along Willow Glen until he reached Barbara's house. This time when he pressed the chimes the woman came to the door instantly. She had put away the crowbar, washed the streaked dirt from her arms and legs, and removed the plaster freckles from the space between her breasts. The bikini pants had been pulled up to conceal the appendectomy scar.

"Oh, it's you," she cooed, trying to shed all signs of the young woman who had told him to go fuck himself a half hour before. "My husband called and said I was such a bad girl to treat you the way I did. He was real mad at me, said it was because I grew up in New York where everybody suspects everybody else. He said I didn't know how to behave in California. He said you want to live in California you got to learn to act like California. He was real mean to me. He said if I ever saw you again first thing I should do is apologize." She simpered at him, rotating her hips slightly to augment the effect. "I apologize."

"You didn't think to ask your husband who he rented the house from?"

"He said he'll be home in an hour; he'll answer all the questions you want himself. Come on in and wait."

Her nipples protruded through the top of the bikini like grapes and she no longer minded his inspection. There was a small dark mole halfway down her left breast.

"An hour is a long time," he said.

"Not when you're having fun." She offered him the simper again. "Come on in. You got to see this house to believe it, it's like wow, man, the whole first floor is the living room, that's got to cover a lot of living. I tell you what, some night I have a party I'll invite you up."

She walked into the room ahead of him and the hips were going like a grandfather clock, ticktock, ticktock, ticktock. Apple-ass, Goldberg thought automatically, and apple-ass, apple-ass, apple-ass, the hips echoed back. Maybe this was the way she walked all the time, but Goldberg suspected at least half the ticks and half the tocks were California hospitality. He wondered how long St. Anthony had spent in the desert, probably more than an hour, but on the other hand Goldberg was no St. Anthony.

"My name is Mrs. Swayne." She turned her head to give him the benefit of her smile and the apple-ass at the same time. "You can call me Myra."

"Goldberg," said Goldberg, thinking maybe he should have cards printed.

"Isn't it a blast?" she said. "You ever seen anything like it? The room, I mean?"

The room ran the full length and breadth of the house, probably a hundred feet by about fifty, and it was painted the bleached bone white of a Mexican courtyard. Color exploded against the white. The rich brown of Mission furniture. The warm tones of glove leather. The jewel beads of antique Indian baskets. The rich blood-red of Navaho blankets. On the far wall a life-size Indian warrior stared haughtily out of canvas. A Mexican Madonna, kidnapped long ago from her cathedral home. Dried flowers. The scent of lemons. The walls were a gallery of southwestern painters.

"You see what I mean," said Swayne. "Some place for a party. I bet you wouldn't believe the things that've gone on in this room."

"You rented it furnished?"

"My husband's going to answer all the business questions," Myra Swayne pointed out a little snappishly, and then relenting, added, "in just about an hour. Gotta take him at least an hour from where he is. You want coffee, or maybe booze, coke, beer, something to eat? We got everything. Maybe you'd like to smoke a joint? Maybe a house tour? You like to see what's upstairs, kitchen, bedrooms, things like that?"

"That would be nice."

"It's a little messy. We have some fixing to do, but you'll get the idea."

As she advanced ahead of him up the stairs, the movement of the nearly naked apple-ass produced a complementary surge in Goldberg, which he rejected severely, reminding himself that what he was watching was gluteal muscle at work, gluteus maximus, gluteus medius, gluteus minimus, maximus, medius, minimus, maximus, medius, minimus. The recitation fell into the rhythm of her hips and did Goldberg no good at all.

"This is the kitchen," proclaimed Myra Swayne, leading him into it.

The kitchen ran along the rear of the house, overlooking the garden below. It had a Garland range, a stainless-steel sink, a seven-foot refrigerator and a matching freezer, a butcher block, wall-to-wall cabinets, quivers of Heinkel knives, copper pots. It was a very serious kitchen; it had

99

been put together as the engine to feed the parties on the floor beneath it.

"You sure you don't want a little lunchie?" inquired Myra.

"I'm not hungry."

"Me neither." Myra grinned at him understandingly. It was clear there was nothing he could say she wouldn't agree with. If she hadn't been so excessively nubile, it would have been merely boring.

"You're not still mad at me?" she asked anxiously.

"Not in the least," Goldberg assured her. "Forgotten and forgiven."

"It makes you like want to cook something." She surveyed the kitchen one last time before turning away from it. "This way to the bedrooms," she announced gaily.

The smaller of the two bedrooms was a little girl's room, shades of pink, frilled and bowed, a mother's vision. In one corner there was an elaborate dollhouse with a little girl's riding helmet perched on the roof, hanging from the chimney by the chin strap. The room was a testimonial to young girlhood, maintained by the force of maternal will. Goldberg remembered how it had been with his own daughter, furniture coming and going in waves as she marched through adolescence, seeking new definitions of herself.

"You like to play with dollhouses?" inquired Myra Swayne, raising an eyebrow as he reached into the center hall to examine a clock that stood there.

"I used to live in a house just like it," he said returning the clock to its place in the hall.

"Different strokes for different folks." Myra Swayne was pleased with herself for having found the phrase. "Come on. I'll show you the big bedroom. It's something else."

If she kept her mouth shut, she'd be dangerously seductive, thought Goldberg, following her down the hall to the big bedroom, but then she wasn't likely to.

"Look at that bed." Myra didn't just speak her opinions, she broadcast them. "You could give parties there without ever going downstairs."

But where Myra saw orgies Goldberg detected hints of chastity, stainless-steel columns, an early-American quilt, white linen bedclothes. There were two Shaker chairs and a chest. The room was filled with pictures of Miranda, Miranda on a pony, Miranda at the beach, Miranda in tights and ballet slippers, Miranda at her kindergarten graduation, Miranda, Miranda, forever Miranda. There were no curtains on the windows, which faced the mountains and nothing else. A window seat had been wrenched from the wall and behind it there was evidence of Myra's burrowing with the crowbar. "A terrible leak through a crack in the wall," she said. "I thought I could fix it myself, but my husband's sent for somebody." Aware that somehow the tour had lost its momentum, she pulled thoughtfully at a wrinkle in the early-American quilt. "Look," she said, "I'll be right back. Why don't you sit down and make yourself comfortable?"

When she returned, the bikini was gone. She advanced across the room toward him, her lips parted, her body softer and rounder and momentarily vulnerable, transformed by nakedness and silence into the Venus of Willow Glen. Even then Goldberg might have put her off if it had not been for the fragrance that rose insidiously from her naked flesh, the scent of irises in a nighttime garden, mingled with even subtler odors that tugged nostalgically at his memory.

Her tongue was in his mouth and the fragrance was in his

nostrils, summoning a word that was like a sigh, a name that would not come. She was unbuttoning his shirt and tugging at his belt and then they were on Barbara's bed and the word, the name, came a little closer, but not close enough. When Myra Swayne bit his neck in her passion, the moment's pain hid another, the sting of a syringe in his left buttock, and it was this second bite that released the name he had been struggling for: Silences, golden script on an incomplete black circle, the fragrance he had seen on Barbara's dressing table in Las Vegas, the one she had worn all the time he knew her. As he tried to roll free he knew it was too late, for Myra had just given him the biggest fix in the world. He grabbed at her flesh, determined to take her with him wherever he was going, but she fought her way free and raced ahead of him down the hall in the direction of the living room. Schmuck, o you great loony schmuck, he cried out to himself as he tripped over a living-room couch and went into the star-spattered revolving darkness.

Deep down in the darkness somewhere he continued to exist dimly, in a cave of flashing light and erupting color. This went on forever, and then after a time that was not like time as he had ever known it before, but rather a smaller infinity, the fragrance, Silences, came back to him in a cloud so enormous it closed everything else out. He floated in Silences, he drifted in Silences, he was Silences, and this odor that had been so wonderful by the fluid ounce tore him and tormented him and threatened to bring an end to him forever. As he was about to disappear for the last time, the sound came through the cloud, like a giant scratching on the earth, huge gnarled fingernails turning up dirt and grass and gravel. Gravel recalled the road that ran around the house, and he knew he was listening to a car's tires grinding and coming to a stop. The front door of the house cracked against its hinge and the screaming started. Even at that great distance he understood the screamer was Myra Swayne. Slowly he put the words together and tried to make sense of them. For a while it seemed to be the same word over and over again, "An hour, an hour, an hour . . ." And then the words slowed down to a point where they began to fit together. "You dumb bastard, that was some hour, more like three you left me alone with the son of a bitch. How did I know how long that dose would last? Some little kid mug you for your watch, or something?"

Goldberg lived a long way back from his eyes. When he decided to open them, he discovered he couldn't quite reach them. He was about to abandon the struggle when the right eye popped open by itself.

They were crossing the room in his direction, Myra Swayne in the lead, the man Goldberg had left behind in the spinning Corvette following her. The Corvette driver had gotten rid of the neon-blue leisure suit and replaced it with a Hawaiian shirt and slacks.

"Slow down," said Myra. "You sound like a sick Singer sewing machine."

"F-f-f-f-uck y-y-you," roared the man she had claimed to be her husband.

"Don't you wish you could," sneered Myra, who was now wearing a dress.

Goldberg's right eye was stuck again in the closed position and the left had never opened at all, but his ears were working fine. His knees banged together on the couch as he struggled to move his legs off the couch onto the floor.

"He's m-m-m-moving," cried the man accusingly.

"He ain't dead. Big one, ain't he?" Myra's voice was

husky with remembered pleasure. "Lucky for you I got him first. He could whip your ass good if he could stand up."

"I c-c-c-could t-t-t-take the s-s-son of a b-b-bitch, the b-b-best d-d-day he e-e-e-ever h-h-h-had in his l-l-life."

"Slowly," advised Myra. "Speak slowly and enunciate clearly."

Goldberg was swinging now in a hammock suspended from a pair of stars, traveling in enormous slow arcs from side to side. In the middle of an arc he banged into an obstacle that hadn't been there before and started to move in a contradictory direction. While he was still trying to figure out what was going on, the stutterer's hammer fist caught him on the point of his jaw and drove him farther, farther, farther out until finally Goldberg disappeared once more into nothingness.

Twelve

Goldberg's night was broken by the lamentations of a mechanical beast, a loud-pitched howl that rose and fell and rose again. It went on and on until it was joined by a distant crackle of trees being chewed by fire in another country. The smoke didn't travel as fast as the crackle, but it arrived soon enough, crawling into his nose and lungs. His throat burned. He was choking. Having died before, he was surprised to be dying again, but he was on the way to his second death when the third one came in the form of rain and he started to die once more, drowning in the torrents that washed in waves over his body and beat at the entrances to his head. Gulping and spitting, he struck out with his arms and legs in a last instinctive effort to swim out of the flood.

It was the swimming that brought him to life, kicking and struggling on Barbara's couch. He was naked. The house was on fire, flames, smoke, alarms screaming from the ceilings, water spurting from the sprinkler system.

He was halfway to the front door, pantsless, shirtless, shoeless, when he remembered the car keys were in his pocket and staggered up the smoke-filled stairwell in the direction of his pants. All around him Barbara's memories and possessions smoldered and spit and charred. In the big bedroom he remembered the neighbor girl, Mavis, in a house not too far away, and, grabbing the telephone, he croaked the fire warning three times before the operator understood what he was up to.

He had to sit on the bed to put on his pants. The car keys were still in the right-hand pocket. He took his shirt and shoes and started to leave the bedroom when it occurred to him to rescue something for Barbara if he ever found her. Filling his empty hand with pictures of Miranda, he moved tentatively, not sure his legs or arms would do what he wanted them to do, toward the stairs. His head hurt, but the pain was the least of it; there seemed to be gaps in his brain, great spaces he had to jump to bring himself from the initiation of a thought to its completion. Looking back at the bed on its four steel columns, he wondered what Myra Swayne had had in her syringe and what else she carried in her pharmacopoeia.

The sprinklers were beginning to beat down the flames

105

and everywhere there was the sound of water turning to steam, the great sigh of a house in its death throes. Placing his feet carefully, not sure each time they would go where he wanted them to, he slid through the devastated living room. If Myra and the stutterer had noticed the sprinkler system, or thought about it, Goldberg would have been dead before they left. Two birds with one stone—they had expected to kill Goldberg and the house together. What did they have against the house? Arson was useful for concealing the corpus delicti, but Swayne's style seemed to run more to kill 'em and leave 'em. Why the house? Because it hid something they couldn't find and didn't want anybody else to find. Whatever it was, Myra had been burrowing for it with the crowbar.

When Goldberg stepped out onto the porch, fresh air startled his lungs. As the new air replaced the old, he staggered, suddenly drunk on gusts of oxygen. Everything was more intense than it had been when he left it, the green of leaves, the blue of the sky, the sun-struck red hood of the Avis Ford. His father, who had always loved red cars, once owned a great brute of a red Stutz that father and son, the boy no more than five, had driven at blistering speeds along the burning white roads of South Carolina. What had they been doing in South Carolina? Goldberg could not remember, but in place of the memory that would not come there came another.

When he left Martha Weir, there had been the promise of something she wasn't quite ready to tell him. She had led him to Willow Glen and now she was going to have to lead him out again. Martha Weir knew a lot more about Angel Barbara and her Pan Am bag full of money than she had yet let on. Maybe this time Martha Weir would love him for his wounds. Or the hot breath of the Swaynes could do the trick. You want them to find her before I do, o Martha mine?

Goldberg struggled into the Avis Ford, turned it around and headed back down Laurel Canyon, at first so slowly that people honked him on, but then, as his arms and eyes and legs began to behave themselves, with more and more confidence. He passed the fire engines on the way up and wondered whether they would find anything in the walls when they pulled the house apart in the search for sparks. He thought he knew what the Swaynes were looking for. The firemen wouldn't find it any more than the Swaynes had.

Even at reduced speed it didn't take him more than half an hour to reach Martha Weir's house, which was exactly the way he had left it, with the MG in the doorway of the shed and the curtains drawn. He rang the bell. Nobody came. The day was degenerating into instant replay, he thought, ringing again and waiting. Maybe she was in the shower, or dressing, or slightly deaf. He gave himself five minutes on the Oyster Perpetual before he rang again. Maybe asleep—she worked nights. He rang the bell three times in rapid succession, but it had none of the authority of Barbara's cathedral chimes. A mouse squeak. He wondered how Martha ever heard it and remembered a pamphlet of domestic accidents his son had brought home from the Boy Scouts: legs broken in bathtubs, ladders off balance, strange paralyzing cramps, rugs that slipped, stairs that broke, epileptic fits. She could be visiting a next-door neighbor, stuck in the attic crawl space, lost in a soap opera, choking on a chicken bone. The longer the list got the surer he was that none of these things had happened to her. Myra's partner, maybe her husband, had been gone for at least three hours, probably longer. Uneasily Goldberg began to suspect where he had been and what he had been doing. He rang the bell once more before abandoning it, and went around to the back of the house, stopping on the way to inspect the shed, which was empty. He rattled the back door, banged on it, kicked it. Inside nothing changed. Through the glass panes he could see into the kitchen. On the stove something had cooked too long and turned the pot black. Picking up a long flat stone, he tapped it against the glass, gently at first and then hard enough to crack the glass. Reaching inside, he opened the door. "Miss Weir," he called as he advanced into the kitchen and turned off the gas jet under the blackened pot. On the counter was the knife with which she had been slicing a tomato. The tomato was still there, half-sliced. "Anybody home?" he shouted, going down the short corridor that led to the living room. "Anybody home?" Then he didn't have to call out any more. Martha Weir was there, in her living room, face down on the rug. Her arms and legs were bound with knotted clothesline to a chair she had carried over with her as she fell. Blood clotted on the rug where her head rested. A linen dishtowel had been wadded in her mouth and fastened in place by a piece of copper wire that was twisted under her ears. There were burn marks, made with a soldering iron, up and down both arms. It was putting them there that had taken Swayne all that extra time, the three hours Myra had been so bitter about. The arms hadn't been enough for Swayne; he'd burned her legs, too, all the way up under her skirt. Craters in the flesh, as though they'd been put there by shrapnel. But she hadn't died from the burns. There were four bullet holes in the back of her head. One to kill. Three for punishment. She had kept her secret until the end.

There are many ways to die, and by now Goldberg had

seen most of them, but being called to your maker in your own living room by a man with face like a side of beef seemed particularly nasty. Goldberg sat in the chair he'd occupied on his first visit, Martha's only mourner, surprised at the intensity of his own emotion. He had barely known the woman, and as a matter of fact hadn't even particularly liked her although he had respected the toughness of her assorted hates and one love. Perhaps the drug was still working on him. Or it could have been the fact the Swaynes had tried to kill him, too, a common enemy being bond enough. At any rate Goldberg wept for the second time in his life, the first having been for his son, the second for a two hundred fifty-pound black woman he hardly knew. Goldberg got his weeping over with and started to search the house, inch by inch, foot by foot, knocking at walls, prying, picking, moving furniture and boxes.

Although not a large house, it wasn't easy to search, for Martha Weir had been an ambitious accumulator, William Randolph Hearst cramped for room. A small armory of weapons, pistols, rifles, revolvers, shotguns, none of which had finally been of any use to her. Three sewing machines. Chests, cartons, trunks of fabric. Closets in which the dresses pressed against each other in an impenetrable wall. Rugs on rugs. Collections: coins, stamps, china doorknobs. Small animals, carved, molded, baked, and blown. Generations of camera equipment. Photographs everywhere, mostly of Barbara, but also a number of stern black women who were Martha's ancestors. There were the sporting enterprises, started, pursued, and abandoned: fly rods, a yachting hat, a marine compass, Topsiders, an outboard motor. Books arranged by subject, mostly texts, biology, physics, chemistry, pharmacology, neurosurgery. The kind of nurse who enjoyed intimidating doctors. Everywhere en-

109

ergy pecking to be let out. A small workshop on the second floor with a band saw, a lathe, a drill press. Hand tools hanging from a peg board. A mason's trowel, chisels, and mallet. A small pile of red bricks set aside for the day when she would find a use for them.

It was clear Martha Weir had aspired to be her own country, independent and undependent, male, female, her own doctor, carpenter, fisherman, hunter. The only outsider she'd ever let in was Barbara, and Barbara had been her destruction. Goldberg repeated the list to himself, knowing he had left something out. Doctor, carpenter, fisherman, hunter, dressmaker, rug hooker. He wasn't looking for any of those. Mason. Mason was it. He remembered where he had seen bricks that were twins to these. He remembered them from the first meeting with Martha. He had wondered then, but idly, how she kept them so clean, and now he went back to look again at the fireplace in the living room.

He removed the andirons and the pyramid of birch logs. The fireplace itself was untouched by soot or dirt; no evening had been cool enough to justify its use. On his hands and knees Goldberg examined the three walls of the fireplace, row on row of red brick, separated by straight white lines of mortar. Strong. Neat. Solid. None of the hesitation marks or patches on patches he associated with his own efforts at home repair. When he pushed the bricks one at a time with his forefinger, he got back nothing but uniform resistance. He lit a candle to follow the ribbons of mortar between the bricks. Martha Weir laid brick the way she did everything else; in the manufacture of your own country there is no room for imperfections. He pulled his head out of the fireplace and looked at the dead woman sprawled on the floor with the chair still strapped to her. God, she was

110

enormous. Whatever she made would be built to her own proportions. Everything extreme. Tall. Wide. Outsize was her size for everything. Goldberg got back in the fireplace and slid his head up tenderly through the darkness of the narrow chimney. Standing on tiptoes and reaching as high as he could he found the handle, a curved steel bar about six inches long. When he pulled down on it, he heard the wall at the back of the fireplace click. On his knees again, he pushed at the wall, which swung open. Behind it was a space the size of two steamer trunks, filled with Pan Am bags. Goldberg pulled three of the bags out into the living room. Each one was swollen to capacity with neatly banded bundles of bright new hundred-dollar bills.

It was Goldberg's first encounter with Barbara's money, and he looked at it with an expert's skeptical eye. He'd seen his share of counterfeit during his working days; the most remarkable thing about most of it was that it had fooled anybody.

Goldberg estimated that he was looking at about six hundred thousand dollars. In the wall behind him there were millions more, upward of twenty he guessed. The most remarkable thing about this money was that it was real. Genuine. Perfect. Paper, engraving, ink, all just what they were supposed to be. If the U.S. Bureau of Engraving and Printing hadn't made this, a lot of people were in for a monstrous surprise.

He crawled into the fireplace again and came out with three bags to a hand, each one containing two hundred thousand dollars. When the knocking started, he had accumulated nearly two million on the rug near his ankles.

Cops have the same knock all over the world. Goldberg had knocked that way himself on occasions, but he'd never been inside listening to it before.

The LAPD came through the back door and the front at the same time, with guns in their hands and the look of curious intensity, eyes slightly squinted, lips tight, that meant they expected to use the guns in the very near future. Remembering what that look felt like on his own face, Goldberg raised his hands over his head.

There was an old woman in the background, trying to battle her way through to Goldberg. House dress with sunflowers. A bosom that swelled from neck to waist. One look and you knew she baked only from scratch. Right now she had no ambition higher than gouging out Goldberg's eyes with her rosy fingernails. "What did I tell you?" she screamed. "Banged the glass with a flat rock and went in cool as you please. I lived here forty years and we would leave the doors open. Now nobody's safe, nothing's safe." It was then she saw Martha Weir for the first time. "Oh, my God. Oh, my God." She started to choke as the vomit rose in her throat and the muffled sound of her retching filled the room.

At that point Goldberg announced that he was an agent of the Secret Service, working for a man named Schoyer, whose office was in the Treasury Building in Washington, D.C.

The LAPD put handcuffs on him anyway.

Thirteen

"You're not going to believe this," began Goldberg.

"Try me," said Schoyer, the words spitting out of the telephone into Goldberg's ear. For years now there had been nothing Goldberg could say that Schoyer would not contradict. In fairness, Goldberg had to concede he was equally bad with Schoyer. "Where are you?"

"The L.A. slammer."

"I believe it."

"That's not the part you're not going to believe."

"What have you been up to now?" Schoyer's snarl had a half-hearted quality that puzzled Goldberg.

"I'm doing your business out here, Schoyer."

"Thanks, but no thanks." Schoyer was worried about something and it was interfering with the purity of his hatred. "What kind of trouble you in now?" Schoyer asked abstractedly.

"I've found some funny money, twenty million dollars worth."

"Counterfeit?"

Goldberg realized there was nothing particularly impressive about the number. Once you started the press rolling you might as well make as much as you'd ever need. "I imagine there's plenty more where it came from," said Goldberg. "But what's funny about this is it's perfect."

"You know better than that. Or have you forgotten?" Schoyer was somehow not as indignant as he should have been. "If it's perfect, it's bona-fide U.S. currency. There's good counterfeit. There's bad counterfeit. There's even very good counterfeit. There's no such thing as perfect counterfeit. It's a contradiction in terms."

"I know. At least I knew until I saw this stuff."

"If it's perfect, how do you know it's counterfeit?" asked Schoyer, somewhat cheered by this new flaw in Goldberg's thinking.

"Because it makes even less sense if it's genuine. You better get out here and look at it yourself. There are things I can't tell you over an open line."

Schoyer hesitated, still caught in that strange paralysis that had taken over from his rage. "I'll send Adams over from the L.A. office. You know Adams?"

"No."

"Doesn't make any difference. He'll be able to find you." Schoyer didn't even bother to laugh at his little joke and that was unusual. Schoyer was operating out of some knowledge Goldberg didn't have, and whatever it was had changed him. Goldberg tried to remember how Schoyer had been before everything had gone wrong. Perhaps this was normal Schoyer, and all the rest was aberration. "I'll be out on the first available plane," said Schoyer. "In the meanwhile, you keep your mouth shut until I get there."

Adams, who turned out to be a lean uncommunicative blond with aviator glasses, negotiated Goldberg's release after some virtuoso string pulling and installed him in an apartment in West Hollywood to wait for Schoyer's arrival.

It was one of those beige days in June that are peculiar to Los Angeles and the dim yellowish-brown light hung in the

114

apartment like depression made visible. Adams seemed immune to the light and everything else. Goldberg estimated his age to be thirty-eight, his height five-foot-eleven, his weight one sixty-five. His eyes were hazel, his shirt white, his unwrinkled suit a pale tan not too far from the color of the air. He was one of those people who seem to come from nowhere. After work he would not go home, he would simply disappear until the next morning when he would show up again, freshly laundered, impeccable, and immune.

One of his immunities was to conversation. He didn't want to know anything about Goldberg, nor did he want to tell him anything, not even the weather forecast, which, for the rest of the month, was hardly likely to include any surprises. Schoyer had obviously instructed him carefully. He never told Goldberg that he was in custody, but on the other hand he showed no disposition to leave him alone. As a concession to hospitality, he mentioned that there was liquor in the liquor cabinet, a plywood rectangle with a sliding door that looked as though Adams had put it together from a kit that morning. The whole apartment, two bedrooms, a living room-kitchen, an aquamarine tiled bathroom, shared that same quality of improvisation. Like Adams it could disappear at the end of the day with nobody the wiser.

Goldberg took some Scotch from the liquor cabinet, showered, and settled down to watch an international soccer match on TV. It didn't interest him much. After a while he went to sleep in the smaller of the two bedrooms. When he woke up, Schoyer was standing over him.

"So," said Schoyer.

"So," said Goldberg, staring up at the familiar jowls and horn-rimmed glasses and the crown of steel shavings that served Schoyer as hair. Goldberg did not feel like getting up. The beigeness of the day had infected him, spreading its insipid gloom to all areas of his body and what passed as his soul. He noticed that, beyond the blinds, beige had turned to a gray-black like ink that had too much water in it. "What time is it?" he asked.

"Ten o'clock," said Schoyer. "But not the day you think it is. Adams tells me you've been asleep for thirty hours." Behind the horn-rimmed glasses the nearsighted brown eyes were worried and appraising. Normal people didn't sleep for thirty hours. If Goldberg was given to sleeping away whole days, he could be as crazy as ever. "So," said Schoyer.

"So," replied Goldberg, sailing in a sea of total indifference. Maybe that's what it was like to get old, caring less and less about more and more, until finally you cared about nothing. "They have lousy accommodations in the slammer," he said finally. "Spoil anybody's sleep." Irritated with himself, he rolled his head on the pillow. "Scratch that. When I tell you what happened, you'll understand the sleeping better." He lowered his hands and pushed himself to a sitting position. "Have you seen the money?"

"Yeah. I've seen it. As a matter of fact I've sent it along to the lab for analysis." Schoyer rubbed his right hand in his steel-gray curls, which immediately sprang back into place. It occurred to Goldberg that in all the years he had known him, he had never seen Schoyer comb his hair; he undoubtedly didn't have to, it was self-combing. "What made you decide it was counterfeit?"

Goldberg got up from the bed and tried to stretch the tightness out of his body. "Listen, I'm just on the outskirts of what's going on, way out beyond Scarsdale, somewhere in the distant suburbs, maybe in the vicinity of Wilton,

116

Connecticut, but I'll tell you what I know and you make up your own mind."

"Thanks. Try to keep it simple enough for my bureaucratic head."

"Let's get out of here." Goldberg, who had gone to sleep in his shorts, pulled on his pants and shirt and led the way into the living room-kitchen, where he poured himself another Scotch and offered one to Schoyer. Adams seemed to have disappeared. "You remember the girl, Barbara?" said Goldberg. "The one in the white evening dress. Of course you remember her, you're the one who saw the guy following us."

"Yeah." Schoyer found himself a bottle of Jack Daniels. "The girl in the white evening dress. The guy in the riding boots. It's a fucking fashion show."

"Take it easy. It took me a lot longer living it than it takes to listen to it. I've been searching for that girl now for six weeks."

"Why?" said Schoyer.

Goldberg looked at him and voted for the easy answer. "She took my money."

Schoyer dipped his beak toward the Jack Daniels, pausing only long enough to say, "Kiss it good-bye."

"A lot of people don't want me to find her. I've been shot at on the freeway, stabbed full of dope up in Laurel Canyon, and left to die in a burning house. Martha Weir, the black woman in Echo Park, was killed because she knew too much about what was going on."

"Which is what?" Schoyer looked tired. It was odd seeing him that way because he had always been inexhaustible, first one up in the morning, last one to bed, painstaking, meticulous, invulnerable. Now he looked like somebody's grandpa playing cop, jowls too pendulous and too gray, the long arched nose aging into a hook, the belly in folds on both sides of the belt. Schoyer was more than tired, he was worried. Fear was turning him into an old man.

"They had a name for the girl in the white dress around the casinos. Vegas, Tahoe, Reno, they called her the Angel. Because she staked busted-out gamblers. She was a bank. Every weekend she was off to one of her places, carrying a Pan Am bag with two hundred thousand in cash. The same kind of cash I found in the chimney and you sent to the lab."

"Doesn't make a helluva lot of sense. It's a guaranteed method of grinding down a fortune."

"Yeah." Goldberg agreed. "Unless the fortune is all counterfeit. Look at it that way, it's just a device for turning bad money into good. At a considerable discount, of course, but you always sell counterfeit at a discount. For what it costs you can afford to be generous."

"Nobody's ever made counterfeit that good." Schoyer was firm about that. "It's impossible. You know that as well as I do. We're not talking about some kind of South American wallpaper. This is U.S. currency we're talking about. Everybody who's ever owned a printing press has dreamed of knocking it off, and plenty have tried. Nobody's ever succeeded. Good enough to fool a guy in a candy store maybe, or a couple of sleepy bank tellers, but good enough to fool an expert, never. You remember that guy Mike Landress, he made pretty good money, only it turned blue in the suitcase." Schoyer laughed at the money that turned blue and put away a little more Jack Daniels in its memory.

"Why you so worried, Schoyer?" asked Goldberg.

"I get paid to worry," snapped Schoyer.

Schoyer reached in his pocket for a cigarette and remembered he'd given up smoking five years ago. He felt around in his pocket anyway and sighed. "We used to be good friends," he said. "You weren't just another guy who worked for me. I always figured you went crazy back there. Now it seems like the whole world's gone crazy. Just tell me the rest of what you've got to tell, and then I've got something for you. Maybe we could work together in a small way. It couldn't be like the old days, of course, but nothing's the same. We'll figure something out."

"There's not a helluva lot more," said Goldberg. "I stumbled into this patch, but you have to assume it's a small piece of something much larger. The piece I've got is a girl with twenty million dollars hidden in a brick chimney, goes up to the casinos once a week to dispose of two hundred thousand in cash—forget why she does it. The guy in the riding boots, Doc Holliday, is after her, probably wants to kill her, tries to kill me. Small in its way. Then it starts to get larger. A thug name of Swayne follows me from Las Vegas, tries to shoot me on the freeway. His buddy Myra gives him a helping hand with a syringe full of junk. They burn Barbara's house in Willow Glen after searching it. Swayne kills Martha Weir with four bullets in the head, but first he tortures her with a soldering iron. They're looking for something. One thing's sure, they're ready to kill anybody who knows too much. Too much about what? *What's* the scary part. How many more girls are there trotting around the country with their little Pan Am bags full of money? How many more Swaynes and Hollidays? If it's genuine, what's the whole scam about? Where does it stop? Right now it seems as if it's all tied into gambling, but that's not much of a limitation. You're not only talking about Vegas, or Reno, or Tahoe, or Atlantic City, or the rest of legalized gambling. There's five hundred billion gambled, bet, won, and lost in this country every year, everything from church bingo to baccarat, horse bets, football bets, you name it. What's the gross national product of Switzerland? I don't remember, and you don't either, but five hundred billion would pay for a helluva lot of watches and chocolate."

Schoyer was slumped down in his chair now, using his belly as a table for the glass of Jack Daniels that he held in his left hand and stirred periodically with a forefinger. He had lost all inclination to argue and for a moment it was like old times when Goldberg would talk and Schoyer would listen and afterward Schoyer would talk and Goldberg would listen. There wasn't much then they wouldn't try out on each other; for Schoyer it seemed to be like that again.

"All right," he said, "I'm going to be straight with you. When they said you were on the phone, I almost didn't answer. When you came on with that wild story about the money, I almost hung up. But if the whole world's gone crazy, you've got to start thinking crazy if you want to stay with it. You say you've got a small piece of something bigger. Maybe I've got another piece way over on the other side."

Schoyer's hands were at his pockets again, looking for the cigarettes that hadn't been there for five years. "Three people were kidnapped in Washington last week," he said. "Same day. Three separate locations. Same green van. Same gang, all young."

Goldberg looked at him curiously. "Kidnapping's usually not your line of work," he said.

"You've got it in one," said Schoyer gloomily. "I get paid to be interested in people like that. They all worked for the Bureau of Engraving and Printing. One engraver. One ink chemist. One printer. All kidnapped off the streets of

Washington, D.C., during the afternoon and early evening. How do you like them apples?" As he became older, Schoyer had become fonder of familiar expressions; he would trot them out periodically, taking comfort in them as though they were mementos of better times.

How do you like them apples? thought Goldberg. Schoyer was going back to his roots, and Goldberg was one of the roots. "If you wanted to make real money, who could do it better than the people who made it in the first place?"

"If you were crazy enough you would figure something like that."

"That money in the chimney's a lot older than last week," pointed out Goldberg.

"I know." Schoyer's face was grim. "I checked. There's no indication of anything like this ever happening before. Of course people quit the Bureau, they resign, they get sick, they retire, they go on sabbaticals. We don't keep track of them after they leave the Bureau. Never would have occurred to anybody before this. I've got them checking now. But you can't think of everything."

Schoyer didn't really believe this: he was convinced that when he was younger he would have thought of everything. His fingers settled on a swizzle stick from a jug on the bar and twirled it like a baton. "You like another drink?" He poured Scotch for Goldberg and Jack Daniels for himself. "You broke?" he asked. "After the girl cleaned you out?"

"No," said Goldberg. "I've taken up winning as a profession."

"Don't play crazy with me, Goldberg, I don't have the time." Schoyer looked Goldberg over, lips pursed in disapproval, jowls shaking. "Where the hell you getting your clothes, out of garbage pails?"

"I've had my mind on other things." Goldberg started to

tell Schoyer about the winning streak, leaving out the dreams and omens and other parts Schoyer would shy away from as crazy, keeping it to places, amounts, and dates.

Schoyer still didn't know what to make of it and finally solved the problem by changing the subject. "You told the cops you were working for me," he said.

"It was all I had on me," explained Goldberg, unnecessarily he thought.

Schoyer accepted the explanation with unusual equanimity.

"How'd you like to work for me again? Like it used to be." But Schoyer knew it couldn't be the way it used to be. "No badge, no pension rights," he said apologetically, "none of that. I'll personally guarantee hospitalization."

Goldberg laughed.

Schoyer was interested now. "What is it you really want?"

"The girl. Alive and well and not in some stinking jail. That's what you're going to give me, Schoyer."

Schoyer's lips went prim for the moment, then relaxed. "You know the problems. What I can do I'll do. Assuming we find her."

"Assuming we find her," agreed Goldberg.

"You want to know your part, Goldberg?" Schoyer prodded his chest with a blunt forefinger. "These people want to kill you. They really seem to have their hearts set on it. You're my bait, Goldberg. At the moment it seems like you're all I got."

Fourteen

The tuxedo was Schoyer's idea. He said it was classy and roulette was a classy game with a great appeal for dames.

Goldberg didn't care one way or the other, but Schoyer was right, there were more women than men at the table and when there was nothing better to look at they looked at Goldberg's rented tuxedo.

The wheel was moving again, gold numbers on red and black and, in two cases, green, one to thirty-six, zero and double zero, each with its own silver-walled compartment called a canoe, all starting to blur while the perfect ivory ball spun crazily against the tide like a salmon swimming upstream. "No more bets," called the dealer at the peak of the blur, just before it began to degenerate into clarity, and then you could start to pick out the numbers while the perfect ivory ball flirted with them, popping into one canoe and out into another, teasing, teasing, until finally it came to rest in a slot that had nothing at all to do with Goldberg. That's what it had been like all evening, the wheel spinning counterclockwise, the ball racing in the direction of time, the hesitation, the pause, and finally the number that had nothing at all to do with Goldberg.

To play roulette you need either inspiration or a system. Inspiration bubbles up from your subconscious with the advice to bet your grandmother's age on the day she married your grandfather. You can buy a system, or if you have enough conviction of your own mathematical gifts, invent one. Either way the house grinds out its five and five-nineteenths percent, but still you flow effortlessly along with the pace of the game until you are broke or desperate enough to quit.

Goldberg had neither inspiration nor a system. His chips drifted lackadaisically out onto the brilliant green baize of the layout, and disappeared inexorably into the croupier's neat treasury. It didn't matter how he distributed his bets, straight numbers, even, odd, red, black, one half the numbers, or the other half, the chips flowed steadily outward in a form of negative luck as improbable in its way as the winning streak. With shrinking patience he waited for the tingle that would announce the reversal, the onslaught of the streak, and in his boredom he found himself staring down the dress of the young woman sitting next to him.

He looked away quickly when he realized she had noticed and was amused. The young woman's name was Lydia Braun and she was one of the five Secret Service agents Schoyer had assigned to him, the trap for which Goldberg was bait. She was a long-legged blonde with the stride of a marathon runner and a bright smiling face she tried to keep serious because she was involved in a serious business. She wore a lavender dress that didn't seem to offer any place to hide a gun, but she must have had a gun. Goldberg, with nothing better to do, speculated about where she kept it; it was not a problem that would have arisen during his days with the Service.

The dealer raked in the losing bets, including Goldberg's, leaving a small tower of sea-green chips on twenty-seven that was quickly joined by a series of larger towers, all sea-green and now the property of an earnest redheaded school teacher from Boise, who was playing a system she tracked and computed in a composition book with a marbleized cover identical to those that had accompanied Goldberg through grammar school.

The redheaded school teacher reminded him of a girl he had known in the sixth grade by the name of Martha Williams, also redheaded, also mathematically inclined, with the reputation of being the smartest kid in the class, maybe in the school. She had confided to Goldberg once that her mother was worried about her marks, too high, they would scare away boys, but evidently she hadn't paid much attention to the maternal foreboding because years later she graduated first in her class from Radcliffe. Goldberg looked for traces of Martha Williams in the redheaded school teacher before he remembered Martha Williams would be his age and a good twenty years older than the redheaded school teacher. Somehow the knowledge made him sad, not so much for himself as for Martha Williams, who would never leave the sixth grade in his head where everybody he had known in childhood remained eternally young while he alone had aged. He smiled at the redheaded school teacher, but she was too busy with her computations to smile back.

It was a slow night in the casino. Even the relentless chug and clink of the slots was muted and boredom hung in the air like smoke. There were reports that Atlantic City was finally draining East Coast business away from Las Vegas. Even the dealers seemed to be having trouble paying attention. His bodyguards were scattered around the casino, trying to blend into the sluggish action but conspicuously eager as they searched for signs of menace. Menace would have been a relief, thought Goldberg, looking down Lydia

Braun's dress again and deciding to bet along with the red-headed school teacher; it would be easier than making up his own mind.

This time her system, which resembled none Goldberg had ever seen before, called for two straight number bets on four and nine and he followed her onto those squares. She lost. He lost. But his mind was in Sicily where he had been part of a signal intelligence team that was supposed to penetrate the Italian lines and tap the telephone communications of the Italian general staff. Since the Italian line was not a line at all but a series of scribbles, it was not difficult to penetrate; the problem turned out to be one that was not anticipated at all in Washington. The Italian telephone system didn't work; you couldn't listen in on it because they couldn't talk on it. The detachment spent the morning in an abandoned Sicilian farmhouse, drinking wine, making jokes about Mussolini, and trying to decide what to do. A master sergeant by the name of Rocco Marcantonio came up with the solution. If the Americans repaired the Italian telephone system, the Italians would be able to talk on it as they were supposed to, and the Americans would be able to eavesdrop as they were supposed to. The Jesuitic clarity of Rocco's logic was irresistible and for the next three days the Americans slaved to give the Italian general staff back its voice. On the fourth day an Italian signal patrol showed up to make its own repairs, and in the ensuing power fight was wiped out. On the fifth day the general staff, discovering the telephones were working again, started to talk on them, but Rocco never knew about that—he was the only American killed in the power fight. A nice boy, who would be eternally twenty-two in Goldberg's head, he had been a star pitcher at A.B. Davis High School in Mount Vernon, New York, which he left to study for the priesthood until

126

the thought of the girls he was missing started to drive him crazy. He got engaged to a Brooklyn girl just before leaving Fort Hamilton for the European theater. His fiancée had married after the war and moved to Alaska, where she had six children.

Goldberg came back from his dream of Italy to find the redheaded school teacher glaring at him. It seemed that while Goldberg's head was mourning for Rocco Marcantonio and the six children he never had his hands had been following the redheaded school teacher through the stations of her system, and each time he had followed her she had lost. Goldberg smiled apologetically, but it was too late for apologies. She stood up from the table, cashed in her remaining chips, and stalked off, muttering. "You son of a bitch," at Goldberg as she passed him.

The trouble with the winning streak was that life was utterly barren without it. For a moment Goldberg wondered what it would be like if you found a game you could play totally in private, a form of solitaire where your winnings rained down from the ceiling and your failures slid under the rug, and he knew it wouldn't do at all. Winning required an audience. When you won in public, you were the star, the center of the entertainment. Privacy was suitable only for losing.

A small man in a straw hat and a seersucker suit that hung on him like a toga placed himself a little behind Goldberg's right shoulder. His nose, like his suit, was too big for the rest of him; it probed the air defiantly, searching for trouble its owner would never be able to handle. He was talking to himself with an intensity that could be justified by no ordinary conversation.

Lydia Braun, who had noticed the tiny man while Goldberg was still lost in Italy, moved her purse slightly to make

127

it more accessible. Concluding that that was where she kept her gun, Goldberg winked at her but she was on duty now and refused to wink back. If you had to cast against character, you could not have made a better choice than the small stranger with the angry nose, but Goldberg found it hard to accept him even as a closet assassin. He looked around for some sign of Myra Swayne and her hog-faced companion; anything would be a relief from the dull work of losing.

"My name's Sy Alch," said the small man when Goldberg's eyes met his. "Sy's for Seymour. Maybe you heard of me?" He removed his hat to make recognition easier. "Sy Alch?"

Goldberg shook his head.

"Then you don't follow the horses. If you followed the horses, you would of heard of me."

"You were a jockey?"

"I wasn't no horse." The nose threatened Goldberg's middle shirt stud and then withdrew as its owner contemplated another course. "Know what I'm doing here? Making mental bets. Last half hour I made fifteen thousand dollars. How much you lose?"

Goldberg ignored the question.

"Tell you what I'm ready to do," declared Alch. "I'll go partners with you. You come up with the money, you get half my winnings." He produced a small thrifty smile beneath the giant nose to confirm the generosity of the offer.

"No, thanks." Goldberg began to scoop up his remaining chips. "I'm cashing in."

Alch watched the chips being turned back into money, brown eyes shining. He clenched his big hands and shoved them into his pockets to keep them out of trouble. "See you around," he called out, somewhere between promise and threat, as Goldberg strode toward the elevators, Lydia Braun a few steps behind him.

"What was that about?" she inquired, pushing her way into the elevator at his side.

Goldberg glanced around the crowded elevator. The crowds in the elevators were bigger than those in the casino; it was one of those nights when the whole population of the city seemed to have dedicated itself to going up and down like vertical lemmings. "Probably just another hustler, looking for a free ride on somebody else's money. It's the oldest gag in the world."

"You sure?" she asked, getting out of the elevator with him.

"No." Goldberg shrugged. "You could have him tailed if you take him seriously enough. You could see if anybody has a file in Washington on a jockey named Seymour Alch. I doubt you'll find anything. Whatever he's done, he's got the look of a guy even the computers have overlooked."

When Goldberg put the key in his door, Lydia Braun was still with him. "I'm your bodyguard for the night," she explained, following him into the room, which was like a sudden plunge into the *Arabian Nights,* silk billowing from the ceiling, an Oriental carpet ready for flight, a sea of pillows and gilt. "We're taking turns." She examined Goldberg a little defiantly. "You look surprised. Is there something wrong with that?"

"No." She looked as though she was about to file charges although he couldn't quite imagine with whom. In fact he preferred her: she was the only one of his bodyguards who didn't treat him like an antique of questionable provenance. "I'm calling down for room service. You want something to eat? Nothing makes me hungrier than losing."

"You can't stand losing, can you? It drives you crazy. I was watching you while you were playing and there were times I thought you would jump out of your skin."

He looked at her, thinking of telling her the truth and

129

then realizing it would take too long. Instead he presented her with an anecdote that rose handily in his head from a course he had taken during his sophomore year in college. "Thomas De Quincey ate opium for fifty years, dying of it when he was seventy-five, and it all started on a rainy Sunday in London. He claimed there was nothing duller in the world than a rainy Sunday in London. That's what losing is like for me—a rainy Sunday in London that goes on forever."

She lit up her face with that remarkable smile and retreated into the bathroom. "You been in there?" she asked when she came out "When they made that bathtub, getting clean wasn't what they had in mind."

"I've already admired it. What would you like to eat?"

"What are you going to have?"

"A triple martini and the biggest steak they've got."

"You can order a steak for me. Skip the martini. I'm on duty."

She sat on the couch with her feet up while Goldberg ordered dinner. When he was finished with the telephone, he sat down beside her. "You run in marathons?" he asked. "You've got the legs."

She raised her right leg, the skirt sliding back over the knee, and examined the leg as though she had never seen it before. "Just little ones. Perrier. Avon. Things like that. The longer ones do too many funny things to a woman's body."

She seemed to be about to explain what the funny things were, but Goldberg, who had never discussed menstruation with anybody in his life and was reluctant to start now, abruptly changed the subject. "Where did you go to college?" he asked, hoping for an innocent answer.

"West Point, but I quit after the second year. West

Point's basically an engineering school and a damn good one. I've been fascinated by engineering since I was a little kid—that's why I went there in the first place—only it turned out I wasn't good at it. I switched to Duke where I got a degree in psychology. Right now I'm working for a Ph.D. in psychology at Georgetown." She put her leg back down on the couch and recovered it. "Do you know anything about Duke?"

"Good school."

"Did you ever hear about the Rhine Parapsychological Laboratory?"

"People guess at cards."

"You've heard about it, but not much." That wonderful grin transformed her face again, asking him not to take offense. "J.B. Rhine was a serious scientist, parapsychology is a serious science."

He should have stayed with menstruation, thought Goldberg, staring up at the draperies that billowed from the ceiling in the breeze of the air conditioner. It was a scene that cried for dancing girls, and what he wound up with was an armed zealot.

Sprawled on his overstuffed couch, she would not be diverted. "When the apple fell, Newton could have turned his head aside and let it go as an accident of the wind, or maybe a momentary aberration of his own eyesight. Instead he went on to explain gravity. When the parapsychologists try to do the same thing on their own ground, the physicists snicker."

Goldberg wondered what was keeping the steaks and in particular his martini. A moment later there was a knock on the door and their dinner rolled in on a splendid cart, pushed by an elderly waiter who had obviously seen everything and refused to look again. He didn't want to see the long lanky blonde. He didn't want to see Goldberg. After positioning the cart and extending its sides he slid the check at Goldberg as though that act had been independently decided on by his right hand. When Goldberg signed the check, the independent right hand picked it up and carried it along with its owner from the room.

Goldberg noticed that there were two triple martinis even though he had ordered only one and he was grateful. He tasted the first martini. It was as good as he had hoped.

Lydia Braun leaned slightly forward into the extended leaf of the cart. "Goldberg," she declared, "I suspect you have extraordinary psychic gifts."

Goldberg went back to the martini with the gloomy conviction that he was on the verge of becoming the subject of a doctoral thesis. He tried to hide behind the martini, but she knew he was there.

To Goldberg's surprise she took a cigarette from her handbag and lit it—even Schoyer had given up smoking and he'd been up to four packs a day. "Nobody really knows what psi is or how it really works," she said, "but the evidence that it does work mounts from year to year. There's telepathy, which is mind-to-mind contact without any physical contact. There's clairvoyance, there have been a lot of experiments with clairvoyance using playing cards—a person identifying cards he can't see and nobody else can see either. Psychokinesis is the ability to make objects respond by simple wishing. Like dice. There's been a lot of experimenting with dice. The fact that it can't be explained yet has nothing to do with it. Apples were falling off trees long before anybody had an explanation."

"Eat your steak before it gets cold," advised Goldberg.

"You're not taking me seriously. You think this is all a joke."

"I'm listening. That's no reason not to eat."

"You fascinate me, Goldberg. You have this great gift and you prefer to believe it doesn't exist."

"Oh, come on. Eat your steak and stop trying to convert me."

"What do you think the winning streak is all about? Why do you think it goes on and on? You have this fantastic gift, this remarkable power."

"It doesn't sound quite legal."

"If the casino operators weren't as cynical as the physicists, they'd stop every game in the place before they'd let you play it."

"Don't tell them." Her ardor continued to make him uneasy; he wished she could think of something else to be passionate about. "What about tonight? If wishing could make it so, my wishes were really malingering."

"That happens, too," said Lydia Braun stubbornly. "A defect of concentration can do it. But didn't it ever occur to you that even the way you lose is a violation of probability? It was more like you didn't want to win, a negative act."

"Okay," conceded Goldberg.

Lydia Braun ate her steak in silence while she contemplated new avenues for attack. "Did you ever have an out-of-body experience?" she asked when her knife and fork had come to rest.

"Absolutely not," said Goldberg firmly.

"Why do you reject the idea so violently?" she asked. "Does it scare you?"

"Maybe." Goldberg finished the balance of his drink. In a flash of memory he saw a football find its receiver in a crowd of defenders, and was struck by the uncanny precision involved. Why did I think of that? he asked himself and decided he was a little drunk.

"I'm going to turn in," he said. "What about you?"

She pointed at the couch. "I'll be here. You don't have a thing to worry about."

Goldberg went to sleep in a bedroom with a mirror on the ceiling. Whenever he opened his eyes, he was confronted by the image of himself trying to sleep, two Goldbergs staring at each other in their lonely golden beds. He briefly thought of going back into the sitting room to escape his own staring eyes, but Lydia would be waiting for him there with more tales of psi. Psi was hers. He didn't want new things to believe in; he was having trouble enough with the old ones.

He fell asleep and heard a voice whispering in his dreams. When he picked up the telephone next to his bed Schoyer was on it, speaking to Lydia Braun. Schoyer's voice was blurred, either drunk or tired. "The early lab tests were inconclusive. I've asked for more. One way or another, we got a real problem on our hands. You people better get something going there and get it going quickly."

"Tell me something, Schoyer," said Goldberg.

"Oh, it's you. Hang up, Lydia." The click of the phone echoed along the line. "What do you want, Goldberg?"

"Idle curiosity. How you doing with the retirees from the Bureau of Engraving and Printing?"

Schoyer hesitated, but he had to tell somebody. "Over the past five years eighty-two of them have picked themselves up and simply disappeared from the face of the earth. No death certificates. No hospital records. Friends, relatives, nobody knows what happened to them. It was as though they all went out to lunch and didn't bother to come back. Nobody packed a bag or made any other preparations for departure. Like that. One at a time they were just another missing person. Put them all together and they're something else. I feel like I'm sitting on top of a volcano and the heat's starting to come through my pants."

"Nice job, Schoyer," said Goldberg and hung up. This time he avoided his reflection in the ceiling and fell asleep quickly, only to have to deal again and again with a blond marathon runner, who leaned across tables of marble and wood and plastic, always with the same message, "Goldberg, I suspect you of having extraordinary psychic gifts."

Fifteen

Goldberg awoke a little before noon to the singing of birds and found himself staring back from the mirror in the ceiling, badly in need of a shave and alone in a Las Vegas hotel room that had never seen a bird that wasn't under glass. The birdsong had come out of a dream of tall mountains, icy streams, and trout that jumped higher than the trees.

He put on his pants before going into the sitting room where his bodyguard was waiting for him beside a table set with fresh orange juice, croissants, and hot coffee. Although she had presumably spent a sleepless night at her bodyguard work, she had the newborn look of a little girl just out of bed on a Sunday morning. As she raised the silvery pot to pour him a cup of coffee, that fabulous full-face grin announced how happy she was to see him.

"Have some coffee," she said. "You look half-dead."

He remembered his own red-eyed face from the ceiling

mirror and, conceding his need with a grunt, sat down. Two cups of coffee later he buttered a croissant that he ate while she studied him speculatively.

No, he said to himself, no more psi, but it wasn't psi that was on her mind. "Frank Walsh followed the little jockey last night after he left the casino."

"Seymour Alch?"

She nodded. "Himself. Turns out old Seymour brings a new dimension to petty crime. One place he palmed some quarters an old lady dropped on the floor after cleaning out a jackpot. He invested fifteen minutes in sniffing a purse a woman left on the next chair at a blackjack table, but she picked it up and was gone before he could get to it. Little Seymour may be more dangerous than he looks, at least he has ambitions that way, he carries a big fold-up knife in one of those baggy pockets. After the purse walked, he tried a couple of shots of bourbon to cool off. He ran an errand for a hooker who needed an overnight bag delivered downtown. About six o'clock in the morning he bet a drunk ten dollars he could make an egg stand on end on the bar and collected. That was the high point."

"The people we're interested in have all the money in the world. If they want some more, they just make it." Goldberg shrugged. "Stealing quarters isn't what they're about."

"There may be more to Mr. Alch than meets the eye. The FBI has a sheet on him. Seems some years ago Seymour was mixed up in a scheme to dope the favorite in the Kentucky Derby. He was fronting for a bunch of gamblers, but he was the one who got caught. In addition to his other character flaws, Seymour is always the one who gets caught. If you needed somebody to take a rap for you, you couldn't find better."

"You planning to sleep?" asked Goldberg abruptly.

"Not in the near future. I dozed a little at my post last night." She gave him the grin again. "Don't worry. A fly on the windowpane would wake me up."

You had to be young to be that invincible, or maybe just a woman, thought Goldberg, the new Myth America. "I'm going to take a shower and shave," he said. "You want to meet me at the roulette wheel in about an hour?"

"I'll wait for you here. Frank brought my clothes while you were asleep. I'll change in the other bedroom."

As he turned to go, he noticed the question in her eye. "Yes?" he said.

"Tell me something."

"Anything you want."

"What's in this for you?"

"What's in it for anybody?"

Unfamiliar wrinkles clustered in her forehead as she worked at her answer. "I'm a professional. It's my job. It's what I do. You used to do it, but it's not what you do now. The way I hear it you left under somewhat of a cloud."

"They called it a nervous breakdown."

"That's bureaucratese for cloud." She lit a cigarette. "You could get yourself killed. In spite of my best efforts. I'm not God."

"Would you believe I'm chasing a girl?"

She looked at him coolly. "The world is full of girls."

"Would you believe patriotism?" he said.

"Ahead of girls. But not very far. This isn't a big year for patriots."

"How old are you?" asked Goldberg.

"Twenty-seven. Why?"

"You kids think you know everything."

The grin started on its mission of radiance and stopped in the middle.

137

"Mr. Schoyer's the one who's really curious," she said drily. "He asked me to find out."

"That's better," said Goldberg. "I hate cynicism in the young. What's the old bastard afraid of?"

She examined Goldberg carefully as though the truth might pop out of an unexpected cranny and momentarily reveal itself if she watched hard enough. "I guess he figured he fucked you once, and he's afraid you're planning to return the favor."

"You figure the same?"

"I don't know you well enough to have an opinion." She scratched her kneecap, raising her skirt to get at it. "It's a little strange these people haven't tried to kill you yet."

"Sorry," said Goldberg. "Maybe we'll get lucky tonight."

Dressed in a lightweight gray tweed jacket, blue slacks, and a blue shirt, Goldberg started playing at three-thirty in the afternoon.

For the first hour his luck was neither good nor bad—it floated in a deadly neutral zone where everything added up to zero.

His eyes began to wander, first picking out his guardians scattered around the room busily blending into the scene, one at blackjack, two at dice, one studying the baccarat table from the tourist's side of the velvet rope, Lydia Braun still next to Goldberg at the roulette wheel. Working with government money for which they would have to account to the parsimonious Schoyer, they were betting modestly except for Seibert who was showing signs of developing into a degenerate gambler at the dice table.

About half the tables in the casino were closed and those that were open were hardly crowded. The torpor was contagious. Except for the dedicated ladies with the gloved right hands who drove the slot machines around the clock, there was none of the frenzy that is the lifeblood of gambling. It was all one great bus tour, betting their budgets and quitting. The recession that might be depression had spread to Nevada, while far away on the Jersey shore Atlantic City was rising from its sandy beaches and splintered boardwalks to drain away a lion's share of high rollers and low.

Goldberg watched the wheel start to spin, gold, red, black, green, silver, the perfect ivory ball racing on its wood running track, and as his attention was drawn into the interior of all that movement, he saw the red and green bucket with which his small daughter had played long ago on the beach at Atlantic City, and he remembered that she was now, wherever she was, twenty-two years old, and his right hand moved without instructions to place the maximum bet, one hundred dollars, on the number twenty-two while all the power of his consciousness focused on the perfect ivory ball, flowing to it, over it, around it. For that particular ivory ball at that particular time the canoe numbered twenty-two was destiny and for Goldberg from the moment his hand made the move there was never even a fractional doubt. Inside him started that humming of the blood and nerves that meant the power was in him, the streak was happening, and he was shedding all the irrelevancies of his life and surroundings to become nothing but a gambler, a man with a single vision of a perfect ivory ball that ran and ran and ran until it started to hop and hop and finally hopped and stayed still in the canoe numbered twenty-two, where it paid off at thirty-five to one, thirty-five hundred dollars rising in a series of towers next to Goldberg's original hundred.

For the next hour the numbers of his life paraded into his head and he bet them one by one.

His father had graduated from dental school in 1918.

Goldberg bet eighteen and won. He bet nineteen and won. He had met his wife in an apartment on East Fifty-seventh Street on April fourteenth, at two o'clock in the morning. It was a meeting that had led to love, marriage, children, death, despair, madness, ecstasy, pain, and even boredom, in an inextricable tangle.

There were sweet numbers and sour, good ones and bad.

Did the events to which they had been originally attached make any difference?

He bet five and seven, lost on five, won on seven.

He deferred the issue with a column bet on which he lost, then returned to the straight numbers with a fourteen on which he won and a two on which he also won.

By seven-thirty he had won over fifty thousand dollars and the word had started to travel. The vicarious gamblers—the tapped-out, the tourists, the two-dollar betters—were swarming around the roulette wheel and throughout the casino the real gamblers were smelling blood and the smell was taking their hands out of their pockets and summoning the money from their wallets.

Goldberg was making the action for the whole room and the sense of that drove him on, a star reborn on every spin of the wheel. He was alive with an intensity you can only know if you've once been dead.

He stopped the play and asked the maximum limit to be doubled all along the line. After consultation with the pit boss the request was granted. He glanced at Lydia Braun. The blue eyes were on fire, and, as lost in the movement of the wheel as Goldberg himself, she had forgotten completely why they were there. It wasn't greed that moved her, but something richer and more obscure: she was participating in his magic. He looked down at his chips that rose in ragged towers like the skyline of San Gimignano

140

and he remembered the day he had first seen those monuments to human vanity pushing against a bright Italian sky. The thirteenth day of June. A Friday the thirteenth.

He bet two hundred on thirteen and won.

Then while he waited for another number to come to him he improvised with line bets, column bets, color bets, low-number bets, high-number bets, and some variations in between, on all of which he came up about even. The straight number bets were what kept him going. The rest were just filler, temporizing while he waited for the numbers to march into his head, the numbers sweet and sad around which his life had clustered.

Fourteen was the number on the football jersey. Ten was the day of his son's birth. Three was the margin by which they had beaten Princeton in the game they were supposed to lose. Nine was the number of girls he had made love to in London. There were three trees around the first house he had owned, the one where they had all been happy.

Seventeen was the day the homecoming queen announced she was leaving him. He bet seventeen and lost again.

It was midnight before he stopped because he had run out of numbers. From beginning to end they had changed the wheel three times without impeding the streak and the dealers a lot more frequently, a kind of funeral procession of gray men who grew grayer as the hours passed.

He had won two hundred twenty-seven thousand dollars in one of the longest streaks on record and as he turned to leave the table he felt hands touching hin.

Two of the hands belonged to Seymour Alch. They crawled over him like giant crabs, tapping, touching, intruding, finally slipping a folded piece of paper into the side pocket of his jacket.

Upstairs he read the note in the privacy of the bathroom. It was lettered in careful capitals with a soft pencil. "I have important information to sell. Meet me in the coffee shop at the Sands. One hour. Alone."

The last word was underlined three times.

On the way out of the bathroom Goldberg paused to pick up the attaché case in which he had taken to storing his winnings.

Sixteen

"So you shook your keepers," said Alch, who had been watching Goldberg's approach through the glass door of the coffee shop.

"What gave you the idea I had keepers?"

The jockey's grin rearranged his dented face. "The Eye in the Sky whispered it to me. You ever seen what the casino floor looks like from the ceiling? They got TV cameras up there would spot a chip wandering into a dealer's sleeve. You think they'd miss that marching band you got with you?"

"You spend a lot of time in the ceiling?"

Alch had a laugh that was as unfriendly as his grin. "I'm a friend of a friend, girl who sleeps with a guy. Says your buddies look like a herd of elephants trying to hide a cactus plant. Vegas is no place you can keep secrets. Half the town gets paid to watch the other half. With all this money around they got spies spyin' on the spies."

Goldberg looked at his watch. He'd left Lydia Braun snoring sweetly on the couch; even her runner's body wasn't proof against two nights in a row without sleep. "You said you got information for sale. What kind of information?"

One of Alch's enormous hands was drawn to Goldberg's forearm in a reluctant caress. "You gotta be the luckiest son of a bitch I ever saw in my life," he said, the hand continuing to probe Goldberg's arm. "The time at the dice table it was like you owned the dice. That's one to a customer, you don't do it twice in the same lifetime, but you did it again tonight. I'll bet they could put you down in the desert and it would begin to piss oil."

The hand continued to worship Goldberg's arm until Goldberg pulled the arm away. "What kind of information?" repeated Goldberg.

"Expensive." The jockey watered his lips with his tongue. "Very expensive." He examined the hand that had touched Goldberg and put it in his pocket. "I saw Barbara go with you that first time," he said spitefully. "Nobody saw me. I'm like wallpaper, nobody ever sees me. Later I heard you were around town asking for her." The incontinent right hand pulled at Goldberg's sleeve. "You want to find her you finally come to the right place." The hand could not resist Goldberg's flesh. It crawled up the sleeve again and fastened itself on Goldberg's forearm. "Jesus," he said, "if luck rubbed off . . ." As he contemplated the possibilities, he stared into the distance on the other side of the glass door and found there a tall man in skintight Levis, a white-and-red-checked shirt, and a ten-gallon Stetson. "Who the hell's that?" he demanded, releasing Goldberg's arm and putting his hand in the pocket where he kept the knife.

"Nobody. A tall nobody in a cowboy suit. If he's got a tattoo on his right hand, he thinks he's the Marlboro Man."

"You better be telling the truth, Jack." The paranoid brown eyes darted from Goldberg to the cowboy and back again. Rage was always on tap in that tiny body and it came out of his face in beads of sweat, while an acrid smell rose from the yellowish armpits of his seersucker jacket. He was like some small poisonous animal in love with its own deadliness.

Goldberg touched the bony shoulder with a forefinger. "Calm down. You want to sell information? I'm ready to buy it if it's any good."

"Not here. This joint's beginning to spook me. I got a place downtown."

"Where downtown?"

Alch laughed. "You'll see. What you afraid of, a big son of a bitch like you, I'm going to do you some damage?"

"This place have a name?"

"Bet your ass. A great name. Ali Baba's Cave. You ever hear of it?"

"Last I heard it was somewhere east of Las Vegas."

Alch shrugged. "Maybe it's a chain. I don't think it's a chain. This one's in Las Vegas all right. I got connections there. Guaranteed privacy."

He led the way to a cab that rattled along the Strip until it reached downtown where it shunted off into the side streets and stopped in front of a ghostly blue neon sign, Ali Baba's Cave.

Goldberg followed Alch through a stone doorway into a white-washed plaster vestibule lit by a single naked bulb. All the doors to the upper floors were barred, but a dead-white stairwell, tight and narrow, led below street level.

The stairs were slate and worn concave by generations of feet. The only sound anywhere was the whisper of the jockey's shoes on the slate.

Turning and turning and turning again, they stumbled into darkness broken only by a single blue bulb that seemed to cast a shadow rather than light. For a beat of two the darkness held; then suddenly there was an explosion of light, a burst of music, a scurry of feet, and Ali Baba's Cave was in full cry. A bartender surfaced behind the bar over which the blue bulb was suspended. To the left of the bar was revealed a rectangular room with a small stage and white enamel cocktail tables, attended by tubular metal chairs.

A girl in a black spangled dress with a rose-shaped pendant that hung down her middle like a third breast hurried past the tables, while a pink spotlight danced promisingly across the stage.

"You're just in time for the show," announced the girl.

"Hold the show," ordered Alch, who was not in the least surprised by any of this, "bring on the champagne. My friend here's got a fairy godmother on his shoulder that pees money."

"That must be nice," said the girl, leading them to a table next to the stage.

"Do they have an audience hidden somewhere?" asked Goldberg as the girl headed for the bar.

"We're the audience," said Alch. "They operate on a very low overhead."

In spite of Alch's instructions the show would not be repressed. The record changed and a small brunette appeared onstage, carrying a very large corkscrew. She took off her clothing conscientiously, as though she were getting ready to brush her teeth, and started to make love to the corkscrew.

145

Averting his eyes, Goldberg sipped the champagne cautiously; it rolled on his tongue like liquid cotton. "Let's get down to business."

"You want to know where Barbara Hall is, I'll tell you where she is. It'll cost you ten thousand bucks. For a man with your touch that's maybe ten minutes at the tables."

Goldberg had an aversion to rudeness, but there was something about the jockey that demanded it. "I don't think you know shit. You're just working me for a couple of free drinks."

The jockey leered at him. "Go on talking, talker. I know things you got no idea, you and your marching band. Who the hell are you anyway? You don't look smart enough to be a crook—you gotta be some kind of cop."

"Sure," said Goldberg.

This was too much for Alch. He spat a mouthful of champagne back into his glass. "Don't try to con me," he warned. "When was the last time a cop won two hundred grand at roulette?"

Goldberg acknowledged the point with a nod. "Okay, now we know who I am, how about you? What would a girl like that have to do with a creep like you?"

Alch's hand shot to the pocket where he kept his knife, then he looked Goldberg over and changed his mind. Summoning the waitress, he ordered another bottle of champagne and a clean glass before returning to his study of Goldberg, which he conducted with his eyes screwed up as though he were dealing with fine print. When the truth came to him, he grunted in surprise. "You poor dumb son of a bitch," he said, laughing. "You're stuck on her."

"What's so funny about that?"

Alch leaned across the table and presented Goldberg a hand like a catcher's mitt. "Meet the lady's daddy," he replied with a simper. "You want I should call you sonny boy?"

Alch had such a good time with the idea he began to choke on his own wit, gasping and thrashing helplessly inside the oversize jacket until the waitress carrying the fresh bottle of champagne rushed up and started to beat him on the back. Onstage the girl with the corkscrew was bringing her performance to a climax celebrated by wild gyrations of the pink spotlight.

Alch choked. The waitress pounded. Goldberg considered the possibility that this gnarled ugly choking gnome had contributed to the making of that tall golden girl. He watched the jockey's seamy face changing shade from pink to dark-red wine and he searched for the smallest hint of Barbara, a misplaced dimple, anything that might confirm Alch's claim to paternity. To his relief he found nothing.

Finally the choking surrendered to the pounding and Alch was free to talk again. "Listen to me, sonny boy. You want proof, I'll give you proof. Barbara Hall, my ass. Real name Emmy Lou Alch, by Seymour, out of Mary Louise, San Diego, 1953. You remember 1953? That was the year Native Dancer lost the Derby to a twenty-five-to-one longshot named Dark Star. Surprised a lot of smart money." Alch's smirk implied he had tales to tell if he chose, but it turned out he did not choose. "Emmy Lou was a lively little filly, started kicking up her heels real early, by the time she was nine she was gone. Takes after Daddy that way, she's always been a rover."

The jockey shook his head in admiration. "Tough little broad. I figured she'd be back on her hands and knees before the week was out, but it was fifteen years before I laid eyes on her again."

He turned to look at the girl with the corkscrew, who, having attained a conclusion known only to herself, was packing to leave. Alch watched her go. "Fifteen fucking years," he ruminated. "Downhill all the way. When I saw that little honey at the dice table, it was like seeing her mother for the first time. Mary Louise, she had the look. You walked down the street with her in San Diego you needed a club to beat off sailors."

Goldberg, the old scar-collector, started to make a list of things his own daughter might say to him if she saw him tomorrow. "What did she say?" he asked for purpose of comparison.

"What the hell would a girl say sees her old Daddy for the first time in fifteen years? 'Hello, you son of a bitch, I suppose you're after the money.'"

"She recognized you right away? Fifteen years is a long time."

"Blood's thicker than water. But it turned out it wasn't as thick as money. She wouldn't give me a nickel. So I figure I'll hang around and see what's going on. Sometimes she saw me watching her. Most of the time she didn't. One night she came up to me and asked how much I wanted so she'd never have to see me again. I made her a price. She throws the money at me. Fine. Any time somebody wants to throw money at me I'll stand still for it. When I tap out, I ask her to do it again. Hit me, honey. She says she's sorry she ever started. I tell her she'll have to kill me before she gets rid of me now. She says that could be arranged, she had friends who do favors like that. I figure it could be— friends like that go with money like that. But I also figure I don't have much to lose. I stick to her like wallpaper sticks to walls. She's in Las Vegas every third week. Where does she go the other two? I track her to the L.A. airport, but I lose her in those goddamn hills. But she don't look like anybody who would hang around the house two weeks out of three. I take a stab at Reno. One week nothing, next week she shows up. I try Tahoe. That's it, one week Tahoe, one week Vegas, one week Reno. You wouldn't believe the money. I know I'm on to something a lot bigger than I would ever see again in my lifetime, and I gotta have a piece of it."

He looked at Goldberg to make sure he understood how badly he had wanted that money. Goldberg nodded his acknowledgment.

"I played me and my shadow with her for six months. After a while she got used to it and didn't even try to hide. The only place I couldn't follow her was into L.A. and I gave up on that. It was like we had an agreement. Stay out of L.A. and you got me the rest of the time. She was still doing that business of hers, banking busted gamblers, but I never figured out how she made any money out of it because her gamblers always lost. It was like the Bank of America put Santa Claus in charge of the loan department, it was starting to drive me crazy. It couldn't have been doing her much good either, because after a while she wasn't hardly paying attention to the banking business, she was playing the tables herself, hundreds of thousands, millions. I seen high rollers before, but they always go home sooner or later, she stayed day in and day out, bucking the odds and losing, bucking the odds and losing. It was like she was trying to make up what she lost in the banking business, only it wasn't working that way, she was pouring out money like Mississippi mud. She was a one-woman gambling boom. When she swept into town, it was like the recession was over."

The music started again, introducing a tall blonde with a

clarinet on which she blew a few discouraged notes before she undressed. She seemed to have a bad cold.

"There was a guy in riding boots following you the night you met her."

"Tell me about him."

"He caught up with her in Tahoe about a month before that. They had a big fight, I don't know what about, but he was madder than spit. He would have killed her except a couple of casino guards threw him out and she disappeared. All of a sudden she wasn't showing up at the regular places anymore, but I knew she couldn't stay away forever. Just about the time you turned up in Vegas, so did she, and she hit the tables like some drunk who's got the word he has one more binge coming and this is it."

Alch tried to concentrate on the girl whose newly exposed nipples were puckering in the cold blasts of the air conditioning, but the memory of the money intervened. "She had a room at the Sands," he said, "and I figured this was Custer's last stand, it was now or never. One way or another she was getting ready to blow and if I didn't get her now I might never see her again. I cornered her on her way into her room. There was a fight. You wouldn't believe how strong that broad is. She decked me with a lamp and I was out like a light." He shook his head in a kind of delayed awe. "That's the Alch in her. All the way back the Alches been battlers. Pow." He slammed his right fist into his left palm, producing a noisy testimonial to the Alches who had preceded him. "When I came to she was gone. Maybe she was sorry for what she done, because she had sprinkled me all over with money." His face darkened. "Tough shit," he said. "Nobody buys me that easy. There was something else on the floor beside me. It came out of her purse early in the fight and I thought to kick it under a chair. You're going to pay me ten grand for it."

150

"Do I get any hint of what it is?"

Alch took a crumpled sheet of paper out of an inner breast pocket and ironed it flat on the table with one calloused palm.

"From here it looks blank."

"Only this side," Alch assured him. "Let's see your money."

Goldberg took ten thousand-dollar bills from his wallet and lined them up parallel to Alch's paper.

Alch turned the paper over carefully and Goldberg found himself staring at a school bill in the sum of seventy-five hundred dollars, one semester's room and board and tuition for Miranda Hall. Alch's broad thumb covered the address of the school that had issued the bill.

"Yeah," said Alch. "Where else would the mother bird run except to her chick? You don't know that about her you don't know anything about her."

Goldberg removed his hand from the pile of bills.

Alch raised his thumb.

Seventeen

In the hills behind Carmel the Eleanor Bowie Ranch School nestles in a green valley that sheltered three generations of Bowies until in 1959, the last of the line, Eleanor, endowed the school that bears her name. Known to the student body as the Horse Nunnery, Bowie was rumored to have the highest concentration of young virgins anywhere in the Far West, a hundred fifty of them every year attending classes in the rambling main house, living in bunkhouses, and riding the range under the supervision of three riding mistresses and an elderly cowpoke who also drove the school bus.

As Goldberg waited in the lofty entrance hall for Miss Morrison, the headmistress, the young virgins were on the move, changing classes, eyes flickering over Goldberg, weighing him, measuring him, classifying him, putting him aside for later discussion. Goldberg remembered a tall gangling, perpetually nervous anthropologist he had known who insisted that during his first class at Radcliffe the students had fixed their eyes on his fly and kept them there for the duration, while he fidgeted anxiously, periodically verifying the state of the zipper with a casual fanning motion of his fingers across his crotch. The anthropologist, whose name was Bowman, had named his first child Lohman, Lohman Bowman, probably in revenge for future anxieties he was confident would be visited on him by his progeny.

"Mr. Goldberg." Amelia Morrison stood at the entrance to her office beckoning him. She was in her fifties and straight as a stick, wearing a severe dress, a severe hairdo, and an expression in her eyes he was not quite sure of: hostility, curiosity, perhaps even a certain interest.

The headmistress's office was as spartan as her dress—oak, antlers, shelves of difficult books. "You're here to inquire about Miranda Hall?"

"I'd like to talk to her."

"It wasn't quite clear on the phone what the relationship is," said the headmistress, trying for frosty and not quite making it.

The lady was worried, thought Goldberg, and she damn

well wasn't going to tell him why. "I'm a friend of her mother's," he said.

That didn't get him any points. A cynical glint surfaced momentarily in the headmistress's eyes and was repressed. "Then what can I add to what you already know?"

"Take a chance," said Goldberg. "I promise not to be bored." He reached out and tapped a slender wrist with his forefinger. "I been a cop too long not to recognize a lady in trouble. Lady, you got trouble, and you want me to help, you'd better speak up."

Miss Morrison adjusted her posture to a new level of severity, but the words were out of her mouth before she had a chance to stop them. "What can I add to what you presumably already know? The girls are bused to San Francisco once a week to participate in the cultural life of the city. This past Tuesday, after attending the opera, forty-nine girls boarded the bus, Miranda did not. She has not been heard of since. No notes, no hints to friends, no warning of any sort. Two days later her mother phoned and then came to see me."

"Did Mrs. Hall leave an address or phone number where she could be reached?"

Miss Morrison was already sorry she had gotten herself into this conversation. As the custodian of rich men's daughters she understood completely the fragility of her position. She could handle declining SAT scores a lot more readily than scandal. Security rather than scholarship was what was important to the average Bowie parent. "No. Mrs. Hall appeared to be in transit. She phoned on Wednesday and Thursday to find out whether we had heard from Miranda, but she did not reveal her phone number or address even though I asked for them. She said she would be in touch with me. I thought perhaps you would know where she is."

Goldberg shook his head.

"Do you have any idea what Miranda's social life was like?" he asked delicately.

"Bowie girls don't have any social life that I don't know about," said Miss Morrison firmly.

"Did she have a boyfriend?"

To his surprise Goldberg detected a glint of amusement, a closet twinkle in some far corner of the headmistress's eyes. "I don't think you understand, Mr. Goldberg. Elizabeth Bowie saw the sixties on the horizon and put her foot down. This place is where she put it down. The girls do not have a great deal of free time during the school year—and virtually no opportunity to form romantic attachments."

Goldberg looked at the difficult books on the headmistress's shelves, and wondered whether she read them. He decided she probably did. Somehow he found that reassuring. "How long has Miranda been a student at Bowie?"

"She's in her third year now. A bright girl. Not a particularly good student, but pretty enough so that a number of the other girls were jealous. I don't know how much you know about fifteen-year-old girls or sixteen-year-old girls or seventeen-year-old girls, Mr. Goldberg, so let me tell you. If any of it gets too familiar you can stop me."

Wrath brought a touch of color to Amelia Morrison's pale cheeks, and for a fraction of a second Goldberg glimpsed an earlier, younger Amelia on whom the headmistress had not yet been clamped down. "The first thing you have to recognize is that they combine the cunning of Talleyrand with the innocence of little Nell, and maybe that's the biggest problem of all, because they don't consider themselves innocent in the least. Their language would raise a blush in a bordello; they know the words for everything, including a few things that perhaps even you have never heard of. The girls at Bowie, which imposes rather severe restrictions on behavior, are like a hundred fifty little pressure cookers bubbling away on a stove, not only ready to blow up, but eager to blow up. The combination of unacknowledged innocence and very real hormonal activity creates a remarkable potential for trouble. My primary educational function is anticipating and preventing that trouble. Until this episode I have been rather successful."

"You make yourself sound a bit like a warden."

"It's not quite what I had in mind when I got a Ph.D. in Icelandic Languages," conceded Miss Morrison drily. "On the other hand, looking back, I'm not quite sure anymore what I had in mind. Icelandic Languages were never a readily transmitted passion."

"Is it your impression then that Miranda disappeared voluntarily, that she picked her own trouble?"

Amelia thought about that carefully. "You should realize Miranda's not your typical victim. She rides a horse like a Valkyrie—and the girls seem to accept her as a kind of leader. Most of the trouble that comes to Bowie arrives by mail, and she's frequently the one the others go to first with their bad news. She is in fact quite a sturdy character, both physically and emotionally. It doesn't seem too likely that she was kidnapped from a standing-room-only performance of *Ernani*. And she isn't the sort to be easily tricked into going with a stranger. I'm sorry, but I can't help you at all."

"How about the other girls. She must have some particularly close friends, somebody she confides in."

"I'm afraid I couldn't permit that, Mr. Goldberg. The other parents are going to be disturbed enough without my getting their daughters involved."

Exasperated, Goldberg lit a cigarette in full knowledge that smoking had to be high on the headmistress's list of sins. "You're not going to get away with pretending it didn't happen. You can help me find her, or I can turn it over to the cops. If there's a suspicion of kidnapping, that's the FBI. They're not going to be nearly as nice as I am."

Amelia Morrison pursed her lips as though she might be planning to whistle through them. She looked at her hands, she looked at her bookshelves, and she made up her mind. "Ellen Mohr is Miranda's best friend; they're as thick as thieves, and you probably can't believe a word she says, but I'll let you talk to her for ten minutes alone in this office."

Goldberg nodded and looked for a place to put out his cigarette. Miss Morrison pointed to a metal wastepaper basket, which was empty. Then she went out into the hall, dug Ellen Mohr out of French class, brought her to Goldberg, and left her alone with him.

Ellen was small and dark and had amber eyes that examined Goldberg as though he were a particularly inscrutable page of French.

"Miss Morrison tells me that you are Miranda's best friend," said Goldberg encouragingly.

Ellen considered this proposition carefully. When she found nothing wrong with it, she answered in a tiny lawyer's voice, "You can say that."

"Good," said Goldberg.

"Why is that good, Mr. Goldberg?" asked the tiny precise voice.

"Because she probably tells you everything."

Ellen decided to be baffled again, examining Goldberg once more with that incredulous amber stare. "There's not a lot to tell at Bowie," she replied finally. "Nothing much happens except the same old stuff."

"Does she ever talk about her mother?" asked Goldberg.

Ellen was surprised by the question. "Not much. Mothers aren't a big topic of conversation." On second thought she decided this was an area in which she could give away a little more. "Miranda thought her mother was trying to turn her into Doris Day. Do you know Doris Day, Mr. Goldberg?"

"Personally?"

"On late-night television."

"I'm surprised Miss Morrison lets her girls stay up that late."

A small smile escaped from Ellen's lips. "Occasionally reports filter through from outside."

"Tell me about *Ernani*."

"An opera by Verdi based on a play by Victor Hugo," Ellen replied promptly.

"Did you enjoy it?"

"I'm not really into Verdi, and as far as I'm concerned, you can box Victor Hugo and send him to the French Academy with my compliments. But it's nice to get out of the Horse Nunnery even if it's just for a ride in that smelly old bus."

"Where did Miranda sit?"

"We generally sit together," said Ellen, recovering her caution.

"When did you notice she was missing?"

"Missing?"

"Her seat was empty."

"She went to the ladies room. I noticed when she didn't come back."

"Didn't that worry you?"

The amber eyes were blank. "Why should it have?"

"Your best friend disappears without a word or a note. It seems to me I would worry. Didn't you even check the ladies room to see if she was sick?"

"Miranda can take care of herself."

157

"That's a funny kind of friendship—you're not even interested in what happened to her?"

"It's our kind of friendship," said Ellen primly. "We stay out of each other's space."

Amelia Morrison was standing in the doorway now, and Goldberg turned his back on her to face Ellen Mohr. "Let me tell you a secret, Ellen."

"What?"

"I don't believe a word you've said to me except who wrote *Ernani*, which, as a matter of fact, sounds as though you've never seen it yourself."

"I've seen it all right," muttered Ellen. "I've got the scars to prove it."

"I know you're not going to tell me any more right now, but I want you to think about it. Unless you're absolutely sure where Miranda is right this minute and you can guarantee she's safe, you could be risking her life by not telling me the truth. I know some things about Miranda even you don't know, even she doesn't know herself. There are people who might want to harm her, people who are perfectly capable of harming anybody."

Miss Morrison was in the room now, looking pointedly at her watch. "It's time for you to go back to your French, Ellen."

"Yes, Miss Morrison."

"By the way, Ellen." Goldberg stopped the girl as she headed toward the door. "If you've got a recent picture of Miranda, it would be a big help."

To Goldberg's astonishment this last request cut to the heart of Ellen Mohr in a way none of his questions had. She turned pale. "I don't have a picture," she gasped and hurried out of the room.

"What was that about?" asked the headmistress.

158

"I wish I knew," said Goldberg. "You don't have a recent picture, do you?"

Miss Morrison reached into the bookcase. "Last year's yearbook is the most recent."

Goldberg took it from her. "If you want to get in touch with me for any reason I'll be at the St. Francis in downtown San Francisco. And do me a favor. If Mrs. Hall calls, tell her that's where I am."

"Did you learn anything from Ellen?"

Goldberg shook his head.

Amelia Morrison smiled. "There's nothing on God's green earth that will separate an adolescent girl from a secret she wants to keep. They study duplicity in their diapers and they refine their technique throughout childhood. They'll lie with a kind of angelic effrontery and a devil's ingenuity, they'll stonewall, they'll conspire on an instant's notice against the whole adult world."

She should have stayed with Icelandic Languages, thought Goldberg. "Remember," he said, "the St. Francis."

"I'll remember," the headmistress promised grimly.

When he reached his car, which was the only one in the parking lot beyond the gate, Ellen Mohr was sitting in the driver's seat. She held a large sheet of drawing paper rolled in her hand. He opened it and saw a pencil sketch of a girl's head.

"Miranda?"

Ellen Mohr nodded.

"It's quite good. Did you do it?"

"No. Somebody gave it to her during intermission. She showed it to me when she got back to her seat and asked me to keep it for her."

"Where was she going?"

"She said it was given to her by this real cute guy, who finished drawing it while she stood there. It was a case of love at first sight and he had to see her for five minutes, or he'd die on the spot."

"So she went off with him?"

"She came back and told me first, then she went."

"Wasn't that a little crazy?"

Ellen sighed. "It's easy to see you don't know much about women, Mr. Goldberg. Who could have resisted?"

"Would you?"

Ellen sighed again, even more gustily. "Do you have to ask?"

"What made you decide to tell me about it?"

"You scared me in there in Miss Morrison's office. It's been four days now and not a word. She would have called me no matter how good a time she was having. Miranda isn't afraid of anything, but she wouldn't forget me. You've really got me scared now, Mr. Goldberg."

"Good," said Goldberg. "Are you sure there isn't something you've left out?"

"She said he looked like a young Paul Newman."

"Anything else?"

Ellen thought and shook her head. "Here, you take this." She handed over the picture. "I'd like it back. It could be my last memory of Miranda." She burst into tears, then remembering something, stopped. "You ought to talk to Ben Watts."

"Who's he?"

"The old cowboy who drives the bus."

"Where would I find him?"

"This is his day off. Probably at the Brass Monkey in Carmel. He says it's the only place in two hundred miles where he can escape from the fresh air."

Eighteen

Goldberg found Ben Watts hooked by the elbows to the bar of the Brass Monkey, a Stetson hat shading his glass. He was a small man, neat hipped in worn blue jeans, a turkey neck protruding from a blue denim shirt. It was hard to tell how old he was; he had passed the point where years made any difference and the mere fact of survival was remarkable enough.

When he spoke his voice was surprisingly deep and resonant. "This is my corner of the bar, feller," he announced. "You want to drink, go someplace else." It was high noon in his watery blues, and his right hand dropped to twitch at his belt although there was no sign of a gun in the vicinity.

"Sorry."

"You oversize bastards are all the same," complained the cowboy. "I pay the same for a suit as you do—but do I get as much cloth? Hell, no, I'm making a contribution to your suit. I don't get any special break on the price of a drink—but you figure you're entitled to stand in my room. Go stand in somebody else's room, or find your own."

Goldberg glanced at the bartender who promptly made himself busy further down the bar. "You're Ben Watts, aren't you?" Goldberg inquired, half turning to get out of the old man's room.

"You got it in one," said Watts, tapping his glass on the bar for a refill. Every move of his tidy body announced he was not impressed by Goldberg or anything else that walked the earth; he had outlived all forms of fear and most forms of curiosity.

"My name is Goldberg."

Watts brushed an invisible fly away from his nose.

"I suppose you were one of the last people to see Miranda Hall alive?"

"Who the hell are you?"

"Name's Goldberg. I'll have a Scotch, bartender."

"Line of work?" demanded Watts. "They already took the census."

"I'm a friend of the family, trying to find out what happened to the girl."

"Why don't you try minding your own business? World's going to hell in a handbasket with people who won't mind their own business. Snoopers, Sunday school teachers, cackling hens—they cause more trouble than the atom bomb." The old man started to detach his elbows from the bar, but thought better of it. Instead he banged for another refill. "If somebody wiped all the snoopers from the face of the earth, it would be a greener place." He had turned away from Goldberg and was talking to his glass. "They all think they're dealing with some school bus driver. Hell, I was riding these hills before there was a school bus, and the only tourists was cows going to market. Chrissakes, now they got a Bach Festival in this town, the sissies are taking over the world." He turned the hat toward Goldberg again, his voice rising to a mocking treble. "The Eleanor Bowie Ranch School. Shit. You're looking at the legitimate owner. That's Ben Watts's ranch sitting there under the Horse Nunnery, and it would have been all mine if it wasn't for that old blue nose, Eleanor."

"I didn't know that," conceded Goldberg, filling his voice with marvel.

"Hardly anybody left knows it anymore, buddy, but I'm here to bear witness. Eleanor Bowie and I was going to be married on Sunday, people was riding in from as far as the Panhandle, and the boys got together to throw me a little bachelor party. Most natural thing in the world, only who shows up at the party except old Eleanor. First party she ever went to off the church lawn, but she had a gift, she could smell booze on an April breeze and hear a girl's pants drop in the next county. She arrives just when the kootch dancer's drawers was coming off." He paused to review the ancient memory, pale eyes glowing. "That was the end of the party, the end of getting married, the end of my ranch."

"An expensive pair of drawers."

"You got the picture," agreed the old cowboy. "One bare ass and I wind up driving the bus for a goddamn nunnery. Eleanor saw to it. She put it in her will. Her idea of a joke." He shook his head inside the hat and sighed. "Me, I couldn't abide leaving the land was rightly mine."

The old cowboy brooded on his loss while he finished his drink and Goldberg honored his grief by drinking along with him. "Miranda," he said finally.

"You got to give it to old Eleanor," said Watts, "she left her stamp on the land, four-square against nature, like all those little girls was made of plaster or stone with ice water for blood."

Watts and Goldberg shared two more drinks and a decent interval of contemplation before Goldberg began cautiously, "I guess you were the only one on the side of nature in the whole school, Ben."

Watts considered this proposition for so long that Goldberg was afraid he might have fallen asleep under his hat;

then the hat turned and the blue eyes were studying Gold-berg. "Nature's on the side of nature. You think an old icicle like Amelia Morrison is going to turn a hundred fifty healthy young females into a hundred fifty tin angels? There's girls in that place would make Willie Sutton look like a choirboy. Cute, sweet-smelling little things. Sure I was on the side of nature. A girl didn't feel like cooling her heels all afternoon at some dumb cultural event, that was fine with me as long as she showed up at the bus before it left. If they let me know in advance, I'd even route the bus where they were going to be and pick them up."

"Was that how it was with Miranda?"

"Why don't you stop worrying about Miranda?" the old cowboy said stubbornly. "That kid can take care of herself if anybody ever could. Nerves of steel and good hands—she could make it as a rodeo rider if that was what she fancied." He glared at Goldberg, the blue eyes clearing momentarily. "Why don't you find somebody else to fret about?"

"She's been gone a long time now," said Goldberg.

Watts ruminated on his lower lip. "Not so long," he said. "If she made up her mind to stay away, she'd stay away good."

"Look," said Goldberg, "I'm not trying to run her life. She wants to stay, she can stay away as far as I'm con-cerned. Only it wouldn't be so nice if somebody's making her."

"Who?"

"People."

"What kind of people?"

"The kind with guns and big muscles who don't mind using them. You been around a long time. You've run into people like that."

The old man's eyes blurred as he searched his memories. "Ever hear of the Houlihan brothers? Three of them. Out of Fort Worth."

"No."

"Crazy sons of bitches," said Ben Watts. He removed his hat, revealing an imperfect ear. "One of them near bit that ear off for me. Mean, all three of them, just as soon kill you as say hello."

"You got the idea. Think of what it would be like if the three Houlihan brothers got hold of her."

The old cowboy went into conference with himself, mumbling arguments for, against, and then finally for telling Goldberg what he knew. Even then he started with a warning. "You better be playing it straight with me, big guy. The Houlihan brother bit this ear didn't bite any other ears after that." He put his hat back on with a flourish and began his story. "I was standing in front of the Opera House, waiting for the girls to come out so I could show them where I'd parked the bus. Miranda was out way early with this guy, nice-looking young feller, and they was laughing. When she saw me she stopped, she always stopped to talk to me, and I told her where the bus was, and she said she'd be on it, not to worry. When she didn't show up at the bus, I waited half an hour, only she'd said not to worry, I figured that meant she'd get herself back to school on her own, it had happened before and nobody the wiser. So I left."

The old cowboy pulled himself loose from the bar, tottered, caught hold, and moved a step toward Goldberg. "Looked like a nice young feller. Smelled of lemons. I stood right next to him. Good-looking boy, height somewhere between you and me, maybe nearer to you, nose had a bump on it like somebody'd tried to change its direction."

165

"Doesn't sound much like Paul Newman," said Goldberg.

"Didn't look like Paul Newman. Maybe a little like when Paul Newman was younger, like Butch Cassidy, you know the look, cause me any trouble and I'll spit in your soup, but nice about it. This kid handled himself kind of like that."

"What color were his eyes?"

"How the hell do I know what color his eyes were? He had one of these blue jackets dudes wear with gold buttons, tan pants, blue shirt. Looked nice. Miranda seemed real happy with him."

Nineteen

It was after midnight when Goldberg reached his room in the St. Francis, too early to sleep, too late to go looking for young men in blue blazers who drew pictures and kidnapped girls. Why was he so sure she'd been kidnapped? Because there were too many Houlihan brothers riding the roads that ran through his head.

Goldberg sat at a long black lacquer table trimmed with gold acanthus leaves. On the table in front of him, reading from left to right, were the sketch of Miranda, folded flat, a deck of Bicycle playing cards, still unopened, a steak sandwich, a glass with ice, a bottle of Stolichnaya vodka, and a Princess telephone. He poured vodka into the glass and studied the picture, a young girl laughing with an exuberance that didn't seem justified by anything in all of Italian opera. It struck Goldberg as being a remarkable piece of work, hasty but drawn with a kind of furious fluency; he could not help believing there was a girl named Miranda who laughed just like that.

He opened the pack of Bicycle cards and started to lay them out for solitaire, but quit in embarrassment after one round. He drank another glass of vodka and that didn't help. How long would he sit here waiting for the phone to ring? All night? All the next day? He tried staring at the phone and giving it from one to one hundred to ring. After five rounds of a hundred each, he dialed Schoyer at his home in Silver Springs, Maryland.

There were three rings and Schoyer caught it on the fourth. He was slowing down, thought Goldberg; Schoyer in his prime was a two-ring man. "Schoyer," announced the gravelly voice.

"Goldberg reporting in, sir."

"Sir? You son of a bitch. Where the hell are you?"

Schoyer's rage was like a familiar stove. Goldberg felt better immediately. "Calm down," he said cheerfully. "This is a social call."

"Where are you?"

"Look, Schoyer, I tell you where I am and you're going to have a blanket of bodyguards all over me so fast I might as well quit. Relax, there's no way you can trace this call, that's why I called you at home."

Schoyer's breath came whistling over the phone. "I wish you would quit," he said bitterly.

"Your age, you got to watch your blood pressure," warned Goldberg.

"I'm only two years older than you are, you old bastard. You still smoking?"

"That's better," said Goldberg. "Now you're entitled to another question."

"Who are you working for, Goldberg?"

"Lydia Braun told me that was on your mind. If it's any consolation, I can't be working for the other guys, we don't even know who they are."

"That's not what I'm afraid of," said Schoyer disgustedly. "Other guys I could deal with. I got to figure you're in business for yourself. The hero business. Last thing I need on my hands is an effing hero."

"Effing?" said Goldberg.

Schoyer got himself under control. "You could always make me mad, Goldberg. It's kind of a gift. Leave your gift at home just this once."

"Tell me some more about the money, Schoyer. It's hard to believe the lab still hasn't figured out how to identify it as counterfeit."

"Oh, that your problem? Don't give it another thought. They've worked out a simple chemical test that identifies it perfectly."

"You don't seem happy about it."

"You know me, Goldberg, hard to please as always. It's as easy as ABC. Funny they didn't figure it out sooner."

"Yeah?"

"Yeah. They've detected a minute difference in the chemical composition of the paper."

"The paper was always tough, the secret that doesn't crack."

"The last line of defense," agreed Schoyer.

"At least that's something."

"It sure is. Only there's a slight catch. In order to make the test you've got to boil the money into paste."

"You're kidding. You boil it down, it isn't money any more, it's porridge."

"You just won the Nobel Prize for Chemistry. That's the catch—in order to test it they've got to destroy it. You want to test all the money in the Federal Reserve System you got to cook it first."

"Oh," said Goldberg.

"You got any idea how much bad money is out there, Goldberg?"

Goldberg shrugged and then remembered that Schoyer couldn't see him. "You tell me. How many people who retired from the Bureau of Engraving and Printing you still can't account for?"

"Latest count is ninety-two," said Schoyer unhappily.

"Unless they're all off on a desert island somewhere having a party, they could have made a lot of money in the past five years."

"How do you know it's five years?" demanded Schoyer.

Goldberg scratched his nose on the mouthpiece of the telephone. "Maybe more. All I know is they've been passing it that long."

"I've got a blanket over every legal gambling enterprise in the country, and we haven't come up with a thing. Maybe it isn't as big as you think," said Schoyer, grasping for any straw he could find.

"Don't count on it, old friend. They've gone underground for the moment. Just until they clean up a couple of odds and ends."

"Like what?"

"Me, for example." Goldberg hesitated, wondering whether he should bring up Barbara's name and deciding not to. "They've got plenty of other places to go. Most of the gambling in the country isn't legal anyway."

"I've had enough of this," said Schoyer suddenly. "You better tell me where you are."

"Good-bye, Schoyer. I'll call again."

Goldberg restored the Princess phone to the far corner of the table and took another drink of vodka. A little later he fell asleep in the chair and began to dream. In his dream the phone kept ringing and each time he answered his wife was on the other end with the same message, the last thing she had said to him on that final desperate morning before leaving with their daughter for Ohio. "The trouble with you is you wanted to be the Jewish John Wayne, only you didn't get it straight and used your son as a surrogate."

It went on like that for a long time. ". . . the Jewish John Wayne, only you didn't get it straight and used your son as a surrogate."

Then he fell into another level of sleep and Barbara Hall was sitting on a rock, as naked as a mermaid, cheering him on while he rowed toward her in short choppy strokes.

At three-thirty in the morning the phone rang again and this time it wasn't his wife. "Yes, Barbara," he said. "I've been waiting for you to call, I'll be right over."

Twenty

The Barbara he found at the Fairmont was no match for the one he had been dreaming about. Hair cut short and dyed black, eyebrows darkened, four-eyed, owl-eyed behind horn-rims, she was nobody he'd ever met. When she held out her hand, he shook it; four o'clock in the morning

working, a bar and restaurant where I'm the hostess and general ambassador of good will. He just walks in and starts talking as though there hadn't been ten years in between. He had a chance for me to make a lot of money. Why me? More money than I had ever seen or imagined or could believe in. But why me? I'd forgotten that one thing about Doc is he's like God, he never answers questions. That strike you funny?"

"I wasn't laughing," said Goldberg.

"Power is Doc's idea of sex," she said. "To take control of me again after ten years of hating him, that was Doc's idea of getting off his gun."

When she stopped, Goldberg waited warily.

"What he told me was he was running a gambling syndicate that had a system for beating every gambling game in the world. Computers made it possible, and they had been cleaning up until the casinos caught on and started to circulate pictures of the syndicate members and bar them from the casinos."

She looked up from the hands she carried folded in her lap. "Doc and his syndicate saw five hundred billion in gambling money changing hands every year, and it was like there was a fence around it, they could win and win and win if they could only get to it. What Doc had figured out was a way to get near it. He would hire tapped-out gamblers to gamble for him, playing the systems the syndicate had worked out. We would supply the money. They would play it for a percentage of the winnings. Big, huh?"

"Big," agreed Goldberg. "But didn't you ever have trouble collecting? Your average gambler figures any money that winds up in his pocket is likely to be his, at least until it's time to gamble again."

"Collecting wasn't my job. Doc had set the thing up like

a spy ring, everything in compartments, nobody except Doc knew more than a little piece of what was going on. There are bankers who find the gamblers and bankroll them. There are collectors who make sure the gamblers cough up their winnings. There are recruiters who recruit the bankers. Nobody knows anybody else."

"What was your job?"

"I started out as a banker, taking my orders direct from Doc. But after a while as the thing got bigger and bigger he promoted me to recruiter."

"Bigger? How big?"

"Only Doc knows how big. It's not just the casinos or the racetracks or betting parlors. There isn't a town in the United States of any size you can't find a regular game. You know that. Clubs, saloons, private houses. Since I've started recruiting I've put more than a hundred bankers to work."

"Jesus," said Goldberg in awe.

"Yeah." She smiled. "Even Doc said I was the best they ever had. And compliments aren't Doc's style."

"One hundred? You sure you're not exaggerating?"

"Not all at once, of course. They come and they go. But one hundred." She picked at the black skirt, removing invisible threads. "I don't know how many bankers the other recruiters put on. I don't even know how many other recruiters there are."

"What was Doc so angry about that time in Tahoe if you were doing so well for him?"

"He caught me gambling. I wasn't supposed to gamble. I started in a small way when I was a banker. A little dice. A little poker. A little roulette. Some blackjack. My job was hanging around the casinos then, and it helped pass the time. A hundred here, a hundred there, maybe a couple of thousand. Then I was gambling my earnings, and pretty soon I was borrowing from the syndicate without their knowing it. It got to the point where I couldn't get through the week without gambling and the stakes got bigger and bigger."

She snapped her fingers in Goldberg's face. "That's how it goes. Before you know it a million is egg money, two million is chicken feed, and you start dreaming of endless zeros, not that you want them, you have to have them. One thing I was sure of, Miranda was never going to depend on any man for anything. No way was I going to stay away from the tables and when Doc found out he went crazy. Nobody breaks Doc's rules and gets away with it."

She picked up her hands from her lap and looked at them in disgust, blaming them for the things they had done with cards, dice, chips, men. She put the hands back in her lap and demanded, "Do you have any idea what I'm talking about?"

"I think I have an idea."

"How the hell would you? You're a winner, I'm a loser— that's two different countries, speaking different languages. I lost money faster than the mint could print it, it was like the dice hated me, the cards hated me, the wheels hated me. That can make you kind of spacy."

"The syndicate's systems didn't work?"

"Sometimes. I gave up on them after a while. What worked on Tuesday didn't work on Wednesday. I figured I had no head for numbers and went on my own. Meet tap city, the genius loser. When I saw you at the dice table, first I hated you, then I thought maybe you were my salvation sent by God, I would borrow your luck. But it was all closing in too fast by then, there was no time left, and I took your money and ran, because I had to get away, I had

175

to get Miranda away, and there was no road back to Martha's chimney, Doc would have closed that road."

"I'm afraid he closed it permanently," said Goldberg as gently as he could. "I'm sorry."

"Martha's dead?"

Goldberg nodded.

She covered her eyes with her hands, but made no sound. When she took the hands away, her eyes were dry. "I can't cry," she said. "She was the only mother I ever had and I can't cry. What's wrong with me?"

"I'm sorry," said Goldberg.

"Sorry isn't enough," she said, and suddenly fierce, demanded the question that would destroy Doc Holliday. "Ask me anything."

Goldberg did the best he could, knowing it wasn't good enough. "Didn't it ever occur to you that maybe Doc's money was counterfeit?"

"Counterfeit?" She looked at him, startled, then rejected the idea with contempt. "Don't be ridiculous. You don't pass counterfeit in casinos. They'd spot funny money while it was still in your wallet."

"Counterfeit," said Goldberg. "That's the thing. The recruiters, the bankers—they were passing counterfeit. What the collectors got back was real, or at least as real as it gets."

Goldberg stood up, his right knee twitching painfully, reminding him that nothing was the way it once was. "Don't open the door for anybody except me—and I'll give you plenty of notice. The best thing you can do for Miranda is don't open that door and don't go out in the street. Just don't do anything until you hear from me."

"When?"

"Soon."

176

He went down into the lobby, all soaring marble, a Gold Rush cathedral, and across onto the steps, now empty, where sometime in the 1970s he had seen Jerry Lewis drive up in a red Lincoln Continental.

The night was fading into fog on Nob Hill and the cold nuzzled Goldberg's bad knee. Somewhere in the distance the first cable car of the day was clanging.

Twenty-one

Petrakis studied the giant crabs with the tender interest he had once devoted solely to girls.

"Good morning, flute player," said Goldberg, his lungs flavored by the salt sea air that blew an iodine high across Fisherman's Wharf.

One of Petrakis's greatest charms was that nothing ever surprised him. He took in Goldberg's presence with the same sympathetic attention he'd been devoting to the crabs. "So," he said, "you have accepted Petrakis's invitation. Good." One hand drew a circle around his restaurant. "Here we bring joy to thousands of bellies every day. It is a splendid activity for one's declining years."

Petrakis, who had always been vast, showed no signs of declining. He patted his stomach in automatic acknowledgment that this was not where he was declining. "I already have a place in mind. We will set you up in your own seafood palace." He nodded to confirm that the matter had been settled, and went on to the next point on the program. "You know I have brought a wife from Greece, a country girl, a young virgin of impeccable character? I will find you such a girl to marry."

"Why do you insist on virginity, a man of your experience?"

"Sexual ignorance is the soundest foundation for a good marriage. Maria is of the opinion that I invented something very special and is eternally grateful to me for sharing my invention with her. Critics have their place, but it is not in bed." He reexamined Goldberg and shook his head. "You did not come here to settle down with a fish restaurant and a young wife, did you? I have never seen a man who was so in need of trouble, Goldberg. Come up to my office and I will listen to what you have in mind."

All around them preparations for the first meal of the day were beginning to accelerate as Petrakis led Goldberg through a maze of Oriental rosewood toward the second floor, where his office looked out on the fishing boats bobbing at anchor.

Petrakis sat behind his desk and reinvestigated Goldberg. "Don't tell me you are still winning at cards and dice," he said finally.

Goldberg nodded.

Petrakis sighed the sigh of a master flute player. "I was afraid of that. Goldberg, you do not have the proper character for winning, which should be simple enjoyment. Instead you insist on converting it into metaphysical questions better left to priests and rabbis. I assume you are still chasing that girl who brought you the bullet in the head."

"I've found her. Here."

Petrakis shrugged. "What can I do for you, Goldberg? I hate to ask."

Goldberg unrolled the drawing he had been carrying in his hand. "I need to know who made this picture."

Petrakis studied it. "A remarkably pretty girl. But why do you come to me with it? If you ask me do I recognize this girl, I do not."

"It was done in this city, probably in the Opera House and undoubtedly by a professional. I want you to put me in touch with someone who might be able to identify the artist."

"What is the nature of your need?" asked Petrakis suspiciously. "This passion for art is new."

"The man who did the drawing seems to have developed a sideline in kidnapping."

"As I suspected," said Petrakis gloomily. "One bullet in the head and now you feel the need for another. Don't be misled by the sweet seductions of San Francisco. We regularly make the top ten in the FBI crime statistics."

"Let me do it my way, Petrakis."

Petrakis pulled a pad and pencil from the top drawer of his desk. "I will give you a list of gallery owners I know. Tell them Petrakis sent you. My name is good for minor favors all over town. But stay away from people who shoot bullets, Goldberg. My influence extends only so far."

As Goldberg headed out of the office Petrakis called after him, "The Princeton game is finished, Goldberg."

"Go to hell," Goldberg replied over his shoulder, one friend to another.

Goldberg found the man he wanted in a small gallery off Sacramento. Homer Wilson by name, he was plump, finicky, and middle-aged, with long graceful alabaster hands into which all the energy of his body had descended. The hands waved and swirled and unrolled the sketch on a countertop, expecting to find nothing and shocked into stillness by what they did find. "So," said Homer Wilson, pursing his lips for a whistle that never came, "where did you get this?"

"Do you recognize the artist?"

The hands twinkled at the absurdity of the inquiry and danced across the sketch to linger in a tendril of hair. "Jack's signed everything he ever did since he was six years old. Out of consideration for the future historians of our culture, no doubt. He was born with a streak of immodesty made only more disgusting by the fact it may be merited."

"Jack?"

The right forefinger tapped impatiently on the curl it had singled out. "You need eyes to see, my friend. When the pencil contradicts reality you have to wonder why. When a strand of hair concludes in a perfect O, Jack Odell's been there, leaving spoor for the cognoscenti. One of the major egos of our time, so big in fact that it races ahead of his accomplishments, which are not inconsiderable."

"You know Odell well?"

"I represent Odell. This little gallery made him whatever name he has. Outside his own head, that is, where his name shines across oceans, and through the centuries. Under that pretty skull of his, Odell walks with Rembrandt and da Vinci, and on occasions he has been known to condescend to Picasso for being unduly commercial."

The agitation of Wilson's hands showed up in his eyes, which were brown. "If you're looking for recent news of the Master, forget it. I haven't seen him in nearly a year. If he's doing any work, I haven't seen it either. Are you a collector?"

"Not exactly," said Goldberg.

The brown eyes brightened with glee. "A detective perhaps? Have no fear, nothing you can say will surprise me. I have always suspected young Jack has a criminal streak that runs nearly as deep as his talent."

"Oh?"

"A degree of physical beauty that I consider a major defect in an artist because it provides too many alternatives to work. Odell is the man who put the horns on San Francisco. He's made a career of other men's wives. Two years ago he toured the Greek Isles with the Grass Widow Everett. He wears a Baume and Mercier watch courtesy of a local banking fortune. The Winterbottom woman took him to Kyoto to celebrate Christmas. Kyoto? Christmas? Sixteen months ago he tried to fly a Maserati off the Embarcadero. I don't know where the Maserati came from, but it didn't come out of a paint pot."

"Do you have an address for him?" asked Goldberg.

"Hardly current. As I said I haven't seen him in more than a year. At that time he had a studio in North Beach, and I'll give you the address, but you won't find him there. Twelve, thirteen, fourteen months ago, something like that, our little Digger Odell struck a new vein of gold that ran deeper and wider than anything he'd ever found before."

The fingers of Homer's left hand did a thoughtful minuet along his chest where the collar of his jacket crossed it. "Cocaine, maybe? Cocaine would do it. Whatever he's got hold of now is too big to be explained by other men's wives no matter how lonely they are. He's gone into some new orbit that's well beyond free trips and gold watches. And as far as I can tell, he hasn't touched brush or pencil since, except maybe for your sketch."

Homer Wilson went to the back of his store and removed a card from a file there. "Here's the last address I've got. Keep the card. I won't be needing it."

Crossing Columbus Avenue just as the city was exploding into lunch, Goldberg headed for the interior of Little Italy and wandered among the small shops where sausage and pasta and sugar-coated pastries were being born in a kind of extended family kitchen. For the first time in days he was hungry, but he kept moving until he found the house on a corner off Bay Street, a Victorian flight of fancy with a witch's hat turret, perched on top of an Alpine flight of stairs that rose and rose and rose until the house itself arrived as something of an afterthought.

Mr. and Mrs. Calabrese were the landlords and, since he had interrupted them at lunch, they invited him to join them. It was not until after the fish that Mrs. Calabrese, a woman of some substance with a sweet smile and an undeniable mustache, raised the question of why he was there. Goldberg explained that Jack Odell had done a drawing about which he wanted some information. When he exhibited the drawing, it was clear that the household was divided on the subject of its creator, with Mrs. Calabrese in favor and Mr. Calabrese opposed.

"A nice boy," said Mrs. Calabrese. "A little wild but still young. A good wife would settle him down."

"Yah," said Mr. Calabrese, forearms rippling. "Maybe his own wife for a change."

Mrs. Calabrese smiled her saintly smile and patted her husband's nearest biceps. "A little wild," she conceded, "but a very good heart, very good manners, flowers on Mother's Day, and a tip of the hat to the ladies."

"Phah," said Mr. Calabrese, "when he wore a hat?"

"When he tipped it, that's when he wore it," explained Mrs. Calabrese, unruffled.

Mr. Calabrese shrugged and returned to the contemplation of his forearms, which rested like twin watermelons on his noble belly. "For a year and a half Mr. Pretty Boy lives in the tower on the top of the house like the king of Naples in his castle. It's a room like gold, all the sun in a thousand miles comes there to visit. He lives up there, he paints up there, he keeps girls up there, he gets drunk up there. Sometimes he breaks his heart and even pays the rent."

"That's not fair," protested Mrs. Calabrese. "Sooner or later he always pays the rent."

"You know something I don't know?" inquired Mr. Calabrese, smiling sourly at his forearms.

"Sounds like a pretty good life to me," said Goldberg. "Why did he leave?"

Mrs. Calabrese started to remove dishes from the table. When she was out of the room, Mr. Calabrese unfolded his arms and rested them on the tabletop. "She don't like to hear about it," he explained. "I threw him out."

"Why?"

"He arrives home drunk once too often. I hear him fall down those steps you come up and it's a long way down, cursing and swearing all the way, and spilling money out of his little suitcase."

"Money?"

"More money than you ever saw in your life, mister."

"Was there something wrong with the money?"

"Yah, there was too much of it. No way he got that much money any way but dirty. Gangs. Rackets. I mind my own business. I threw him out."

"You got any idea where he went?"

"I wouldn't want to know," said Mr. Calabrese disgustedly. "Pretty boy."

In the distance Mrs. Calabrese was talking volubly, a sound like crooning with interruptions, and when she came back into the room the hospitality started all over again, more coffee, which in turn required more pastry, and in turn more coffee to go with the excess pastry. It was a cycle that might never have been broken if Goldberg had not gotten to his feet. And even then she insisted on taking him up to the tower room to see what splendor had surrounded her boarder.

Twenty-two

From the top of the steps Goldberg saw the Porsche 928 squatting at the curb like a great black toad a hundred yards up the street. Behind the steering wheel there was a blur of head and shoulders, features concealed by the flash of sun on the windshield. A gun could be somewhere inside that blaze of light, but it would take more than a handgun to reach him and anything larger would have to come poking through an open window before it could be used.

At the foot of the steps he stopped, undecided whether to go after the car, or let it come after him. It was Dr. Porsche's idea of a luxury car, designed to cruise at a hundred MPH or crawl at five without throwing up. Goldberg decided to let it crawl.

He marched toward Beach Street, looking neither left nor right but managing an occasional glance behind him as though uncertain of his direction. When he reached the corner, the Porsche left the curb and moved slowly after him. I've got a Porsche on a string, thought Goldberg, stepping out to the music of a small whistle somewhere in his head, striding along briskly in the cold sunshine toward his destination where he would lose himself among the tourists but not so completely that he would be difficult to find.

When Goldberg reached Ghiradelli Square and slipped into the concealment of the ex-chocolate factory, a warm feeling of contentment swept over his back, which had spent the previous fifteen minutes anticipating bullet holes his head had assured it were not in the cards. He sampled the chocolate in the old-time ice cream parlor, shopped for an antique cane he decided reluctantly not to buy, browsed in the bookstore for a book he could not find, paused to examine Benny Bufano's nearly life-size bear, and wandered genially from level to level among galleries and plazas, smiling at children who sometimes returned his smile. When he decided the owner of the Porsche had had enough time to park his car, he stationed himself by the mermaid fountain in front of the olive trees and waited. In a little while a young man passed him, scowling.

About six feet tall, broad-shouldered, and athletic. The nose had been shifted by some violent contact slightly to the left. The eyes were his claim to being a Newman lookalike, a blue so brilliant you would remember them when all other details of his appearance had faded from memory. A muscular, determined, self-indulgent, movie-actor's face.

The mermaid fountain was as popular as the clock at the Biltmore had been in the days when Goldberg waited there for girls. The young man was busy waiting now, glancing at his watch, pursing his lips, and pacing. Three times the pacing took him around the fountain, each time a little closer to Goldberg whom he elaborately did not see.

On his fourth circuit Goldberg stopped him. "I believe we're waiting for each other," he said pleasantly.

185

Odell, caught by surprise, fell automatically into an exotic posture of defense that Goldberg recognized as deriving from one of the martial arts although he was not quite sure which one. It would have a name, he knew, some bit of Oriental whimsy like Grasp Bird's Tail, or perhaps Carry Tiger to Mountain, the only fragments of Tai Chi he remembered from a paperback he had consulted in a dentist's office. Could this be Tai Chi?

Odell went through several revolutions of whatever he was doing while Goldberg studied him. He was not so much threatening as admonitory, putting Goldberg on notice he was dealing with an expertise so arcane he could hardly expect to cope with it.

"Are you sure you've got that right, son?" inquired Goldberg.

After due consideration the arms returned to their normal position and the legs straightened. "Don't try to find out," Odell said a little huffily.

"All right, if that's the way you feel about it." Goldberg explained about the dentist's office and Odell relaxed, reassured now that he was dealing with an aging, if rather large, eccentric.

"What do you want from me?" he demanded.

"You followed me here," pointed out Goldberg, but quickly decided that Odell was too easily confused for that kind of play and desisted. "I'm interested in your picture," he said, unrolling the sketch of Miranda.

"How do you know it's mine?"

"You signed it."

Odell shrugged, on the verge of boredom. "A bad habit. I should confine my signature to important work."

"This could turn out to be more important than you think," suggested Goldberg. "Why don't we go somewhere and discuss it?"

Odell glanced at his watch, a Baume and Mercier with eighteen-karat gold studs and eighteen-karat gold links. A lot of eighteen-karat. Very masculine. Very expensive. He was getting impatient with Goldberg now, convinced that whatever had been worrying him before was nothing to worry about. "What makes you think it's so important? I have a business appointment in exactly twenty-two minutes. That's important."

"A good-looking watch," said Goldberg. "You get it recently?"

"What the hell business is that of yours?"

Goldberg put out one hand to clasp the wrist that held the Baume and Mercier, putting enough force into the movement to alarm Odell. "Gently, gently," said Goldberg. "I should warn you, I'm wearing a gun under my jacket and I was using it long before you put on your first pair of Pampers."

"Jesus, a holdup," said Odell, looking around for help, but finding himself surrounded by so much innocence he might have been alone in Paradise with a mugger.

"I don't want your money. I don't even want your watch. What I want is some information about a young girl who has disappeared. The girl whose face you put down on this piece of paper."

Odell tried to separate his arm from Goldberg's hand until Goldberg released it, leaving no doubt he could have kept it if he had wanted it. "Who are you?" Odell demanded.

"Goldberg's the name."

"The world is full of Goldbergs. What does this one do that needs a gun to do it?"

Goldberg hadn't had a good answer to this question for some time and, as a result, his response varied with the inspiration of the moment. "I'm a retired cop doing a favor for a friend," he decided. He liked the sound of it—not too threatening and yet with some promise of effectiveness. "Mostly I do favors for friends. In this case the mother of the girl in your picture."

Odell curled his lips for spitting. "Mothers burn my ass."

"You can tell me about it on the terrace next to Benny Bufano's bear," said Goldberg soothingly, locking one arm around the painter. "At a nice table over a cup of Irish coffee. Maybe you'd like something to eat."

"Jesus," said the painter, but he went without further protest, and, once seated, began to recover himself, or at least what he considered himself to be. He had the petulant look of a man who had gotten what he wanted so often he no longer knew what to want. He was embarrassed at having been afraid of Goldberg and infuriated at having been manhandled by him.

"Nice woman, Mrs. Calabrese," said Goldberg.

"Fuck Mrs. Calabrese." Odell leaned forward, elbows sliding across the table, the designer haircut swinging over his ears. "Do you have any idea who you're talking to?"

"Yes," said Goldberg, "you're the man whose ass is burned by mothers."

"In 1980 *ArtNews* described me as a major talent," proclaimed Odell, who seemed to be working out of a prepared defense. "I'm not exactly unknown. The demand for my work is international." He noticed Goldberg looking at the Baume and Mercier. "I'm even better known in Europe than I am here," he explained.

"It's a funny background for a kidnapper," Goldberg agreed.

"What are you talking about?"

"The girl in your picture was kidnapped."

Odell was genuinely amazed and then he was equally

genuinely amused. "That was the least-kidnapped girl in the history of the world. Call it a jailbreak and you'll be closer to the mark."

"Tell me about that."

"What's to tell? Divorced parents. The mother had her locked up in a place they call the Horse Nunnery, a sort of rich girls' reform school. Daddy and daughter wanted to meet and I was the carrier of the airplane tickets. Anything illegal about that?" Odell was suddenly glib and terribly relieved. "It was my good deed for the year, a fast five points on the pro bono scale, busting a prisoner out of the Horse Nunnery."

"Why didn't her father just mail the tickets?"

"They censor the mail," said Odell happily. "Would you believe that? Besides, I was the cover story. Ran away with an unknown painter she met at the opera. Her mother would take that a hell of a lot better than the truth. Divorce is like taking a lid off an oil well. Pow. Two people who've hated each other for years suddenly have a license to blow each other up."

Goldberg had an uneasy feeling that the painter believed every word of his own story. "You a friend of the father's?"

"I'm a friend of freedom everywhere. Think of me as a patron of liberty."

"Forget liberty for the moment. What do you know about her father?"

"Never saw the man in my life." Odell was practically singing his relief. "You're pissing in the wind, whoever-you-are. Even where you come from, wherever that is, delivering airline tickets is hardly a felony."

"You weren't worrying about airline tickets when Mrs. Calabrese tipped you I was looking for you."

Odell gave Goldberg his best enigmatic smile, accompanied by a flourish of the designer haircut. "You figure that out." And then, in case Goldberg hadn't, he added, "Half the husbands in town would pay prize money for my cock."

Back to the nutcracker, thought Goldberg, the painter was starting to slide away. "You realize what the penalty is for kidnapping in this country? Ever since the Lindbergh baby there's been federal legislation: cross a state line with the victim, it's the death penalty. Just one little toe across and you got the FBI on your ass. You think I'm unreasonable, wait'll you deal with them."

"You deaf or something?" said Odell. "I told you . . ."

"I know what you told me. Now tell me where the girl is."

Odell's petulant lips pulled back from the impeccable teeth, and his voice started to slide upward toward soprano. "I don't know where the girl is."

Goldberg decided it was time to change the pressure points. "I want to make a phone call. It will probably take about fifteen minutes. You could leave this table while I'm calling and disappear. If you do I'll have to turn your name over to the FBI. From then on you'll be a fugitive. Everything you consider part of your life will be out of bounds, because it's history that catches fugitives, old girl friends, old houses, old occupations, old coffee shops, everything you're used to touching, smelling, eating, doing. No more articles in *ArtNews*, because the FBI will be taking out a subscription. You decide."

Without looking back Goldberg went in search of a telephone. When he found one, he dialed the Horse Nunnery, and asked for Miss Morrison. She was on the phone within thirty seconds. "Hello, Mr. Goldberg. Have you located Miranda?"

"No. But I've got a small idea. Can you tell me whether she has received any long-distance phone calls in the past month?"

"Her mother?"

"Not her mother."

She knew what he wanted all right, but she was reluctant to give it to him; Miss Morrison had grown up on the principle that anything you said might be held against you. She hesitated again. "It was about two weeks ago. I couldn't help overhearing, because Miranda was screaming into the phone and she's not ordinarily a screamer. 'Who? I don't have a father.' That's all I heard, it was not my intention to hear anything at all. The second call I heard nothing, but when she came out of my office she had that grin of hers spread all across her face. It's a look I've seen before and it generally meant she was planning something particularly reckless."

"Thank you," said Goldberg.

"I hope it's been helpful."

"More than you'll ever know," said Goldberg.

When he returned to the table, Odell was sitting with his elbows on it, cradling his head. He looked up at Goldberg. "Well?"

Goldberg dropped into his chair and started to stare at the painter as though trying to memorize him. "You know," he said at last, "you may be the unluckiest man I ever met."

Odell began to construct an airplane out of a cocktail napkin.

"I figured you had to exist, only I never expected to meet you."

The painter, absorbed in the aerodynamic potential of his napkin, refused to take the bait, and Goldberg sipped the last of his coffee while he considered how unlucky Odell really was. When he had considered long enough, he went on. "You do much gambling?"

Odell looked up from his construction. "Sorry. I don't play games. At least not that kind. What makes you ask?"

"I was working on a theory," Goldberg explained. "I've been on a roll for three months. Dice, poker, roulette, doesn't make any difference, the luck rolls on. When something like that happens to you, you really start thinking about it, you walk around it and examine it from every angle, you try to understand what it is and what makes it work, and what might happen to stop it. Look at it this way. All probability says is that over a certain number of events a certain pattern of frequency will establish itself. Throw a thousand dice and you get a certain number of sixes. There's nothing that says Goldberg has to throw the thousand dice; people are working at that day and night in Vegas, Monte Carlo, and the gambling pagodas of Thailand. All you need is a losing streak for every winning streak—and the laws of probability are restored to instant sanity."

Odell abandoned his airplane and began to smile. "So you're a gambler. So that's what this is all about. Where'd you hear about me?"

"Around," said Goldberg, thinking here it comes.

"You're a gambler and you're broke and you need a stake. All that talk about kidnapping's a lot of bullshit. You're looking for a fairy godmother. Why didn't you say so in the first place, you dumb son of a bitch?"

"So you're the guy." Goldberg leaned back and sighed his relief.

The painter was like a walker lost in strange country who suddenly spies a familiar landmark. His eyes glistened. The shoulders enlarged inside the navy-blue jacket. His fingers strutted across the table in front of him. He was a man restored to his idea of himself. "In San Francisco I am it," he proclaimed, a barker starting his spiel, "the gambler's friend, balm for the busted, a fresh pocket for the tapped-out, loser's safe harbor, the door that's open when all others are closed, the banker with the heart. If you're a degenerate gambler, cousin, you've found a home."

Twenty-three

When he got back to the Fairmont she was still wearing the black suit that was the uniform of her anxiety. The blouse with a collar that tied around her neck. Black shoes, black legs. If she had thought of it she would have been wearing black gloves. Vestal Mama, black and impregnable. Later Goldberg blamed the suit for the abruptness with which he blurted out the truth about Miranda.

"Miranda doesn't have a father," she said as though that would make it all go away.

"The guy on the other end of the phone had a different idea."

"The son of a bitch," said Barbara, her pale skin paler than ever. She pulled at the high-necked blouse as though it was choking her. "I don't believe it," she said without specifying what it was she didn't believe. Her fingers could not stay away from the neck of the blouse. "He tricked her and she fell for it. She ran to her father." Her lips turned up in the way that was always a part of how he remembered her, a defiant grin that proclaimed she was not about to be taken in by anybody or anything. "Do you know how I feel?" she said.

"Yes."

"No you don't." She reached behind her and released the tie that held the collar of the blouse against her neck. She went to the sideboard and found herself a glass of Scotch. "How I feel is silly," she said and took a gulp of the Scotch. "All those years. All that work. All that pain. Silly." She lit a cigarette, but it didn't do any good, and she crushed it out in an ashtray. She took another drink, put down the glass, and removed her jacket in order to get at the blouse. She untied the collar, but that was not enough. She took off the blouse and that was not enough either. Nothing was enough until soon she was pale all over except for the amber fire between her thighs, the color of Scotch, thought Goldberg, wondering why that had never occurred to him before.

His wild joy took him by surprise, but he was even more surprised a little later when he realized that he was thinking most of the gambling, more and more of the gambling that would take place that night.

The toadlike Porsche arrived in front of the Fairmont at eleven o'clock with Odell inside it.

Odell, who was dressed in evening clothes, looked Goldberg over critically. "You clean up pretty good," he said finally, reaching over to straighten Goldberg's skinny black tie. "You're going to meet the cream of San Francisco society tonight. Not too many people could get you in. Yacht

194

people. Limousine people. People with houses that when they die become museums."

Goldberg noticed that Odell was wearing another watch, thin as a potato chip, with diamond numerals. "I'll be nice," he promised.

Odell reached into the rear of the Porsche and brought back a black leather attaché case. Goldberg opened it. It was full of new hundred-dollar bills. "The limousine people usually carry this kind of cash?" he asked.

"The limousine people carry whatever they want. They got credit would take your breath away. You don't. If anybody asks, you come from Texas."

"What if I lose?"

"You still come from Texas."

"I lose I won't be able to pay you back."

"You follow the systems I gave you you can't lose. You memorized them?"

"Like my Social Security number."

Odell looked over at him suspiciously. "That was awful quick. Most people take longer."

"I've got a photographic memory." Goldberg glanced at his own watch; it was twenty minutes after eleven. "You beat the tables often with these systems?"

"Why do you think we have to keep bringing in new ringers? If the systems didn't work, we could walk in anywhere and play. New faces is what we need and you're a new face."

Goldberg had gone over the systems carefully. They were no sillier than anybody else's. "You gamble much yourself?" he asked curiously.

"Enough to look legitimate. Nothing real big. I can't afford to make myself unpopular. This is a business with me."

195

"Good business?"

"The best."

"Could I get into it?"

Odell laughed scornfully. "You got to be gamblingproof to do what I do. A couple of long streaks and you'd give the whole scam away. You be satisfied with what you got. A couple of big evenings on me and then you're on your own."

The surest sign of aging is an irresistible urge to advise the young, thought Goldberg. He went ahead anyway. "Seems like a funny business for a painter."

"It's the perfect business for a painter. You're free all day when the light is good and you work at night when you couldn't paint anyway. People like to forget artists have to buy frozen food and pay for gas just like anybody else, they expect you to live on the prospect of immortality. They don't take immortality at the supermarket. Besides, I'm not going to do this forever. One more year and I'm home free."

"Maybe you could quit sooner," suggested Goldberg.

"Maybe you could mind your own business."

Odell was tapping the steering wheel with a forefinger. Goldberg had noticed before that the painter seemed to have trouble keeping his whole body still at once. If it wasn't a finger it was a foot, or sometimes one leg folded over the other jerking and tapping, keeping time to some hidden anxiety. "If it's such a good business, why are you so nervous?" asked Goldberg. "Why don't you think of it that way?"

"In just a minute I'm going to dump you out of this car, I don't care how big you are. Who the hell do you think you are anyway, Solomon? Couple of minutes you'll be sawing babies in half."

196

Goldberg subsided into the roller-coaster landscape of San Francisco, reminding himself that he was an ex-father as well as an ex-cop, and began to concentrate on the gambling. It would be his first time with play money and he wondered whether that would make a difference to the streak. He could detect no sensation in his body that gave any hint one way or the other, no bubble, no excitement, no premonition. It was all flat and a little stale, but he had felt that way before and it had meant nothing.

Their destination turned out to be a private club in a high rise on one of the two crests of Russian Hill. At least it was billed as a private club on a discreet brass plate to the left of the front door. If it was a club, Goldberg was a member a couple of seconds after he arrived, his induction consisting of a whispered conversation between Odell and a swarthy man in evening clothes who was introduced as Mr. Victor and could easily have passed for the young George Raft.

The Pumpkin Club occupied the top two floors of an apartment house that was a long-drawn-out Alhambra. By any name it was a gambling casino with another one of those spectacular views that San Francisco keeps coming up with just when you figure the city fathers have finally run out of scenery. South you looked down on the skyscrapers of the financial district; north you had the bay, the Golden Gate, and the hills beyond, and everything except the hills contributed to the festivities its own pattern of light.

The first floor of the Pumpkin Club was a single enormous room dedicated to roulette, dice, and blackjack. Three sides were glass and two enormous ebony bars filled all of the fourth wall that was not required for exiting and entering. It was a highly professional layout, worthy of any casino in Las Vegas, but strangely sanitized and refined. It was like a gambling room in a dream, white walls, white carpets, wheels turning, dice flying, no sound. The throb was missing, the battleground noise of slot machines and the pressure of desperate flesh torn with the need to win or lose before time ran out. The patrons of the Pumpkin Club did not sweat or encourage the dice with loud cries. You could lose your money in a room like this with the sense that you were fulfilling a social obligation. Chinese waiters in red velvet jogging suits glided steadily between the bars and the thirsty. Near the entrance the cashier sat at an Empire desk, conscientiously unprotected. If there was any security in the room, it was concealed behind bland smiles and ruffled shirts. Tranquility was part of the decor in Mr. Victor's little kingdom.

In the center of the room there was a circular ironwork staircase. "What's up there?" asked Goldberg.

"Special rooms," said Odell indifferently. "Baccarat, bridge, high-stakes poker. You'll find as much action as you can handle down here." In his shrug there was the implication that Goldberg would never make it upstairs.

Goldberg wondered about that. Odell seemed to be as happy as a clam serving two masters, the one who made the money, and the one who took it. There had to be a bullet or two in the arrangement somewhere, but all the painter saw was his personal retirement plan in flower.

When Goldberg turned his attention to the dice table, he understood the painter's shrug. They were playing money craps, the high roller's game, the fastest way to lose money ever invented by the mind of man, money on the table in trim packets of ten thousand, five thousand, twenty-five hundred and one thousand dollars. The game could devour Goldberg's stake in under thirty minutes, and there was no question in Odell's mind that it would. The layout was the same as in Las Vegas but without the proposition bets—the only betting spaces being the lose line, the win line, and the box numbers.

Goldberg slipped into the circle to the right of the shooter and settled down to wait for the dice to reach him. He bet cautiously, not so much out of prudence, but because he knew by now that the bugle in his chest blew only when he himself held the dice.

There were eleven men at the table and one woman, on Goldberg's right, who would be the last shooter before the dice reached him. She wore a dress the color of wet sand, a liquid-silk jersey, enormous shoulders, two fan shapes embroidered in gold beads on the belt. The neck of the dress was rather high, but the dress made up for the modesty of the neckline by the immodesty of armholes so deep you could see the flash of naked young breasts through them. Chunks of sculptured gold dragged at her earlobes. Dark hair, tawny skin. Emerald eyes. A slightly aquiline nose. Maybe twenty-five and beautiful in a way you would remember long after you had left her. The man on her right was her husband, twice her age, but handling it well, over six feet, lithe, a yachtsman's cross-grained skin, hair that was not merely white but sterling silver. There was something wrong between them that was more than one night old, a marriage going bad for a long time and by now as bad as it could get before it blew. When the woman noticed Goldberg looking at her breasts through the movement of the sleeve, she gave him an accident-prone smile.

"Good luck," whispered Odell as he slid away, leaving Goldberg with the impression he didn't mean a word of it. The dice were cold and so was the atmosphere at the table, which looked more like a board of directors' meeting than any crap game Goldberg had ever seen before. A lot of black tie and bankers' eyes; there was nobody whose baby needed new shoes. There had to be a big bookie in any collection of high rollers, but if there was one here, he had gone underground in a Bond Street suit.

Cold dice, waiting for Goldberg, passed around the table in a wrong better's dream—until they reached the silver-haired yachtsman whose name was Hugh. Hugh and Charlie, Charlie being the girl whose breasts twinkled at Goldberg when she moved her arms. Each time Goldberg was surprised, but he was beginning to suspect it took a lot to surprise Charlie.

"Okay, honey," she said sweetly, "cast the bones and see if you can do anything right," and, leaving no doubts about her expectations, she bet five thousand against his passing.

It turned out the dice had not been waiting for Goldberg but came alive in the yachtsman's hand. He held them for a little less than ten minutes while the neat green packages of money flowed across the darker green of the baize cloth in a tidal wave.

Goldberg looked at Charlie, Charlie looked at Goldberg. Hughie slung the dice with the growing assurance of a man who finds he can do nothing wrong. During that nearly ten minutes Goldberg and Charlie became allies. When the dice turned cold on Hughie, Charlie refused her turn and let them pass to Goldberg.

Goldberg called for fresh dice, picked a pair from the choice of five offered by the stickman, and cuddled them in his palm while he waited for their message. There was no message. It was possible that in some obscure malfunction of destiny his streak had touched down on Hughie and would pass Goldberg by completely.

Knowing nothing, he made his first pass with the dice. An eleven. That was the beginning and from there on it was like being lifted, carried along and driven by some monstrous roaring wind that shut out everything else, Charlie's breasts, Hughie's needle eyes, the board of directors that came and went, betting with him, or against him, Odell trying to pluck him from the table, the stickman who seemed to get taller and the dealer who seemed to get shorter and squatter, Mr. Victor contracting inside his suit until he was all sharp edges like a stiletto in pants. It all started a little after eleven and stopped shortly before three when Mr. Victor declared the table closed. In that time Goldberg had won somewhere around eight hundred thousand dollars—the exact amount was never going to be any clearer than that—some from the board of directors but a great deal from Mr. Victor himself, who, as the house, had taken the brunt of the betting when the bankers' eyes began to say no, no, and no again.

Twenty-four

"Jesus," said Odell, a little short of putting the Porsche into a tree in the early-morning fog, "Jesus, Jesus, Jesus."

"Half of eight hundred thousand can't be that bad," said Goldberg.

"Tell me about it, Santa Claus. Give me chapter and verse on how lucky I am." Odell half turned in the driver's seat, letting the Porsche find its own way in the fog. "I'm a dead man, and a fucking dice degenerate put me in my coffin."

"We'll both be dead men if you don't look where you're going."

Odell shrugged. "Sooner or later, what the hell difference does it make?" But he turned his eyes back toward the windshield. "I should have started running the minute I laid eyes on you. Anybody ever tell you you look like the ace of spades?"

"No," said Goldberg, but he thought about the question for a while after he'd answered it. "Mr. Victor mad at us?"

"You bet your ass, Mr. Victor is mad at us."

"He let us walk."

"Mr. Victor runs a nice place. He doesn't believe in killing his meat on the premises."

"Why don't you run?"

"Didn't you notice? I'm running."

"Right into the next tree is where you're running. You think you've got some obligation to do Mr. Victor's killing for him? Stop the car and let me drive."

"I'm no criminal," said Odell, who by now was talking to some third party in his head. "What did I ever know about dealing with criminals? I'm a painter, that's what I am, an artist, living in a country where nobody gives a shit about artists. That's the God's truth. I was trying to make a buck so I could paint in peace. A major talent is what they said. What'll they say now? Grab his pictures, they're bound to go up in value, there's nothing the market likes like a dead major talent. If Mr. Victor doesn't get me, the other guy will. It's a kind of race, and I'm first prize."

The Porsche was sliding around curves, climbing hills, bucketing down them, finding its own way in the fog as though it had an instinct Goldberg lacked. Maybe the painter had superhuman vision. Goldberg hoped so. It occurred to Goldberg that he had not spent any of his winnings: they slept in a valise like a collection of old newspapers. He thought he might spend some of them now, but he couldn't think of anything he wanted enough to buy. All of the things he had bought in the past—homes, educations, cars, food, orthodonture, music lessons, riding lessons, summer camps, fur coats, cloth coats, dresses, suits, pants, sheets, jewelry—had nothing to do with him now; the only thing that mattered was winning.

"What the hell, it didn't hurt anybody," Odell explained to the windshield. "The other guy wanted to put money in, Mr. Victor wanted to take it out. The other guy didn't seem to mind if he lost, Mr. Victor was happy as a clam because he always won. It was hand in glove. What was wrong in working for both?"

You should have stuck to painting, thought Goldberg, if that was your idea of hand in glove, working as a kind of pusher for a gambling house, introducing pigeons and undoubtedly working on a commission, the only oddity being that he supplied the money the pigeons lost, an irregularity made even odder by the fact that the money was counterfeit.

Odell was the first to hear the warbling in the distance. "What the hell's that?"

"Police car," said Goldberg, grateful for anything that would stop the Porsche before it went off a cliff.

Stopping was not part of what Odell had in mind. His foot hesitated a fraction of a second on the accelerator pedal, and then sent the Porsche plunging forward blindly into the fog.

"Goddammit," said Goldberg. He fiddled with his seatbelt, not sure whether he wanted it tighter or off completely. He decided on off; he didn't like drowning and he liked burning even less. "Why the hell run from the police? You trying to protect a perfect driving record?"

"How do you know it's the police?"

With his head turned Goldberg saw the prickle of lights trying to flash through the fog. "They've got a police car," he said. "Police cars have radios. You run long enough they'll figure they've flushed a coke dealer and every car in the area will be closing in on you."

"On us," said Odell.

"Damn right us," agreed Goldberg. "My half says stop running."

"You and your fucking winning streak," said Odell bitterly. "I should have listened. But how could you expect me to buy that kind of garbage?"

"Listen now," advised Goldberg.

For another sixty seconds Odell thought things over, then let the Porsche drag slowly to a halt as though he still hadn't really made up his mind, but was surrendering to inertia.

Goldberg sighed. He felt better than he'd felt for the past half hour. When the police car pulled up alongside them and the redheaded cop got out and peered through the driver's window, Goldberg was prepared to like him. It was not an easy face to like with its big broken nose and assorted scar tissue. He didn't seem to like Goldberg's face any better than Goldberg liked his. He had his gun out of its holster, hanging at his side. "You all sons a bitches. You all come on outta there," he said. It wasn't a real Southern accent, more something he'd caught from a Southern sheriff in a made-for-TV movie and liked the sound of. Two more guys in cop suits were getting out of the patrol car. They also had their guns drawn. The fourth man didn't have either a gun or a uniform. What he had was a look that left no doubt what the guns were for. It was Mr. Victor.

"Motherfucker, motherfucker, motherfucker," said

Odell to the dashboard of the Porsche. He turned and looked at Goldberg. "Do something," he said. "You're the one with all the luck." His lips were trembling.

There was a cop on Goldberg's side now, tap-tapping with the barrel of his gun. He was a very fat cop with a belly the shape and just about the size of a keg of beer. His navel protruded from the too-tight shirt like a very large doorbell. Goldberg held up his hands to show they were empty, lowered them to release the door lock, then raised them again, see, still empty. He wondered where they had gotten the police cars, and the uniforms, and the guns. If he had liked Odell better, he would have apologized to him. "I'm getting out of the car, officer," he said carefully to the phony cop with the beer-keg belly. "You can see I've got my hands up and there's nothing in them."

Mr. Victor's personal police force had no feeling for the conventional amenities. "How you like I stick this thing in your ear?" he said, running the gun up the sideburn Goldberg presented to him.

Goldberg didn't like the idea at all, but he decided not to bring that up.

On the other side of the Porsche, two of Mr. Victor's cops were collaborating on the removal of Odell, whose strategy was to go limp in the driver's seat. For a moment Goldberg thought he had fainted, but his eyes were open and staring through the windshield. When the cops had wrestled him out of his seat, he went limp on the road, his face buried in the macadam. One of the cops kicked him twice in the right kidney. Odell grunted, once for each kick, but he kept his face down, his big hands cradled over the back of his head.

The cop with the exposed belly button escorted Goldberg around the Porsche and lined him up next to Odell for Mr.

Victor's inspection. The gambler, still in black tie, came over and kicked Odell with a size-eight patent-leather shoe that elicited a yelp from the painter. "You better get your ass out of that road before we bury you right there," suggested Mr. Victor. "I give you a count of three."

Odell was on his feet at two, dented and dusty and somehow shorter. None of his clothing seemed to fit anymore.

Mr. Victor stuck a small, sharp finger into Odell at the bottom of the vee where the two halves of the tuxedo's collar met. The painter screamed as though he had been stabbed and Mr. Victor withdrew his finger as though disgusted with where it had been. "You scream like a little girl," he said, leaving Goldberg with the impression that at one time or another he had heard and evaluated all kinds of screams. Mr. Victor was nothing if not experienced.

Mr. Victor did most of his business according to rules that had been laid down a long time ago. Only rarely did anything come up that required fresh thinking and when it did his black eyebrows slanted down toward each other with unfamiliar effort. His eyebrows were slanting now as they dealt with the spectacle that was Odell. "You're too disgusting to kill," he said eventually.

Odell heard this news with a twitch of relief that did not otherwise affect his slump; he was being careful not to make himself any less disgusting.

"I tell you what I'm going to do," said Mr. Victor. He pointed at Goldberg. "I'm going to let your partner here kill you. He looks as though he could manage it nicely."

"No," said Odell.

"You don't like that idea?" Mr. Victor did some more of his heavy thinking until the eyebrows nearly met. "Tell you what. You got a chance, too. You kill him first and we call it quits, you and me. I get back my money, you get back your buddy's body, and we're all even." He looked Goldberg over carefully. "It's a lot of body. You win it, you've earned it. How's that for a deal?"

Odell, a little taller now, sneaked a glance at Goldberg, and shook his head.

"Come on now," coaxed Mr. Victor. "You don't kill him, he's going to kill you. Ain't that the truth, big guy?"

Goldberg didn't say anything.

"Take my word for it," said Mr. Victor. "Big guy here looks like he might have done a patch of killing in his own time. Take my word for it, Odell, I know the look."

Mr. Victor was beginning to enjoy himself, but he wasn't a patient man, and the enjoyment wouldn't last without a little action. He did a dance step up on his toes. Maybe he thought he was George Raft. Or maybe he was getting a little cold. The fog was nothing you'd want to stand in for very long. Goldberg felt it on his hands and on his face and through his shirt where it wasn't covered by the jacket. He moved his arms a little and considered the possibility of picking Mr. Victor up in them and using his doll's body as a shield against the guns. Mr. Victor danced out of range as all three guns came up. "Maybe you're right," he said to Odell. "It wouldn't hardly be a fair fight. Nothing I hate worse than not a fair fight." He reached in his right pants pocket, pulled out a switchblade, opened it, and threw it at Odell's feet. Open, the blade was between six and seven inches long and quite narrow. Black handle. Brass trim. A serious-looking knife. Mr. Victor didn't keep it to shape his nails.

Odell looked down at the knife, then looked at Goldberg. He shook his head. Mr. Victor stooped and picked up the knife. "Maybe I better give it to Mr. Lucky here. I ain't got all night." He started to offer the knife to Goldberg, whose hand went out for it. "Too fucking eager, big guy," said Mr. Victor, dancing back out of the way. "You could break him in your hands. You're not entitled to a knife." He turned on his heel like a man in a clock and skipped out of the beam of light that came from the police car. When he came back he had the knife in his left hand and a stylish little Beretta in his right. He stuck the Beretta into Odell where his finger had once been. "You got twenty seconds," he said. "Either you use the knife, or I use the gun."

Goldberg automatically started counting. Mr. Victor was giving short change. On the count of fifteen he was pressing the little gun deeper into Odell as though he wanted to make sure it would reach a vital part. "Time's up," he said. "One of you leaves here alive. It's up to you which one."

Odell reached down for the knife. Once he had it, it seemed to be pulling him toward Goldberg, at first slowly and then, when he'd covered half the distance between them, in a headlong rush, the knife held out in front of him like a horn on a charging bull.

At the last minute Goldberg stepped aside and chopped at the knife hand. When the knife hit the road, Goldberg gathered it in with a long right arm and turned quickly, still in a crouch, looking for a piece of Mr. Victor, not quite sure what he was going to do with the piece, but hoping to put it between him and the three phony cops.

At that point Odell, who had a very confused idea of his allies, probably saved Goldberg's life by charging into him and sending him sprawling. Odell wanted the knife more than anything he had ever wanted, fame, gold watches, money, other men's wives. He kneed Goldberg in the left ear and aimed a kick at his groin that made Goldberg grunt and drop the knife. Goldberg blamed himself for dropping the knife. The kick had been a little off target and delivered in patent-leather slippers that were a lot softer than football cleats.

Goldberg rolled away from the knife that Odell was once more trying to shove into him, rolled to his knees behind the painter, and got to his feet, half throwing, half pushing Odell at Mr. Victor, who had come closer to get a better look at his private gladiatorial contest.

Mr. Victor took one step back and neatly shot Odell with his little gun about an inch above the bridge of the painter's nose. Odell straightened up and stood at attention, staring at Mr. Victor in surprise. Mr. Victor seemed equally surprised at what the little gun had done.

The fog was all around, holding them in place like china dolls in a Christmas box, Odell, Mr. Victor, the three fake cops with guns hanging and their mouths open. Then Odell started to crumple and Goldberg was gone, over the side of the road into a terrain of sliding rock and bushes that tore at his pants. He tripped and rolled thirty yards into a gully and got up and ran again.

As he ran he heard the shots behind him. One shot. Two. A volley of six. The three gunmen were making a show for the boss, but Goldberg was gone in the fog.

Twenty-five

When he knocked on the door, he knew what she was going to ask and what he would answer.

"How'd you make out?" she would ask.

"I broke even," he would answer, very cool in the shredded tuxedo.

But she never asked and he never answered. When she opened the door, her blackened hair was swinging around her face like enemy fire. A forefinger darted out to stab his chest. "Where in God's name have you been?" she demanded. "Hell breaks loose and you're out to lunch. Why aren't you ever where you're supposed to be when you're needed?"

"I don't know the answer to that," he said.

"You drunk?" she asked, pulling at his jacket. "Whose blood is that on the sleeve?"

Goldberg took off the jacket and threw it on a chair. There was more blood on his shirt. "I'll let you know as soon as I get down to skin," he said.

Whatever was bothering her, she still had time for a sneer. "Here comes macho man. Gone all night and now you're brave as a bull. Suppose I was dead. You ever try being macho to a corpse?"

Goldberg looked around the room; everything was in

one piece and in the right place. Whatever had happened hadn't disturbed the furniture. He felt the scar the thorns had made on his right calf beginning to throb.

At that point she decided to be calm. "I heard from Miranda," she said, her chest rising and falling inside the black silk blouse as she struggled to control her breathing.

"How?"

She looked at him with contempt. "On the telephone. How the hell else?"

"Sit down," he said. "We could waste the next two hours hating each other, or you could just tell me what happened."

Anger was good for her skin. She looked better than she had in days. When she moved, there was a snap to the movement, a sense of energy boiling inside her. She was out of mourning and into something else. "I picked up the telephone and there she was, she might have been around the corner. I didn't even yell at her. I said, 'Oh, my God, Miranda.' She said, 'I'm sorry, Mommy.' She hasn't called me Mommy since she was seven years old."

"Did she say where she was calling from?"

"She didn't know where she was calling from. She was babbling. I think she was on something."

"How'd she know where to call?"

"She's no fool. I always stay at the Fairmont in San Francisco." She looked at Goldberg with renewed contempt. "You've never been a mother," she pointed out.

He shrugged.

"Mother and daughter is fire and water, fire and fire, water and water."

Jesus, thought Goldberg, but, knowing he'd have to listen anyway, kept quiet.

"She hates me because I meddle. She'd hate me even

more if I didn't. There wasn't any question in her mind I'd be in San Francisco looking for her and staying at the Fairmont." The look she gave Goldberg now left no doubt he was a fool for asking.

Barbara Hall, that's all, he thought, the most beautiful woman in America had turned into a mother. "She knew where you were, but she didn't know where she was?"

"That's right."

"Look, I'm not attacking her I.Q. But didn't she give you a hint?"

Barbara was crying now. He watched the skin under her eyes grow slick with tears and the breath rasp in her throat. "The son of a bitch," she said at last. "The son of a bitch has her." She started to cry again but thought better of it. "It was like I'd gone crazy. Miranda talked to me for maybe five minutes and then there was the sound you get when the telephone is dropped and somebody's trying to keep it from dropping and it's swinging by the cord, a whole basket of bangs and scrapes, and then the phone was dead. Ten minutes later it rang again and it was Miranda and she was saying word for word what she had said before and then I was listening to myself saying word for word what I said before, and I thought maybe I was dreaming and this was a nightmare. But then I knew it was a tape playing. Whoever invented the tape machine had Doc in mind. Mr. Bug. He never lived anywhere from the time he was eighteen where he didn't put a bug on the telephone. His idea of paradise would be listening in on every conversation in the world and nobody would have any secrets except him.

"The tape cut off while I was hearing myself yell at Miranda for being a fool, and then it was Doc on the line. He had been listening all along. He was laughing. Doc really gets off on things like that. I asked him what he wanted from me. He said he didn't want a goddamn thing from me or anybody else in the world. He said it was all over."

"What was all over?"

"It. How do I know what *it* was? If I ever understood anything at all about Doc, I would have started running the minute I first laid eyes on him. He was crazy then. All I thought was he was a genius and he probably was. Still is. But crazier. For a long time now I figured he was going to blow something up, but it would have to be very big to be worth the trouble. I think he's found whatever it is that's big enough, and I don't think he gives a damn about anything, not even if we find him."

Goldberg went to the bar and poured himself a Johnnie Walker Black. When he held the bottle out to her, she shook her head. "If Doc knows you're here, the sooner we leave the better." He poured a second drink, saw himself in the mirror above the bar, and wondered whether the dice had started to lie to him. He watched Barbara in the window. She was combing her hair with the scrupulous calm of a neurosurgeon at work. "You sure you haven't left anything out?" he asked. "Doc must be sending us a message, but I haven't heard the message yet."

She thought through everything again and found what she had left out. "Philadelphia," she said, "I left Philadelphia out. A man and a woman met her at the airport. They said they were from her father and brought her to a car. Suddenly she didn't know anything, and then the next thing she was in a room with a high ceiling and plaster cherubs on the ceiling and windows covered with tin. She thinks there must have been at least a day between going to sleep in the car and waking up in the room."

Philadelphia was the message, thought Goldberg, Philadelphia and a car ride and plaster cherubs on the ceiling and windows covered with tin.

Twenty-six

"Where are we?" asked Barbara, opening her eyes. She had fallen asleep as soon as the plane had left San Francisco.

"Deep in the heart of Texas. Dallas, to be precise," said Goldberg. "I'm getting off to make a phone call."

She looked at him suspiciously. "Who do you have left to call? All your friends wind up dead."

"Don't be nasty." Goldberg stood, looking at her, then shook his head and wandered off down the aisle.

In the airport he slid into a bank of telephones between some love beads and a Stetson. "Mr. Schoyer, please," he said on reaching his number. "Tell him it's Goldberg."

When Schoyer got on, he was amazingly mild. Goldberg had been with him in good times and bad and both had seemed to exacerbate his temper. His new meekness was without precedent and Goldberg didn't know what to make of it.

"Hello, Goldberg," Schoyer said in that new polite voice that even he didn't seem quite sure how to handle. "Hello, Goldberg," he said again, trying it out for the second time.

"Are you sick?" asked Goldberg. "You didn't even ask where I am."

"Listen," said Schoyer, getting some of the reassuring

savagery back into his voice. "On the list of my problems, where you are falls pretty low. Where are you?"

"I won't be here for more than ten minutes, so what difference does it make?"

The young man in the love beads slammed his phone down into the receiver and said, "Fuck you, too," to Ma Bell, to Dallas, or maybe to all of Texas.

"I think I'm on to something," said Goldberg cautiously, not sure whether or not he was lying, but thinking perhaps he was on to something that would reveal itself more clearly in the near future. "I can't talk where I am."

"Airport? It makes noises like an airport."

"Is there anything I should know?" asked Goldberg, glancing over at the Stetson. "I can't talk, but I can listen fine."

The new mild-mannered Schoyer thought that over for a minute. "I'm going to tell you something, Goldberg. God knows why I'm going to tell it to you, but the way things are going I'm ready to try anything, even you. Only I'm warning you if this ever gets beyond you I'll track you down to the last airport on earth and fix your wagon like it's never been fixed before."

"I've been accused of a lot of things one time or another, but having a big mouth was never one of them."

"Our friends with the printing press got something new going," said Schoyer. "Whole new line of merchandise, it would blow your mind. Me it's given an ulcer on my ulcer."

"You really got an ulcer, Schoyer, or are you just showing off?"

Schoyer's only response was even greater mildness; maybe he really was sick. "There's a road called the Atlantic City Expressway," he said. "It runs from Philadelphia to Atlantic City and it's a pretty good little road if you want to go from Philadelphia to Atlantic City, which more and more people want to do these days."

He stopped to let that sink in. While he waited, Goldberg examined the man in the Stetson, who seemed to be having more luck with Ma Bell than the wearer of the love beads. He was smiling at the telephone as though he would like to do something even more tender to it.

"You listening, Goldberg?" demanded Schoyer.

"You bet I am."

"Tuesday there was an accident on the Atlantic City Expressway. A nice neat little panel truck, brand-new, suddenly went out of control at about sixty miles an hour, and cracked into a semi. The driver of the panel truck was killed, the driver of the semi got shook up pretty bad, and five more cars managed to get themselves involved. It was a real mess, I can tell you." Schoyer inaugurated another one of his pauses and held it for at least thirty seconds. "You got any idea what was in that panel truck that was scattered all over the Atlantic City Expressway, Goldberg?"

"Yeah, I got an idea."

"You think you got an idea, but you don't. It was the new fall line, fives, tens, twenties, and fifties. Hundred-dollar bills aren't enough for our friends anymore, they're into some new phase I don't even want to think about."

"Good stuff?"

"As good as the hundreds. Near enough to perfect so it makes no never mind."

"Son of a bitch," said Goldberg.

"Son of a bitch," agreed Schoyer. "There was a hundred million in that truck, and God knows how many other trucks just like it didn't have an accident. Which is another funny thing."

Again the pregnant pause. Again Goldberg encouraged him with a "yeah."

"That was no accident, it was more like an execution. Somebody had worked out on the front axle of that little money truck with a hacksaw."

"Jesus," said Goldberg. "Did the press get hold of it?"

"We were lucky this time," said Schoyer. "But we're running out of that kind of luck. God knows what'll happen next time."

They were calling Goldberg's plane. Turkey lurkey, the sky is falling, he thought as he hung up. He remembered his son repeating the words to him in the big bed he had shared with the homecoming queen.

Twenty-seven

She had gone to sleep in San Francisco a mother in mourning. She woke up in Philadelphia a gypsy queen grasping for her castanets. "I've got to get out of this dress," she said defiantly. "I don't care how much of a hurry you're in. I'll change in the ladies' room."

He looked at her in surprise, not sure whether he was dealing with some new trick, or another one of those mysteries of female chemistry that so frequently eluded him.

When she came out of the ladies' room she was wearing a red linen dress he had never seen before. Revenge on Miranda for conniving in her own kidnapping? When he looked more closely, he realized that her eyes had the same desperate glitter he had mistaken for passion in the hotel room in Las Vegas, and he wondered whether she had taken advantage of his absence to make a phone call.

"What's wrong?" she asked. "Don't you like the dress?"

He shook his head. "The dress is fine. I was thinking about Atlantic City. The last time I was there I played on the beach with a red bucket and a green shovel. My parents were in their twenties, and it would never have occurred to them or to me that they would grow old and some day die."

She grimaced. "At least that's one advantage I have over you, Goldberg. I travel light. Nothing to remember. Everything to forget. The biggest thing I ever wanted when I was a kid was a lock on my bedroom door and we never could afford it."

All the way to Atlantic City she sang Cole Porter songs that, she explained, she had learned from an aging singer who was one of her first lovers after Doc left her. Goldberg had never heard her sing before. She had a pleasant voice. There had been a time when he had been unreasonably disturbed every time she dug up a new lover from her old kit bag, but he listened now to the full repertoire of the aging singer without a qualm.

The problem was he couldn't decide whether to count Mr. Victor for the streak, or against it. It was clear enough that Goldberg had won gloriously at craps, but Mr. Victor had canceled the arrangement with his little Beretta. Touch me, dear. Am I hot or cold?

Some cities slumber into extinction. Others jump. Atlantic City went to sleep with the departure of the Army and Navy after World War II and soon there was hardly anybody left who even dreamed about its early grandeur. It was well on its way to becoming a vast seedy parking lot for the dispossessed when the gamblers came to town and began to grow their glittering towers in the rubble.

218

It was a city still charred by the wave of arson that coincided with the discovery that scorched land was more valuable than the Victorian relics encumbering its surface. It was the city that appeared on the late-night news when its majestic old hotels were blown sky-high, once at full speed, bang, and then rising and falling one final time in a slow-motion memorial to the passing of brick and marble.

It was the place where salt-water taffy was invented and Miss America was born.

Goldberg hardly remembered the place at all and it didn't think kindly of him either. There was not a room to be had anywhere along the Boardwalk.

"What are you going to do now?" challenged Barbara in the lobby of the Tropicana where a solicitous young woman in a tuxedo jacket and black skirt had just closed the last door on them.

"Gamble," said Goldberg.

"That's your answer to everything. I was planning on a bed. And a little privacy. This place makes me nervous."

"I'll win a bed," promised Goldberg.

Goldberg won the bed around two-thirty in the morning behind a silk rope at Resorts International. It was a long time coming. There are two different times for losing and winning and most of the night Goldberg had spent on loser's time.

When your rhythm goes, the more you think about it, the harder it is to get it back, and that's how Goldberg was with his luck, worrying it from dice to cards to wheels, and when changing games didn't work, he tried changing places. Golden Nugget. Tropicana. Playboy. Caesars. Bally. Claridge. Sands. Resorts. In an assortment of sequences, each one punctuated by the trip along the Boardwalk. They could have traveled the back streets in cabs, but

Barbara would have no part of them. In the casinos you could scream, on the Boardwalk you could run, in a taxi you were a prisoner; she stuck with screaming and running and Goldberg was too preoccupied with his luck to argue with her. He was obsessed by the sheer ambiguity of the episode with Mr. Victor. When you couldn't tell whether you'd won or lost, you were in a new kind of trouble.

Somewhere between Lady Luck Shoes and the Great Tee-Shirt Factory, on the swarming Boardwalk, Barbara dug her nails into his arm and pointed to the figure of Mr. Peanut in front of the Peanut Shoppe, a Planter's Peanut kind of Mr. Peanut, top hat, pale shell torso, monocle in the eye, black trousered and leaning snappily on a cane.

"What's wrong?" said Goldberg.

"Look at his little feet."

Goldberg looked at his little feet. They were tapping.

"Did you see that?"

"His feet moved."

"He's alive." She took her hand back. "I didn't realize he was alive. I thought he was a statue." She looked around the crowded boardwalk and shuddered. "It looks so innocent, old people in little trains and babies in strollers, but Doc's people are all over the place with guns stashed in picnic baskets and knives in their socks."

Goldberg shrugged. "The easiest way for us to find them is for them to find us."

Through black shadows on the land side and dark blue by the ocean, the Boardwalk carved a long funnel of light out of darkness. Las Vegas had grown from a gangster's hunch and never lost the touch of the sinister that flourished like some flesh-eating cactus on the hot desert breeze. The new Atlantic City was founded on a marketing proposition, a city where the Gideon Bible would never have to turn its face to the wall, where showgirls wore brassieres, and Charles B. Darrow, the father of Monopoly, smiled benignly from a bronze plaque on Park Place. Even the withered wood beneath Goldberg's feet whispered of domestic values. The Ritz was rumored to be offering condominiums at one million and more, but this was still the land of salt-water taffy and the hot dog. Although prosperity might not have brought full employment to the shadowy slums behind the Boardwalk, that deficiency was being paved over with bright young faces from Omaha and St. Louis and Milwaukee. Across the way from Convention Hall, where the Miss America Pageant was promised for September fourteenth to seventeenth, John F. Kennedy's bronze hair was turning the color of cornflakes.

"Do you think she's here?" asked Barbara suddenly.

"Who?"

"Miranda."

"Probably."

"I don't know what to believe anymore. For years I was sure a girl who looked as though she had been invented by Laura Ashley was all sugar and spice and everything nice. Now I don't even believe the sweet smiles in my photo album. I remember how I was. It starts when you're so small all you've got going for you is tricks against the giants. Outsmarting the big folks. Once you know you can do it, it's like candy, you just can't stop. It's a dangerous game and the danger gives it a nice little extra edge. Who knows what Miranda's up to now?" She dug her heels into the wood with a ferocity that carried her several steps ahead of him. "It's hard being a mother," she said. "Too close for comfort."

Goldberg refused to compete.

"I think we're being followed," she whispered.

"Probably," said Goldberg, but in his mind he was already tending toward baccarat, which, while the rules were harder to follow than a legal brief, offered the best odds in the casino. He thought about asking her if she'd made a phone call in the Philadelphia airport, but the odds against a straight answer were too great.

"Look at me, goddammit," she said. She stepped in front of him and turned, arms akimbo. "There was a time not so long ago when you couldn't stop looking. Or other things, too. When are we going to get that bed?"

Goldberg looked at her. So were other people. Other people were always looking at her. Dressed or undressed, she was still the most conspicuously beautiful woman he had ever known. He wondered how he could have forgotten. "Soon," he said, "we're minutes away."

It took a little longer than that. In the beginning the cards were true to the evening's form, flirting, teasing, and failing, but about one o'clock, with the arrival of a new dealer, a blond girl with a cynical, amused, intelligent face, the cards turned in his favor and the naturals began marching in. When he quit at two-thirty he took with him sixty-eight thousand he hadn't brought, and a sense that the trumpets were blowing again. The rhythm was back, and, in his gratitude, he shared his luck with the cynical, amused, intelligent dealer to the tune of ten thousand dollars.

A woman in her early forties, wearing a demure black suit that looked as though it had been issued with an MBA from Wharton, met him outside the shiny rope, quickly determined that he was roomless, and reproached him for not having identified himself as a high roller before. Fifteen minutes later he was enjoying his just deserts in a suite so resplendent with gold lamé that even Barbara was cheered. The sheets had already been turned back on a bed like

Baker Field, but first there was a discreet knock on the door.

"Probably Dom Perignon," Goldberg reassured her.

Instead it was Schoyer, looking like his own grandfather now, anxiety engraved in deep pouches beneath his eyes. "So," he said, pushing his way into the sitting room where the gold lamé seemed to reject his rumpled presence. "Somebody in the other room?" he demanded, knowing damn well there was somebody in the other room.

"Don't worry about it," said Goldberg. "An old friend like you is welcome any time of the day or night."

He poured Schoyer a Jack Daniels and Schoyer drank it like Coca-Cola. "Where the hell you been?" He ran one hand through his steel-shaving curls. "The whole world's ready to blow up and all you can think of to do is make jokes."

"Sit down, calm down. Give that drink a little breathing spell or you're going to choke on it."

Schoyer sat down. This time he approached the Jack Daniels as though finally recognizing what it was. "Once I would have depended on you for my life," he said sadly. "What the hell happened to you?"

"Now what?" said Goldberg.

Schoyer shook his head.

"Worse than the truck full of fives, tens, twenties, and fifties?"

"Oh, shit." Schoyer looked as though Goldberg had reminded him of something he would have preferred to forget. "We've got a little more rundown on the dead driver," he said. "He was wearing silk jockey shorts."

"I didn't know they made them in silk."

"Not real jockey shorts. You know. Knitted underpants. Imported from Italy. Everything on him was silk. Shirt. Pants. Socks. A platinum buckle on his belt. An emerald ring cost maybe forty thousand on his little pinkie."

"Look at what he was riding in front of. If he had wanted to, he could have bought the Trump Tower to hang his silky things in."

"Even criminals don't have any discipline anymore," complained Schoyer. "He was a kid named Scarfoglio, thrown out of the Marine Corps for peddling dope. Carried a big chip on his shoulder, claimed he'd been framed, and took that as license to steal anything he could lay his hands on. Two years ago he disappeared from sight. Just vanished from the old neighborhood. Abandoned his mother, his girl, and ten thousand dollars worth of stereo equipment. Shows up dead on the Atlantic City Expressway."

Goldberg looked at him suspiciously. When Schoyer ran on this long about anything, he usually had something else on his mind.

"All that time not a peep to anybody in the old neighborhood," said Schoyer.

"I know, not his mother, not his girl, not his ten thousand dollars worth of stereo equipment. What's really on your mind, Schoyer?"

"It suddenly occurred to me, suppose he wasn't making a delivery, suppose he was just running away with a hundred million dollars."

"Okay, Schoyer, consider it supposed."

"All right, then tell me this: why was the axle sawed half through?"

"Punishment for running away?" guessed Goldberg.

"That's what I was thinking. But why would anybody who wanted to punish him for running away let the money get away? Why not just shoot the simpleminded son of a bitch?"

Goldberg shrugged, "I don't know, but I suspect you're going to hate the answer when you find out."

Twenty-eight

Atlantic City has a population explosion every morning around ten o'clock when the day-trippers, mostly in the fullness of their years and mostly women, fall out of their buses onto the hotel sidewalk, forty-five to a bus, three hundred thousand buses per annum.

Goldberg was walking along an empty sidewalk when three buses flashed to the curb and he was buried in senior citizens, laughing and calling out and racing to the bathroom. The fourth bus looked like all the others, but it wasn't. It had come a longer way and something had happened to it that hadn't happened to the others. The first woman at the doorway was so big she seemed to have trouble getting through it. She stood there for a moment, like a cork in a bottle, nearly six feet tall, maybe three hundred pounds, wearing a red velour top and white slacks, her head wreathed in flashy chestnut curls. She remained poised on the top step for another second as though astonished by what she saw, and then, letting out a whoop that echoed up and down the street, barreled her way through the crowd and disappeared inside the hotel.

The rest of the passengers came out more slowly, each one carrying a neatly wrapped package the size of a pound cake. The packages had been distributed by a cadaverously thin man in his middle thirties who had gotten on the bus with the rest of them in front of a funeral parlor in Staten Island, carrying two suitcases. Somewhere in Jersey he had stopped the bus, distributed his packages, and departed in a green Mercedes that was waiting for him at the side of the road.

Each pound-cake-size package contained ten thousand dollars.

The driver of the Mercedes looked like a weightlifter with a face like a slab of raw beef and close-cropped pale yellow hair.

Schoyer sat at the counter and did the arithmetic on a cocktail napkin. He did it over on a second napkin—three hundred thousand bus trips times forty-five passengers times ten thousand dollars for each passenger. The zeros came out the same way each time. "If they gave ten thousand to each bus-tripper on each bus, that would amount to a hundred thirty-five billion in a year," said Schoyer, shredding the two napkins and dropping the shreds into his coffee cup where they turned mud brown.

"They're not going to do that, Schoyer."

"How do you know what they're going to do?"

"The whole rhythm has changed. Doc never passed money before and now he's giving it away. They never gave it away before."

"You telling me he's gone crazy?"

"He's always been crazy. Now I think he's dying—you heard how the bus-trippers described him. He's showing off his money before he dies."

"That's all I need," said Schoyer. "Who knows how much of it is out there already, buying bread or diamonds or apartment houses, and flowing into banks in savings and going out in loans and coming back in deposits, in and out of the pipelines all around the country and beyond the borders into Europounds and petrodollars, buying gold and stock and Swiss francs and commodity futures, the whole world spinning and turning on play money or box tops or baseball cards?"

Schoyer stood up abruptly. "Come on outside," he said. "I don't want to talk in here anyway."

Outside the sun smiled on the crowded Boardwalk. A breeze blew from the ocean. The sky was cerulean touched with gold, the water a darker blue with here and there a languid whitecap. A freighter trudged along the horizon on its way home, while sport-fishing boats rocked in the middle distance. On the beach more sleepers than swimmers. All in all a Chamber of Commerce kind of day, and Goldberg and Schoyer stood side by side against the sea rail inspecting it.

Schoyer held out a hand, palm down, cupped it, and turned it over. He smiled happily at the hand. "In fifteen minutes I'm going to have them right there in the palm of this hand." He took a gulp of briny air deep into his lungs and pointed. "Do you see that thing sticking up out there? That's the Central Pier. The flat space on the side is a helicopter pad and in fifteen minutes there's going to be a 'copter sitting on it. Normally it's a commuter service running high rollers out of New York, Philadelphia, and Washington, D.C. Right now it's under contract to me."

Schoyer whistled "The Easter Parade" all the way through. It was his only music and he reserved it for significant highs and important lows. "I'll bet you a thousand you can't guess who's going to be on that whirlybird."

Goldberg thought the offer over. "You win," he said finally. "I can't guess."

"Damn right you can't guess. It's a girl named Frannie Warburton."

"I still can't guess."

"Frannie Warburton was Scarfoglio's girlfriend. Tony Scarfoglio being the guy who died on the Atlantic City Expressway, the kid who was thrown out of the Marine Corps for dealing drugs. Frannie knew about the sawed axle, and she knew who did it and why they did it, and maybe she figured she was next. She was pregnant with Tony's baby, and they were planning to elope with a hundred million in homemade cash, but somebody got wind of their plans and that was the end of Tony Scarfoglio."

Schoyer shielded his eyes against the sun and peered into the sky. "Frannie's been playing it real cozy. The less she tells us the more important she is to us, and the more she's got left to bargain with. On the other hand, she's a real airhead. Unless they're crazy they wouldn't trust her with any of their more intimate secrets. As pretty as a flower and just about as smart. Tony recruited her in a singles' bar six months ago and brought her home with him. That was the beginning of the end for Tony."

"Did she say that?"

"No. I said that. Frannie babbles. Half the time she doesn't know what she's saying."

Goldberg heard the sound of the rotors beating and then the helicopter scuttled out of a hole in the sky and began to descend toward the Central Pier. Goldberg hated helicopters; the blades beat in his head, stirring up memories of the helicopter war and making him tremble. He looked over at Schoyer to see if he had noticed the trembling, but Schoyer was totally absorbed by the incoming flight.

"Here comes Frannie," muttered Schoyer. "Frannie. One thing I didn't tell you about Frannie: she's not very good at names and numbers, but she never forgets a face. Her six months with Tony the only thing she really learned was the faces. That's what she's going to do for us in Atlantic City, she's going to pick out the faces." Schoyer couldn't take his eyes away from the helicopter, hovering now in the sky above the Central Pier. "Whatever they're staging, they must all be in town for it, or damn near all. And Frannie's got their faces stored away in that pretty little head."

He was smiling at the helicopter when it belched the first little puff of smoke and the smile was still on his face but fading when the whole thing came apart into metal shards and flames and one final great puff of smoke. "Oh, my God," he said, but Goldberg barely heard the thin wavering voice, because all his powers of sensation had gone into his eyes, and the sky was streaming blood. Goldberg felt his own flesh burning. It was his son falling out of the sky.

When he let himself into the gold-lamé room, a grotesque woman was standing there, adjusting her hair in the mirror above the bar. She towered and swayed on platform heels like a figure out of the Macy's Thanksgiving Day Parade, a great swollen bosom and mammoth hips, encased in a loose tweed sack designed for some monster maternity. Black hair streaked with gray, which she patted and pushed and shoved into place. When she finished with the hair, she went to work on the bosom, swatting it peremptorily into fresh arrangements.

"What do you think?" she said, simpering, as Goldberg advanced into the room.

Grunting, he reached past her for a bottle of Johnnie Walker.

"Would you have recognized me?"

He looked at her again. "If a haystack could walk, that would be you. Except for the voice. What the hell are you trying to do?"

"I'm going cabin crazy," complained Barbara. "If I don't

229

get out of here soon, I'm going to go over the edge altogether. I sit here with my eyes open and have nightmares about Miranda. Mostly I feel guilty. What have I done so wrong I have to feel guilty?"

"You're not going to find her on the Boardwalk."

"At least I could look. This way I'm just waiting for you to do something and I can't see you're doing anything except gamble."

The Scotch didn't have any affect on him at all. Was it guilt? he wondered. Who the hell knew who was guilty of what anymore? "You really think you need a disguise?" he asked. "How many of them know you?"

"Doc knows me. The people who burned down my house know me. Doc has pictures of me. Every one of them would know me by now if that's what he's got in mind."

"How many of them do you know?"

She reached inside the mammoth bosom and began to remove wads of Kotex from it. "I worked for Doc. That was all I knew. Doc and more money than J.P. Morgan dreamed of in his wildest dreams. That was all I wanted to know and it was all Doc wanted me to know."

She pulled the tweed sack over her head and stood revealed in swollen knickers and a brassiere like a hammock in which the remainder of the Kotex still swung. "Don't look at me," she said. "If you laugh, I'm going to crown you with this mirror on the wall." Then she saw his face for the first time since he had entered the room. "What happened? Does it have something to do with Miranda? Oh, my God, if it's Miranda, I'll never forgive you."

He told her about Frannie Warburton and the helicopter and Schoyer, and he told it all in a matter-of-fact reporter's voice, but this time he didn't fool her.

"There's something else," she said, and finally he told her about his son dropping from the sky.

By now the brassiere had fallen away onto the floor where it lay in a litter of pure-white Kotex, and, stepping down from the platform shoes, she shucked the billowing knickers. Naked, she approached him and put her arms around him. "Oh, you poor man," she said, "holding it all inside you and you weren't going to say anything. My God, it must be hard to be a man, all stiff upper lip and shaking knees."

She took him into the bedroom and undressed him and pushed him down on the bed, where she made love to him until they both fell asleep.

It was just beginning to get dark when he awoke and listened to her breathing on the pillow next to him. "You can't argue with God," said a voice in the dream from which he was just recovering, and he got up and showered and dressed.

When he left the room, she was still asleep.

Twenty-nine

The ticktock hips had a familiar rhythm. Apple-ass. Apple-ass. Apple-ass. They passed the window of the jewelry store, stopped, and turned.

It was Myra Swayne, who had left him to burn in Willow Glen, her giant nubile body coated in pale Italian silk. She came back through the shopping arcade as though on an invisible string and entered the jewelry store. When Goldberg looked through the window, her index finger was ranging across the top of a showcase, summoning jewels from their resting place. She moved with the feverish haste of a refugee packing supplies for a dangerous and unanticipated journey, fingers gobbling diamonds and rubies as they arrived on the counter and stuffing them in her bag while the clerk stared at her in astonishment. When the girl started to protest, Myra quieted her with a roll of cash.

"Hello, Myra," said Goldberg, moving in beside her. Without looking up, she grabbed the bag and tucked it under her arm like a football, but there was nowhere to run except into Goldberg.

"You're supposed to be dead," she said when she recognized him, her nostrils flaring as though with the memory of smoke, and for a moment she and Goldberg faced each other, remembering what it had been like in the burning house. "Everybody thinks you're dead," she said, her lips rounding into a giant pout.

"Everybody?"

"Everybody who counts." There was something wrong in the green eyes, connections broken, links gone, a brain that didn't work quite the way other brains worked. All the junk in the world had gone to fix those eyes. Somewhere the screen between public self and private self had slipped, and she no longer knew the difference. "It's impossible this man's not dead," she said. "I've gotta get out of here." She grabbed Goldberg's arm in her strong fingers. "You can't blame me. It was George."

Goldberg wasn't sure whether she was talking to him or explaining herself to the world. "Where's George?" he asked.

"Around. Away. Who knows? Am I George's keeper? I've got myself to worry about before I get killed."

"Who's going to kill you, Myra?"

She closed her eyes almost all the way but not quite, like a child pretending to be asleep. "None of your business," she said, peeking out at him through half-closed lids. Something shifted in her befuddled head. The tip of her tongue crept between her lips and brushed them from right to left and back again. "It's the town boob-inspector," she said, beginning to weave her hips, Venus's-flytrap getting ready for capture. "I'm glad you're not dead."

"I would never have guessed," said Goldberg.

She moved a little closer, flesh to flesh. Goldberg wasn't wearing much and she was wearing less. He could feel her nipples pressing into his chest. "I liked you from the moment I set eyes on you, hon. You know why?"

"No."

"Because of the way you looked at me. You got bedroom eyes. The way things are going these days it's hard to find a man with a serious interest in women. I was really sorry George came back when he did. We could have had ourselves a real good time." She shivered against him. "Why don't we go upstairs. Standing around in the open makes me nervous."

Stepping back, Goldberg put a hand under her elbow. "Collect your change, Myra," he said, pointing at the wad of bills in the salesgirl's hand.

She took her change in a wrinkled lump and offered it to Goldberg. "You want it? You want more? I'll give you more money than you've seen in your life. There's nothing in the world you can't buy with the money I'll give you."

"Put away your money, Myra. People will start to talk."

"Where are we going now?" she asked when she had stuffed her change in the big purse.

"You're going to help me find George."

She tried to take her elbow back from Goldberg. He kept it. "You don't want to find George any more than I do," she said. "Unless you're crazy."

He wrapped an arm around hers, feeling the rich flesh surge in protest.

"Go find George by yourself. You don't need me."

"Of course I need you."

She twisted to face him, head to head. "We'll both be dead before morning."

"You got me to protect you, Myra."

"Protect me. Shit, man, you can't even protect yourself." She groped in his armpit for evidence of a gun, followed the line of his body down to his waist, found no gun and started to continue the exploration deeper into his trousers when he stopped her. "Not even a gun," she said, "not that it would make much difference with George, he's bulletproof." She looked at the exploratory hand, which Goldberg was still holding. "What ever happened to fucking?" she wailed. "I remember you, you got the inclination. Why don't you just let yourself go, man?"

Goldberg moved them along the arcade in the direction of the escalator. In his free hand he swung the attaché case in which he carried his gambling money. Before leaving the gold-lamé room he had also included the gun Myra had been looking for in his armpit, a Beretta .380 auto, thirteen shots in the clip, given to him by Schoyer, who had recommended it with some bitterness. "Can you imagine Daniel Boone with an Italian gun, or Davey Crockett packing an Uzi? That's what it's come to."

"How did a sweet kid like you hook up with a mad-dog killer like George?" asked Goldberg, guiding her onto the escalator.

She accepted the phrase as Goldberg's invention and

234

rolled it around on her lips. "Mad-dog killer. Mad-dog killer. Man, you got it, little Georgie is one mad animal; people have nightmares friendlier than he is, standing there bare-ass in front of the mirror, watching his muscles move like a basket of snakes and grinding his teeth." She shuddered. "Sometimes I wake up in the middle of the night and he's staring at me like I'm a walnut he's planning to crack in his teeth. Man, you don't want to find George."

"You haven't answered my question."

The disconnected green eyes stared at him, lost. "What's the question?"

"Why'd you ever start with George?"

She shuddered again. "He gave me a peek at all the money in the world and before I noticed anything else it was too late."

"Counterfeit money."

"Counterfeit money?" That seemed to be news to her, but the news didn't faze her in the least. She shrugged. "I thought maybe it was drugs. That's when I thought about it at all. All I know is I got used to it real quick, you don't need practice being rich, it comes as naturally as breathing. And what difference would it make anyway? Citibank don't turn it down, nobody turns it down. Just as pretty as any other money, works just as good."

The memory of all the things the money would do started a small fire in the blurred green eyes. She licked her lips greedily as though she had discovered crumbs of chocolate icing on them. "Let's go find a room," she said.

"What about George?"

"We won't tell George."

"Where is George?"

"If we work it right, we'll never find out."

Goldberg understood now that he was in possession of

the ultimate witness. It was like playing a slot machine; there was a big payoff in there somewhere, but if you ran out of quarters before you dug it out, that was just too bad.

Her nipples moved under their Italian-silk gloss. The fire was still burning in her eyes. "You must have a room, this place is nothing but rooms. You won't be sorry. People tell me I'm pretty fantastic."

Goldberg was embarrassed to notice that while his head wasn't interested at all, certain familiar stirrings nearer to the floor demonstrated once again that his head didn't necessarily run things. "I came out tonight to gamble. It's like a Gurkha's promise to his knife. Once he draws it he has to use it before he puts it back."

"Shit," she said, the fire going out in her eyes, "you don't look like no Gurkha. If you gotta gamble so bad, why don't you let me go?" She examined his face as though she had never quite seen it before. "All you want is George? What's so special about George? So he tried to kill you. You got away as good as new."

"Somehow I keep remembering that old black lady in Echo Park. She didn't get away. I might have gotten to like her if I had known her long enough."

"Put an ad in the paper. Make new friends."

"Old friends are the best," said Goldberg. "Let's go gambling."

There's nothing unusual about shooting craps one-handed, but when the other hand is busy with a hundred-seventy-pound woman whose greatest ambition is to disappear you lose the easy movements that tickle and excite the dice. Nasty little plastic cubes the color of cheap candy, the dice snapped back at him like discarded mistresses, deadly snake eyes peering at him evilly, threes rolling into sight, snickering, only to be replaced by the crunch of twelves; he crapped out in every way available, and then started all over again. Every time the dice arrived at his position they stayed for a single pass and then flirted on, whoring after more exciting palms.

Eskimos have sixty-seven words for snow, drunks have even more for what happens to them, but gamblers, who live on hope, have a limited vocabulary for losing. Cold? Goldberg was ice, dry, drowned, hooked. The winning streak had gone into a losing streak without a backward glance; Goldberg was losing the way you lose blood from a broken nose; and yet the greatest surprise was that he felt nothing. Olympian, he looked down on the losing as though it were happening to somebody else.

He remembered a girl long ago describing the loss of her faith; it had been there one day and gone the next and once gone it was as though it had never been, a track, a trace, a spasm that could be reflected on with wonder or regret or even self-reproach, but never taken seriously again. Once Goldberg might have felt that the Power had abandoned him; now he knew it didn't exist and his only memory of it was a mild disbelief in his own brief credulity.

Meanwhile, Myra Swayne, the disconnected green eyes restlessly on the watch for George, took on herself the role of goodwife, the voice of domestic thrift, of egg money, of a-penny-saved-is-a-penny-earned.

"You could just as well have thrown the money in the sewer," she said and for a moment Goldberg heard his mother's reproachful tones, dealing with one of his father's ill-fated investments. "You coulda bought a Rolls-Royce," Myra announced a little further along, "you coulda bought a yacht," and then as his losses grew and her imagination dwindled, she tried to price-out items beyond her direct experience, a king's palace, Radio City Music Hall, and finally the state of Rhode Island.

"Shut up, Myra," said Goldberg, staring at a small red-faced man for whom the dice had suddenly grown hot.

Goldberg bet the "don't pass" line like a man in love and the red-faced man passed and passed and passed. Finally Goldberg switched to the "pass" line, stopping the red-faced man dead in his tracks.

He felt Myra's hand tremble in his and glanced around quickly for George. There was no George. "I gotta pee,". whispered Myra desperately.

Goldberg looked at the dice scrambling around the table, considering the strategies available to a dice player in his predicament. You could put on the horns and change your position at the table. You could rub or touch or somehow adore a rabbit's foot, a saint's medal, or some more personal talisman, lucky socks, a propitious belt buckle, an especially fortunate necktie. Or you could leave.

Goldberg escorted Myra to the ladies' room.

Goldberg had been at the blackjack table for more than twenty minutes when he noticed the Chinese girl. Black silk dress. Embroidered collar. Spine straight as a plumb line. She sat on her stool as though it was the imperial throne, commanding the cards with her eyes, and the stacks of hundred-dollar chips grew like young trees in front of her.

When the shoe was exhausted, she stood up, the black silk skirt falling away to midthigh, tipped the dealer, collected her winnings, and moved on, her eyes engaged by a mysterious middle distance in which she found something that brought a quizzical smile to her lips.

"Man, you look like the cat that swallowed the fortune cookie," said Myra Swayne, still attached to Goldberg's left hand. "You never seen a Chinese lady before?"

Goldberg motioned to the dealer for another card,

238

busted, and continued to stare, more interested now in the Chinese girl's luck than his own. She had just split two queens and he watched her win on both, accepting the local celebrity that accompanied her rising tide of chips with the same minimal smile that might not have been a smile at all.

Did she feel the way he had felt when he was winning, the power running through her like an electric current, the rhythm waltzing, all the rules off and everything under control, the winner's high than which there is nothing higher? Her eyes were black as jet, her skin a pale gold, and she won and won and won until this shoe, too, was empty.

When she stood up, once more she tipped the dealer, at least her right hand tipped the dealer, the rest of her was totally absorbed in something else.

Three tables over a plump young man with a cherub's smile rose, sighing, and pocketed the few chips in front of him, half in the left pocket, half in the right. Noticing a spot on his right sleeve, he went to work on it with a handkerchief he dampened on the tip of his tongue. A lot of tongue. A little rub. Less tongue. More rub.

When the Chinese girl took the place abandoned by the now-spotless young man, the shoe was about halfway down, and she immediately began to bet as though she owned whatever was left. This new shoe turned out to be even hotter than the one she had just come from, and in the next twenty-five minutes she won seventeen thousand dollars.

Goldberg waited for her next move, sure now that the Chinese girl was the big player for a team of card-counters, the one who moved in with the serious bets when the coolies had run down the decks sufficiently to identify what was left as pay dirt. Goldberg was trying to reconstruct the code, the chips in each pocket, the business with handkerchief and tongue and sleeve, when he felt the movement against his back, accompanied by a violent tug from Myra Swayne. He hung onto Myra, but there was no getting rid of the gun in his spine.

"I g-g-got a present for you," said the voice behind him.

Goldberg looked at the dealer, whose left eyebrow was rising into a circumflex. "Hit me," said Goldberg.

George had the gun inside a silvery Tropicana laundry bag. "Can't it wait?" asked Goldberg.

"N-n-no." George smelled as though he had been doing laps in an Aramis lagoon, but right under the surface there was the acrid stink of a thousand locker rooms. On both sides of Goldberg the players were shifting uneasily out of the way.

Goldberg considered the possibility of shoving his chair back into George's groin, but one look at that muscle-bound face changed his mind. "Why don't you give it to me here?" asked Goldberg.

"You're g-g-g-going to have to come outside to c-c-c-collect it. It's too b-b-b-big to bring in here."

"Give me a hint. Maybe I don't want it."

"It's b-b-b-black," said George. "Like a h-h-hearse. And you w-w-want it."

Thirty

The three of them sauntered along the Boardwalk to Goldberg's execution, their pace regulated by the night people, who never went to sleep, just walked a little slower.

George's face had an expression of deep concentration as though he were psyching himself up to lift a weight that had always baffled him before and his little fish eyes gleamed with the effort.

"I thought you'd never get here, George," Myra whined experimentally.

George shifted the muscles inside his shirt like a man moving salamis and made a sound that might have been a chuckle. The gun in the laundry bag shook a little against Goldberg's kidney.

Look at it this way, Goldberg advised himself, you've been searching for him all night, now you've got him.

Goldberg's feet lagged but everything else was working overtime. He could feel the warm splintery boards reaching through his tennis sneakers to caress and scratch at the soles of his feet. He smelled vanilla custard turning in vats, popcorn frying, chocolate fudge oozing, sunburn lotion drying in the cold night air. He choked on the Aramis winds blowing off George. His eyes read the fine print on tee shirts.

What would be the last thing he thought of if George pulled the trigger in the laundry bag? Something he should have done but hadn't; his life was a laundry list of things he should have done but hadn't. Suppose he jammed George now, tramped on his foot, kneed him, spun him, knocked away the gun. His own gun, the Beretta, was still in the attaché case in his right hand, and he swung the attaché case casually, playing with the idea of putting it into George's throat while he took the kidney out of the reach of the laundry bag. It was not the kind of thing you could think about; once you started thinking it was already too late.

They went past a boarded-up construction site that promised the tallest hotel in town and showed a boat-tail Auburn from Harrah's collection, past Sunglass City, past Louis's Artist Village, past bars and grilles and pizzas whirling in the air, past plastic hoagies and paper salads, past shoes and hats and dubious jewels glittering behind glass, past a seating pavilion occupied by old men and older women with their backs firmly set against the Atlantic Ocean. The three of them slow-marched to Goldberg's funeral, the gun holding them together like glue, and fell into step behind a baby in a stroller pushed by a blond girl in shorts and a halter with another baby beginning to show in her tan belly.

Three women who might have been sisters, as dark as gypsies with wild straggly hair and gold hoops in their ears, glared at them from the shadow of a dumpster. Two showgirls on their break went by shining in their greasepaint. A young black woman pushing an old white man in a wheelchair. Three big-bellied men in straw hats and Hawaiian shirts, looking for trouble or a convention, whichever came first, gaped recklessly at Myra. Goldberg contemplated shoving George in among their paunches, but twins in a double stroller intervened before he had a chance.

"Why don't you just walk away?" Goldberg said to Myra. "No way he's going to take this gun out of my ribs. You got a free ticket to anywhere."

Myra hesitated, licked her lips, looked over to George, and was lost. "I don't have to run away from George," she said hopefully. "It's you he's mad at."

George leaned against the gun that ended in Goldberg's side. "Asshole," he said. The arm with the gun grew muscles, some of which Goldberg had never seen out in the open before.

"You ever compete with Schwarzenegger?" asked Goldberg, not sure where he was going but figuring that anything was better than where he was now.

"S-s-schwarzenegger, s-s-shit," said George.

"What's your position on steroids?"

"Steroids, sh-sh-shit." George's jaws went to work on some huge cud of rage.

"Just trying to make conversation," said Goldberg. "How much can you lift, Georgie?"

"L-l-l-lift *you* and th-th-throw you, one hand." The idea brought the nearest thing to an expression Goldberg had yet seen on George's face. "C-c-crack your b-b-back," he added for good measure.

"You really think so, how come the gun?" Privately Goldberg suspected that George was underestimating himself. "Man could accomplish all that doesn't need a little steel pipe with bullets in it."

"You trying to make me m-m-m-mad?" The smell coming off George now was pure locker room. He filled his chest with air and then let it go again. "You don't g-g-g-gotta try to make me m-m-mad, I'm m-m-m-mad enough already."

"What'd I ever do to you, George?"

"You're s-s-supposed to be d-d-dead. You make me look like some kind of a sch-sch-schmuck you're s-s-supposed to be d-d-dead and you're walking around."

"That's embarrassing."

"Embarrassing, sh-sh-shit," said George, turning abruptly and sweeping Goldberg with him down a ramp; at the bottom of the ramp there was a barricade of boards surrounding a demolition in progress.

The building that was going down was one Goldberg remembered from his childhood as a palace of the old Boardwalk, built in the late nineteenth century to stand forever, of rock-face granite and slate and copper, with turrets and dormers and terra-cotta ornaments and a princely English name that had been obliterated as the first act of demolition.

There was a capricious quality to the demolition that puzzled Goldberg, one row of windows gone, the next intact. Two large window areas, at street level, had been replaced by painted canvas on which palms leaned toward a tropical sea. There was rubble everywhere, but the building was a lot less destroyed than it looked at first glance.

George had a key to an iron door that must once have led to a two-story service area projecting from the lower part of the hotel. He gave the key to Myra while he kept the gun on Goldberg.

"You first, Myra," he said when she had the door open.

"C'mon, Georgie. You don't trust me? *Me*. This is Myra talking."

"I know who you are. I'm not as-as-asking s-s-something real big. I'm just as-as-asking you to go in the door first."

"I know that look. When you get patient. The only time you get that look is when you're going to kill somebody. I'm not one of your jobs, Georgie. All we been to each

244

other." She tried to find a word for what they'd been to each other but couldn't. Instead she grabbed his monumental left arm, the one not occupied with Goldberg.

The arm twitched like an elephant's trunk and Myra flew through the doorway.

"In," growled George at Goldberg, urging him along with the gun in his kidney.

The long hall went black when the door slammed behind them, and George took a flashlight from the leather purse he wore slung over his shoulder. The beam found Myra's face low down on the wall against which she had fallen.

"You got some nerve, George," she whimpered. "After all we been to each other." The disconnected eyes were trying to make some connection that wouldn't quite come together. Her lips were fumbling with a prayer she had learned in childhood but could no longer get straight.

"You shoot that thing, somebody's going to hear it on the Boardwalk," Goldberg pointed out.

"P-p-people don't chase l-l-l-loud noises," replied George with the condescension of long experience. "Maybe they c-c-call the cops. By the time the c-c-cops show up you're g-g-gone."

But he had another kind of problem. He didn't want to take the gun away from Goldberg long enough to use it on Myra. Goldberg found that reassuring, even a little flattering, but muscle against muscle he didn't give himself much chance against George. Remembering the left-arm twitch that had sent Myra flying through the doorway, he revised his estimate downward; no chance at all.

"Get up, Myra," said George.

"I can't. You hurt me too much."

He nudged her with a foot. "Get up, Myra."

She got up. Something went on in her eyes, a connection

245

made that she had been missing all along, and suddenly she
bent from the waist to start pulling at the hem of her dress.

"What the hell do you think you're doing?" demanded
George nervously.

"What does it look like I'm doing?" she shouted, the
Italian silk now above her hips and rising. When she had it
over her head, she was naked. She stood there, showing
him her body in the glow of the flashlight.

"For ch-ch-chrissakes," he said.

"Take a good look. The body's not going to be any good
to you at all once you put holes in it."

"You k-k-keep t-t-trying to make it p-p-p-personal,"
complained George. "There's nothing p-p-personal about it
at all. You think this is my idea?"

"Whose idea is it then?"

"You been officially c-c-condemned as a t-t-traitor, a b-b-
b-bungler, and a m-m-money m-m-maniac."

"I'll bet you really stood up for me, Georgie."

"I wasn't a-a-asked what I th-th-thought."

"You volunteer for this job, Georgie?"

George was beginning to sweat; Goldberg could smell
him in the darkness. "N-n-no, I didn't v-v-volunteer. Why
should I v-v-volunteer? I'm the executioner, that's what I
do. G-g-get going, M-m-myra."

She marched ahead of them down the hall, her naked
hips glowing in the darkness like an erotic pendulum. Tick.
Tock. Tick. Tock.

The hall, which led directly into the interior of the hotel,
had been skinned of its plaster walls and wooden floors.
The ceiling trailed lath and broken plaster and twisted elec-
trical cable. A mean and nasty death, thought Goldberg,
choking to death on its own rubble. But then they passed a
giant firedoor and were into another category of devasta-

tion: the main lobby soared above their heads like a bombed cathedral, stripped of the marble and rich wood and lacy ironwork that had been one of the glories of Goldberg's childhood, but awesome in its granite nakedness. It was so quiet you detected within it sounds you would otherwise have missed, the slithering of snakes, wings beating, rat feet, and something else for which there was no name. The hair stood up on Goldberg's arms.

"P-p-p-put your d-d-dress back on," said George, half pleading.

"You worried I'll catch cold?"

"P-p-put it on."

"I was born naked—I'll die naked." But she had found a small advantage, and she was no longer completely convinced she was going to die. "What's wrong, Georgie, you never killed anybody naked before?"

She began to twist her hips and roll her belly in the flashlight's beam, grinding out a promise of incredible delights, Delilah, Little Egypt, Mata Hari, every woman who had ever seduced a man with an unspoken and unspeakable invitation to paradise here on earth. And while she danced she accompanied herself with a kind of chant. "What's this remind you of, Georgie boy? What's this make you think of? You're never going to find another like me, Georgie, you so big and strong, where you going to find a woman big enough and strong enough and crazy enough for you, Georgie boy, you never found anybody like me before me, and you'll never find another after me."

George grunted, a deep angry sound that shook his mammoth body.

"Why don't you kill the gambler and let me go?" George hesitated and she went on, "What's wrong, Georgie? Nobody told you to kill the gambler? And you don't do anything unless you're told? Is that your secret, Georgie, you don't do anything except what you're told?"

George grunted again as though she'd penetrated this time to the seat of an old wound, and he pulled the gun out of Goldberg's side and held it out toward the naked woman. A single bead of sweat rolled down her belly, like a tear, into her navel.

Goldberg chopped at the arm holding the gun. It was like chopping at an iron railing, but the gun wavered as it went off, and Goldberg dove into the darkness beyond the flashlight's beam, rolling and twisting on the broken floor until he was stopped by a pile of rubble. He came up from the floor with a brick in his right hand, hefting it as he sought the balance, and, still in a crouch, throwing one of those bullet passes that had been a personal trademark years ago, flat and straight and deadly, feeling as it left his fingers the trueness of it homing in on its target at the center of the flashlight's beam, right into the space between George's prognathous jaw and massive collarbone with a thud like a slaughterhouse mallet. The scream had hardly started through George's throat when it stopped.

There was a moment of darkness as the flashlight clattered on the floor and broke, immediately followed by an explosion of light that illuminated the huge, devastated cathedral-like space, revealing in its glare, Myra, naked and upright, and George sprawled at her feet, his neck bent at an unreasonable angle.

There was a shout, and then there was a second explosion of light, and a third, with the difference that the final one was entirely within his own head.

Thirty-one

Inside his head twelve scale-model Goldbergs danced on a giant roulette wheel in order to stay alive. Down went a Goldberg and then there were eleven. Down went a Goldberg and then there were ten. The roulette ball whizzed by as though it had been shot out of a cannon—jump, Goldberg, jump—and half the remaining Goldbergs went down together. He was running out of Goldbergs, but there was no way to quit the game.

When the light came through his eyelids and began to screw its way inside his head, Goldberg shifted his attention momentarily from the wheel. "You're in there somewhere, Goldberg," said the voice that accompanied the light. "Come on out unless you've got your heart set on dying with your eyes closed."

Goldberg knew he ought to get back to the roulette wheel, but he was distracted by fingers groping in his scalp. When the fingers uncovered the scar made by the bullet in Las Vegas, they went away and the voice came back like a needle in his ear. "You got the kind of head bullets bounce off of, cowboy. Anybody wanted to do you any permanent damage would have to find a better way in." A gun barrel roamed over Goldberg's belly, stopping periodically to make commas and semicolons in the vulnerable flesh. "You don't quit playing dead, friend, you really will be."

The voice had brushed against and been neutralized by all the regional accents of America, but the flat wah-wah-wah of Nebraska kept breaking through. Mr. Colt. Doc Holliday. The man he'd come all this way to find. Goldberg opened one eye.

The counterfeiter had traded in the Colt for an Uzi with which he was punctuating Goldberg's belly.

Goldberg opened the second eye and tried to sit up. He was on the floor of what had once been a hotel room, a torn Oriental rug under him, a cracked chandelier over him, canvas bags of money behind him, around him, and stacked head-high against the walls. Some of the money had gotten loose onto the floor where it had picked up footprints.

Goldberg stopped trying to sit up when Holliday raised the barrel of the Uzi and pushed it into his chest. Something deep inside was eating away at Holliday and all that was left was the fury that made his hands shake. A blue-eyed stare as brittle as dry ice. Dark puddles of skin around the eyes. Scuffed boots. Shabby suntans. He had "handle with care" written all over him.

Goldberg issued a small groan as a warranty of his helplessness and rolled around a little on the rug, testing his arms and legs. He could get up now if he wanted to, but he decided he didn't want to.

"I should have killed you in Las Vegas," said Holliday.

"Don't blame yourself," muttered Goldberg. "You gave it the old college try."

Holliday smiled, a dead man's grin, all teeth and anguish. In his hands the Uzi looked like some deadly kitchen instrument, the latest thing in noodle-makers gone wrong. "This time I've got a Jewish gun," said Holliday. "Just keep up the jokes, comedian."

If Holliday wanted to kill him, he certainly wasn't in a hurry, thought Goldberg, and decided to settle down on the rug to find out why. As he located the strength in his arms and legs, he rolled his head slowly from ear to ear in an affidavit of agony.

"I could have stayed a minute longer," said Holliday, still rethinking Las Vegas. "One more second, one more bullet, and none of this would have happened." He raised the gun to see what Goldberg looked like in the sights. "You can stop groaning, you son of a bitch," he said. "In addition to everything else, you're a lousy actor."

But still he didn't shoot. He had something else on his mind and maybe he didn't know exactly what it was himself; he fumbled with the Uzi as though he was searching for inspiration through his fingertips. He started slowly. "If you had half a brain in your head, Goldberg, neither of us would be here now. Anybody else goes to bed with Barbara and comes out saying good-bye, you gotta chase her all over the U.S.A. Anybody in his right mind finds twenty mill in a dead lady's cellar he doesn't call in the Secret Service, he takes the money and runs."

"It was counterfeit," pointed out Goldberg in his own defense.

"Just because it wasn't made in Washington? My money's as good as the money the government makes any day of the week."

With the Uzi on the rise Goldberg decided to change direction. "It sure fooled me," he said.

"God save us from the experts," sneered Holliday. "What you are, Goldberg, is you're dumb, dumb but lucky. Dumb is bad enough. Lucky is worse. What you are is an insult to the intelligence."

Holliday picked up a bundle of hundred-dollar bills and

scattered them over Goldberg. "You could spend that money in heaven," he said. "You could buy senators with it." The electric-blue eyes crackled in their dark pockets. "You could buy this hotel with that money." He giggled like a mad little girl. "The Victoria Regina Imperial. I bought it with my own money."

The Victoria Regina Imperial. The soaring magnificence of the name carried Goldberg back to his childhood when his parents had taken him to a Fourth-of-July lunch in the Victoria Regina Imperial's Rudyard Kipling Room, which made an impression so great he had promised himself guiltily that as soon as he got home he would read *Stalky & Co,* a birthday present almost a year old and located, unread, between a hockey stick and a pair of boxing gloves under his bed. When the little cakes came at the end of the meal, there was a red-white-and-blue flag stuck in the middle of each one, and those little cakes with their little flags had haunted Goldberg's memory for years, showing up at the most improbable times to remind him that he had not forgotten them.

The bullet exploded into the chandelier, sprinkling crystal shards over Goldberg. "You listen to me, Goldberg," said Holliday, lowering the gun. "You want to live a little longer, you listen." The crazy blue eyes were moist with rage. "There should be history books about what I've done and if Mr. Schoyer had his way I wouldn't even make the eleven o'clock news. For five years I owned this country, and he thinks I'll disappear like a bankrupt shoe clerk. That's not my way, Goldberg, I do things big. Nobody makes me small."

With his left hand Holliday reached into the pocket of his suntan shirt and pulled out a piece of paper. "This is a copy of a letter," he said. "The real letter is in the mail where nobody, not even Schoyer, can stop it."

He glared triumphantly at Goldberg, who was touched by his faith; everybody had to believe in something even if it was only the U.S. Postal Service.

"This letter," said Holliday, "is written by me and addressed to the president of CBS, the president of NBC, the president of ABC, and the president of *The New York Times.*"

"Big players," said Goldberg.

"The biggest," agreed Holliday, "I don't fool around." He cleared his throat. "I'm going to read it to you, Goldberg, but don't you get ambitious, I've got peripheral vision that just won't quit, you make a move and I'll nail you to that rug."

Opening the letter, which was folded in four quarters, he began to read. "'Dear Sir, the undersigned is the founder head of an organization that for the past five years has been competing with the U.S. government in the manufacture of money. Our money is not only as good as the government's, it is absolutely the same and *undetectable.* This is because it is made by people who used to do the same for the U.S. government. As the founder, it was my idea to do it that way and in your reporting you should give me full credit.

"'It was also my idea to distribute the money through the U.S. gambling enterprise, legal and illegal, which amounts to five hundred billion a year. You can check that number, and you will find it is true.

"'Through the gambling we have passed hundreds of millions into the official money system. You probably have some of my money in your wallet right now. Look and you won't even know. What it all means is I have, single-handedly, destroyed the official U.S. money system. No conspiracy no matter how high up can keep this a secret forever.

"'It is your responsibility to tell the truth of all that I

have done. To prove that I am not just another nut or jerk and that I know whereof I speak, just watch the Boardwalk in Atlantic City. By the time you get this letter the Victoria Regina Imperial will blow into the sky. I am doing this because my work is done and I am taking with me Mr. Schoyer of the Secret Service and all his people who have made my life miserable for nearly a year now, including Mr. Goldberg and the people who made the money. Their work is done, too.

"'Tell this on the airwaves. Put it in your newspaper, Mr. Times. It is all true and the blowup on the Boardwalk proves it.'

"Signed 'Very truly, Doc Holliday, Chief Executive Officer and Founder.'"

"Good letter," said Goldberg. "Only one thing."

"Damn good letter. What one thing?" Holliday had both hands back on the Uzi and he was not in the mood for criticism.

"Great letter," said Goldberg. "Only why didn't you send it to the *Wall Street Journal?* Biggest circulation in the country and nobody's more interested in money."

"Oh, shut up," said Holliday. "They can watch it on TV like anybody else." Suspicious of Goldberg's flippancy, he pointed to a metal box resting on a table of bagged money next to him. "You think I'm kidding about blowing this place up? That's radio control, baby. One big bang and off we go. It's my hotel and I'm taking it with me." He laughed. "When they blow a hotel in Atlantic City, it always makes the eleven o'clock news. How do you like that, Goldberg, it's you and me on the eleven o'clock news?"

"What about your people?" asked Goldberg. "They buying into all this?"

"Sent them away," said Holliday. "The ones that didn't

254

run away. Not that they were worth much. The money drove 'em crazy. All they could think of was spend, spend, spend. Except Georgie. And you got Georgie." The electric-blue eyes flickered. "The only thing we have to wait for now is Mr. Schoyer."

"How would he know where we are?"

"I called and made an appointment," said Holliday sardonically. "The minute he arrives in the lobby it's off we go into the wild blue yonder. Hardly even time enough to be surprised. You believe in prayers you can start saying them now."

"I'll make you a bet," said Goldberg.

"What you got to bet with?" demanded Holliday contemptuously.

"I'll bet you didn't spell 'undetectable' right," said Goldberg. "It's one of the most commonly misspelled words in the English language."

"What you got to bet with?" repeated Doc Holliday, but his eyes went automatically to the letter in his lap, searching for the offending word, and in that instant of distraction, Goldberg flipped over the barrier of money bags on his left and sprang up carrying in his embrace what his son would once have called a humongous bag of money, half buffer, half weapon. "I'm placing my bet," he roared, feeling the shock of bullets thudding against money and stopping, and then more bullets, one, two, he couldn't count, tearing at his arms, but Goldberg, the human tank, was running for paydirt now and nothing could stop him.

As he crashed into Holliday, he heard the terrible sound of bone and cartilage cracking and knew that he had won his bet.

Thirty-two

He had been in the hospital for three days, dreaming war dreams, with the needles in his arms and the tube in his nose and violent daylight all around him, and then they had taken out the tube and some of the needles and rolled him into another room, where he slept peacefully until they brought in the visitors, who were Schoyer and Barbara and Miranda, in that order but together. Schoyer escorted Barbara to the side of the bed with the slightly vainglorious air of a man paying a debt nobody had really expected him to pay.

Barbara was wearing the white dress in which Goldberg had seen her during the first big run of the dice, and she carried yellow roses in a tissue-paper cone. Putting the roses on the bed, she reached back to bring the girl to her side. "This is my daughter, Miranda," she said. "Miranda, you know Mr. Goldberg."

The girl looked at him coolly. She was taller than her mother and stood very straight in a linen dress the color of seawater. She was biding her time, waiting for her mother to release her from childhood, but she wouldn't wait much longer. "Of course I know Mr. Goldberg, he's the man who killed my father."

She made the statement coolly enough—she was all in all

the coolest young woman Goldberg had ever met—but everybody in the room understood she had just taken a position from which she would not retreat.

"Honey," said Barbara, only the way she said it was *honeee,* "we're going to go far away and never see any of these people again."

Schoyer started to pat Goldberg's shoulder, then was afraid he might be damaging it, and took his hand back. "You've seen the letter?" he said.

"He read it to me."

"Craziness, pure and utter craziness." Schoyer shook his head in disbelief. Disbelief was one of his better expressions and he spent a little time on it. "Naturally, nobody in his right mind would believe a word of a letter like that."

"Of course not," said Goldberg. "The man said he was going to blow up the Victoria Regina Imperial and there it stands the way it's stood for a hundred years." Sitting up in the bed, he leaned toward Schoyer who glanced anxiously at the tube trailing from Goldberg's wrist. "Just tell me one thing."

"Maybe," said Schoyer.

"Was that box really rigged to blow up the building?"

Schoyer contemplated the question with the reluctance of a man who has just been invited to waltz in a minefield. He inspected his shoes. He fondled his nose. He glanced uneasily at Barbara and her daughter who were engaged in some intensely private conversation near the door. Finally, sighing, he leaned over and whispered, "Goldberg, you've got to be the luckiest man alive."

257

For a complete list of books available from Penguin in the United States, write to Dept. DG, Penguin Books, 299 Murray Hill Parkway, East Rutherford, New Jersey 07073.

For a complete list of books available from Penguin in Canada, write to Penguin Books Canada Limited, 2801 John Street, Markham, Ontario L3R 1B4.